Little Josephine

MEMORY IN PIECES

Valérie Villieu & Raphaël Sarfati

Little Josephine

Memory In Pieces

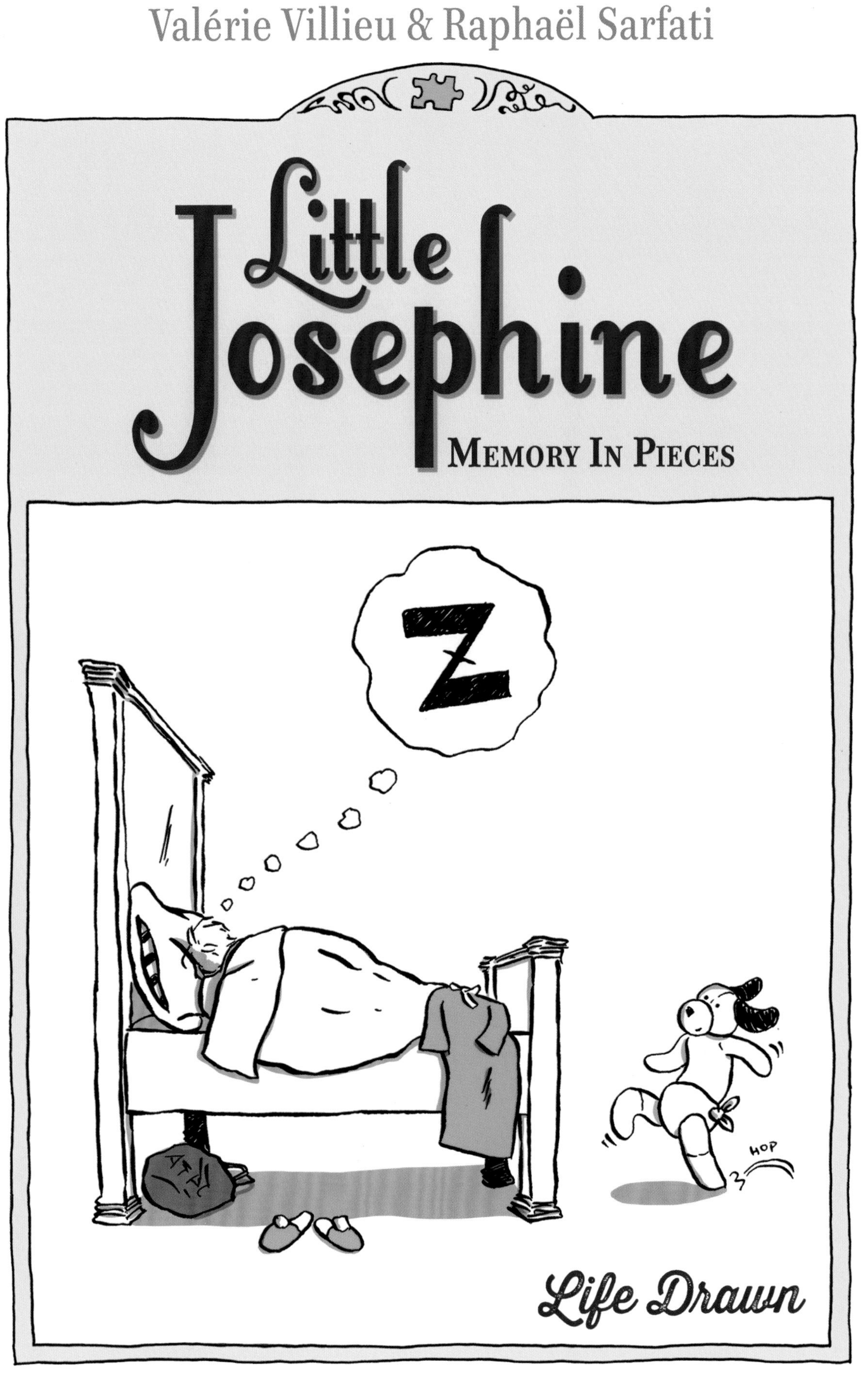
Z
HOP

Life Drawn

Valérie Villieu
Writer

Raphaël Sarfati
Artist

•

Nanette McGuinness
Translator

•

Fabrice Sapolsky
US Edition Editor

Amanda Lucido
Assistant Editor

Vincent Henry
Original Edition Editor

Jerry Frissen
Senior Art Director

Fabrice Giger
Publisher

Rights and Licensing - licensing@humanoids.com
Press and Social Media - pr@humanoids.com

LITTLE JOSEPHINE
This title is a publication of Humanoids, Inc. 8033 Sunset Blvd. #628, Los Angeles, CA 90046.

Library of Congress Control Number: 2019916180

Life Drawn is an imprint of Humanoids, Inc.

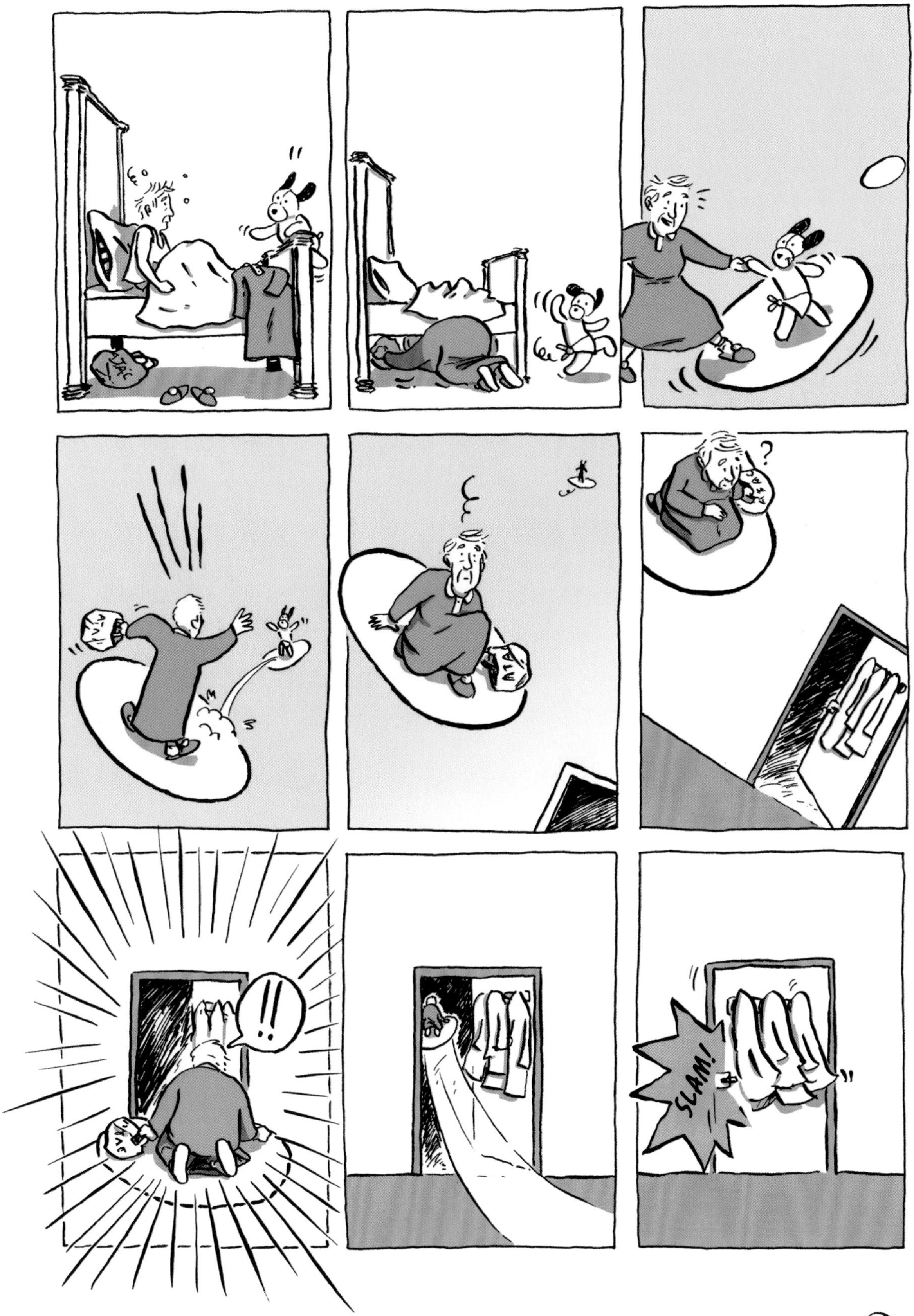
!!
SLAM!

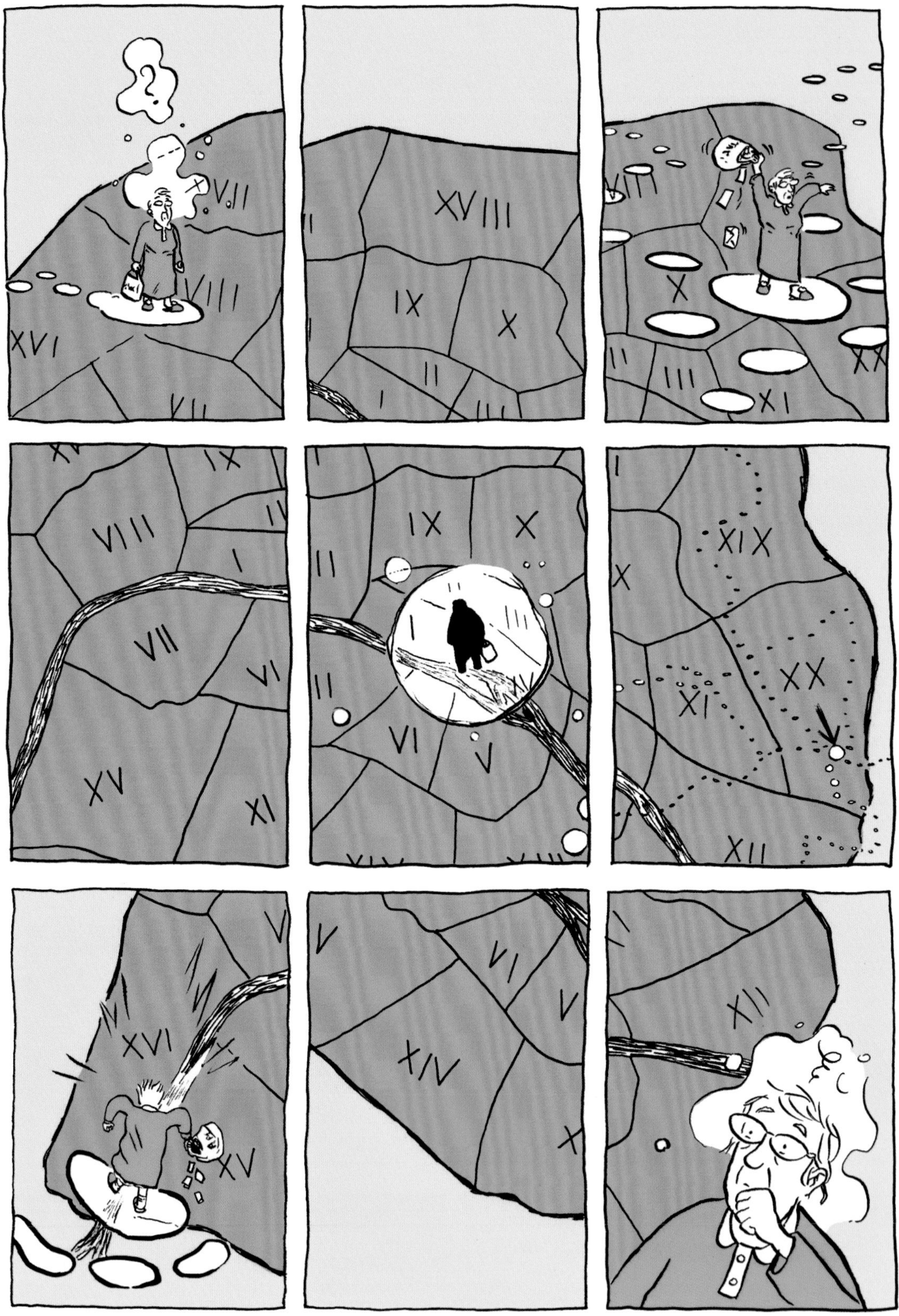
?
VII
VIII
XVI
XVIII
IX
X
X
XI
XX
VIII
VII
VI
XV
XI
IX
X
VI
V
XIX
XX
XI
XII
XVI
XV
VI
XIV
XII

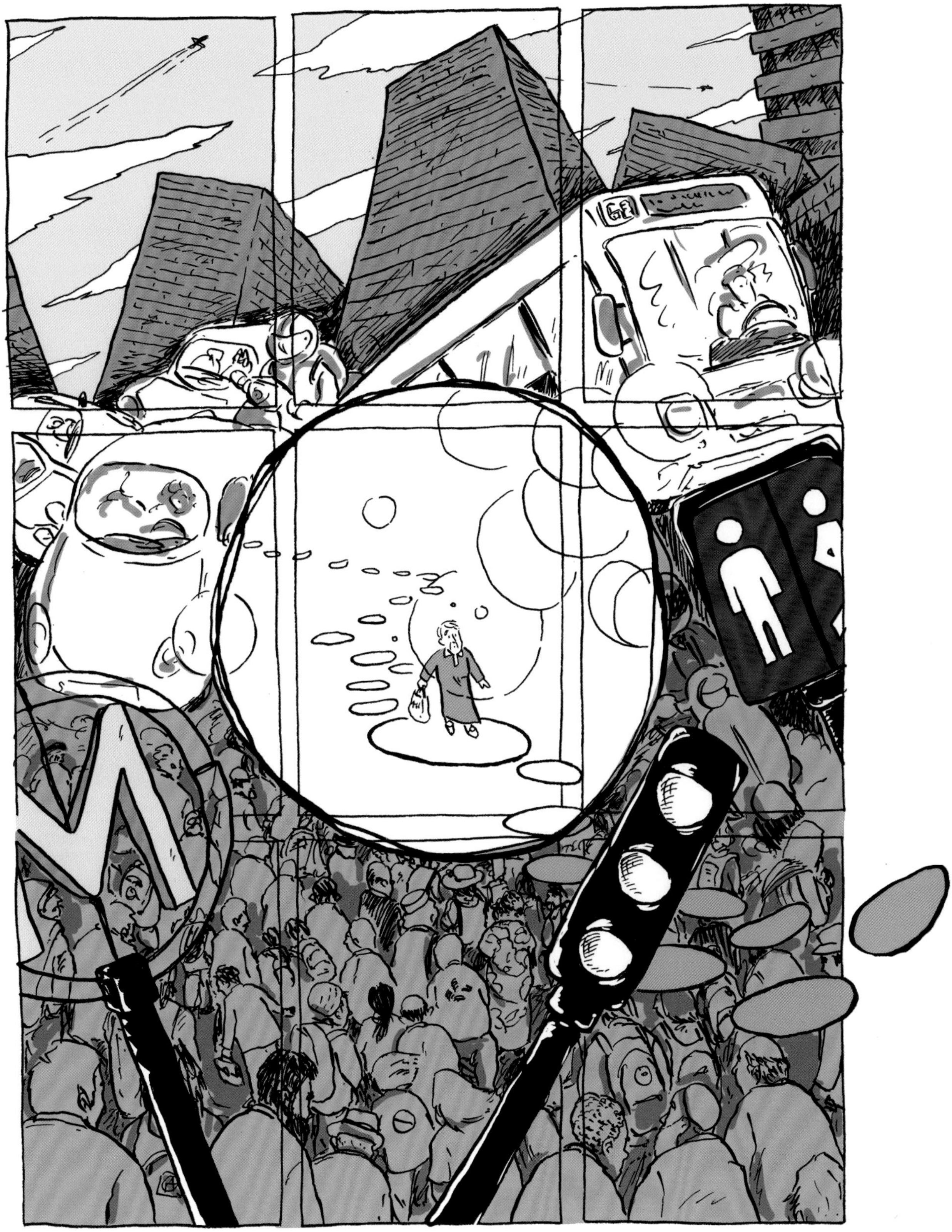

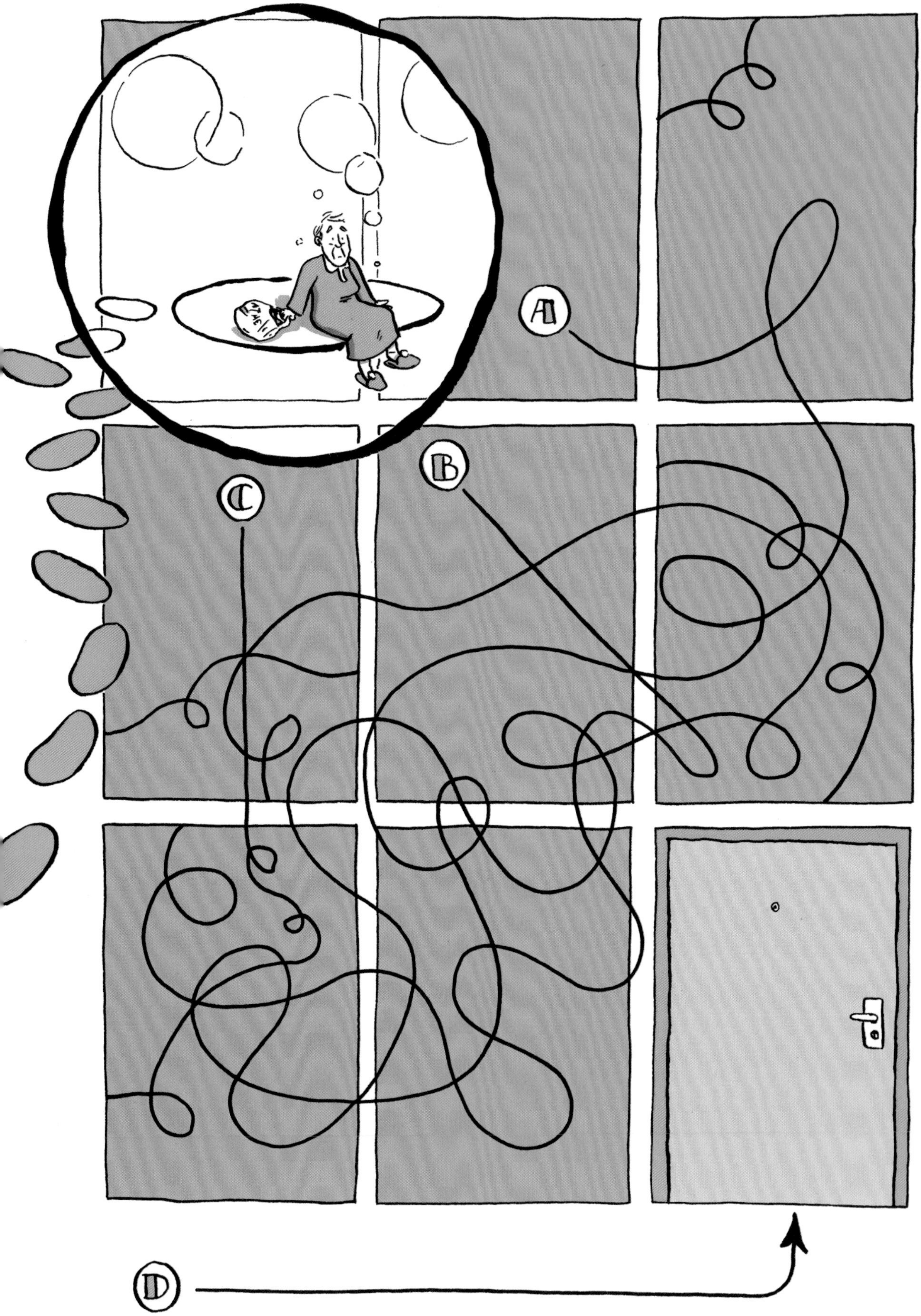
A
B
C
D

First Impressions

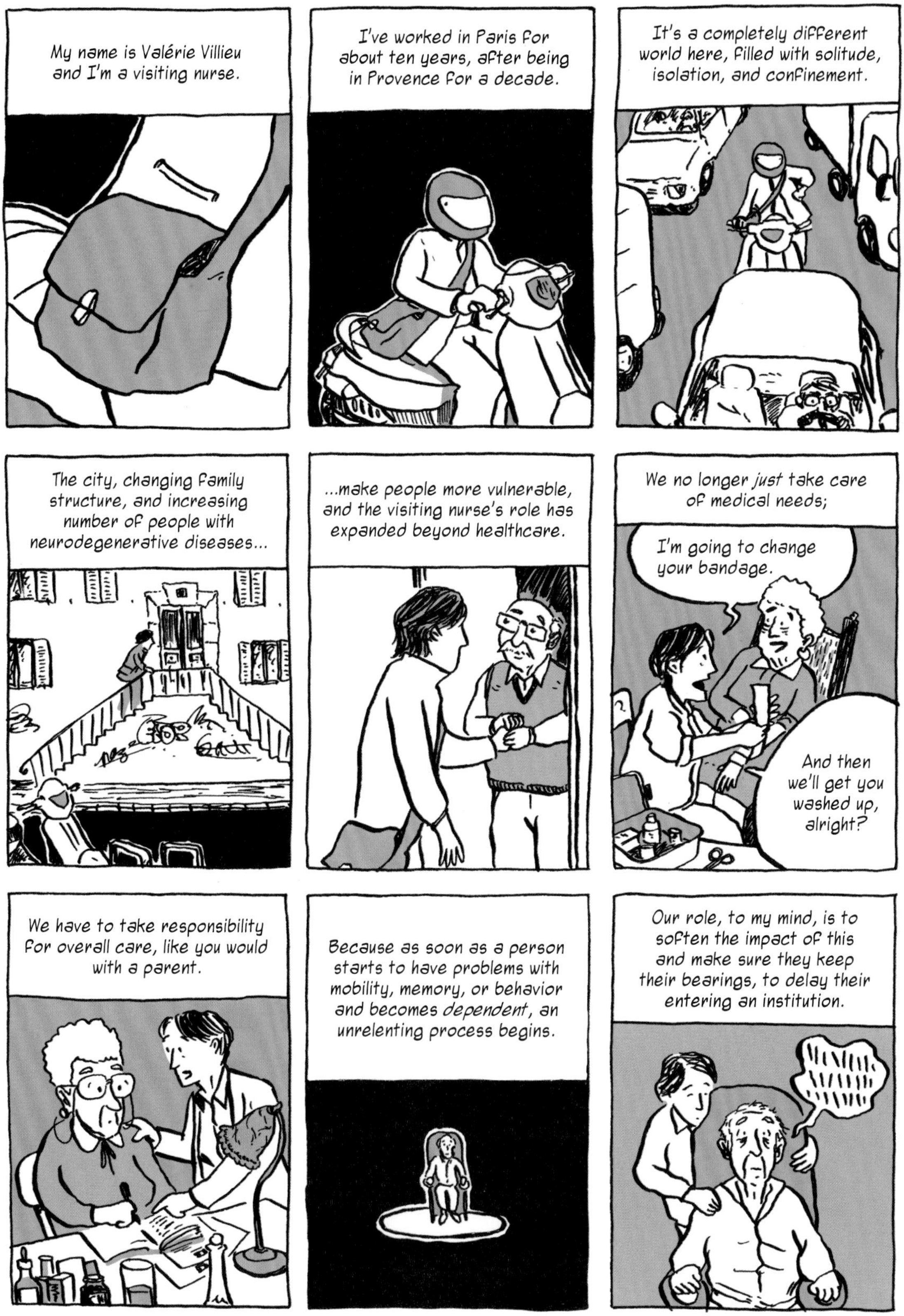
My name is Valérie Villieu and I'm a visiting nurse.
I've worked in Paris for about ten years, after being in Provence for a decade.
It's a completely different world here, filled with solitude, isolation, and confinement.
The city, changing family structure, and increasing number of people with neurodegenerative diseases...
...make people more vulnerable, and the visiting nurse's role has expanded beyond healthcare.
We no longer *just* take care of medical needs;
I'm going to change your bandage.
And then we'll get you washed up, alright?
We have to take responsibility for overall care, like you would with a parent.
Because as soon as a person starts to have problems with mobility, memory, or behavior and becomes *dependent*, an unrelenting process begins.
Our role, to my mind, is to soften the impact of this and make sure they keep their bearings, to delay their entering an institution.

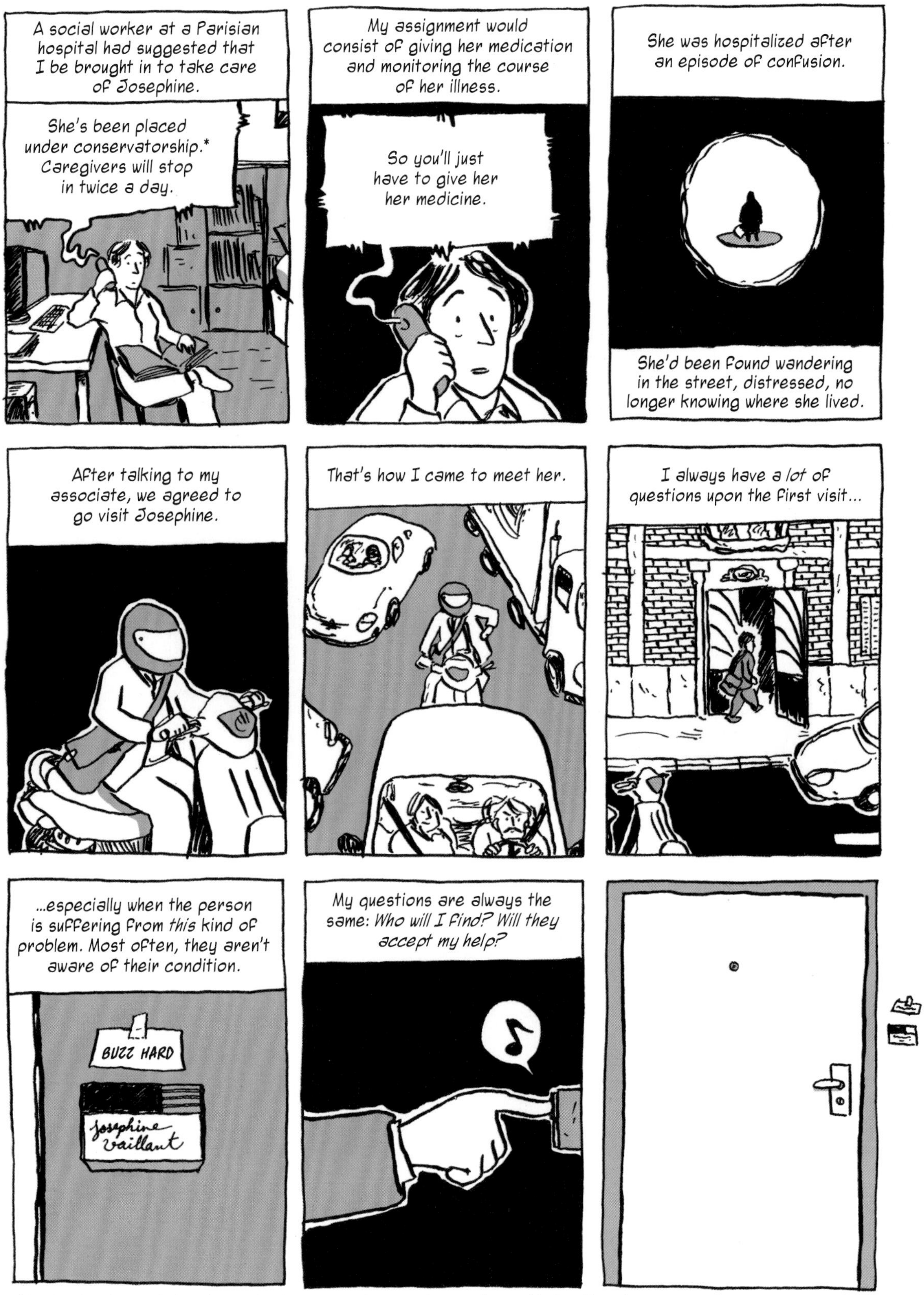
A social worker at a Parisian hospital had suggested that I be brought in to take care of Josephine.
She's been placed under conservatorship.* Caregivers will stop in twice a day.
My assignment would consist of giving her medication and monitoring the course of her illness.
So you'll just have to give her her medicine.
She was hospitalized after an episode of confusion.
She'd been found wandering in the street, distressed, no longer knowing where she lived.
After talking to my associate, we agreed to go visit Josephine.
That's how I came to meet her.
I always have a *lot* of questions upon the first visit...
...especially when the person is suffering from *this* kind of problem. Most often, they aren't aware of their condition.
BUZZ HARD
Josephine Vaillant
My questions are always the same: *Who will I find? Will they accept my help?*

*This is a legal state induced to protect someone who cannot properly provide for his or her own personal needs for physical health, medical care, food, clothing, or shelter.

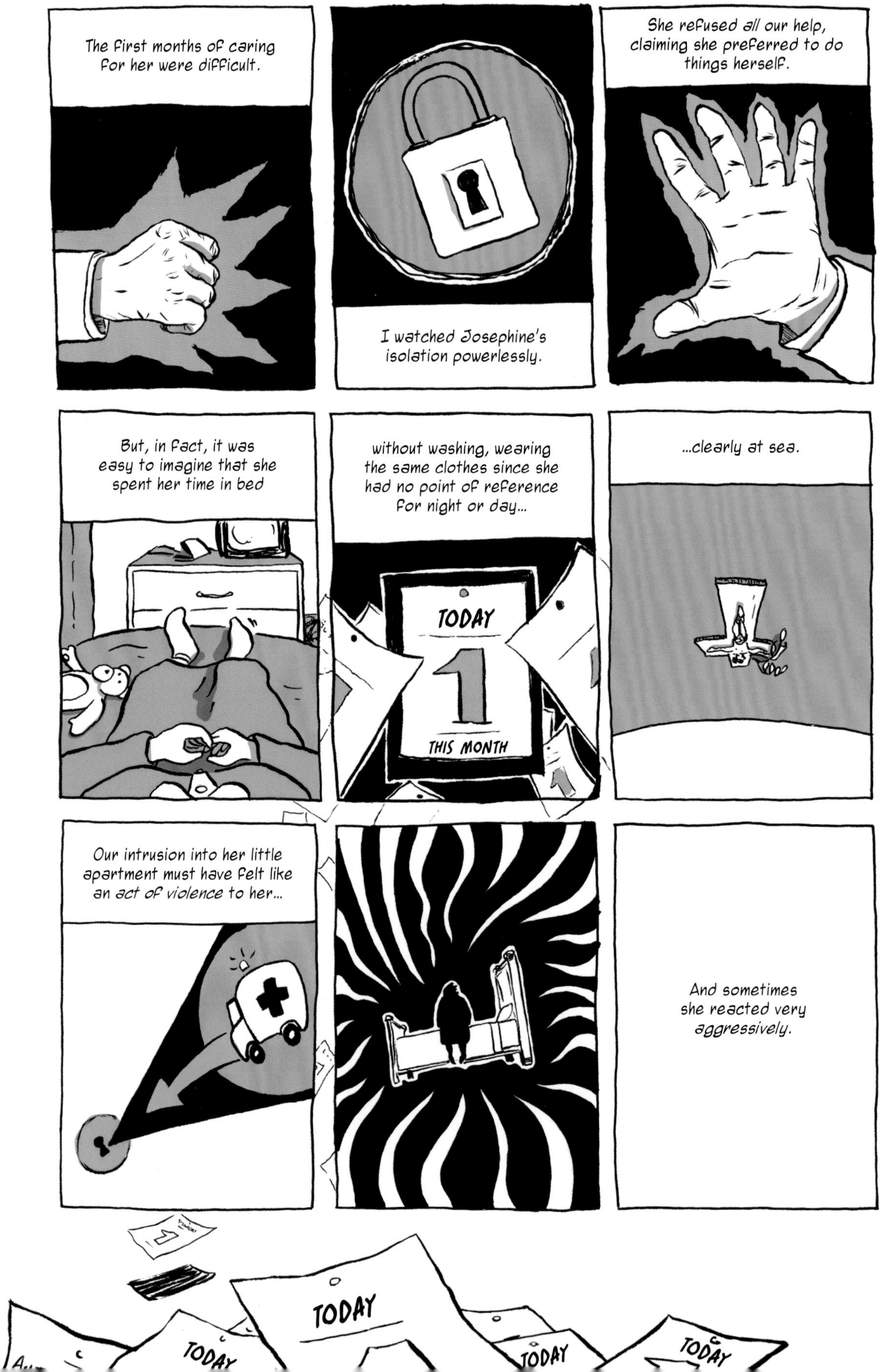

The first months of caring for her were difficult.
I watched Josephine's isolation powerlessly.
She refused all our help, claiming she preferred to do things herself.
But, in fact, it was easy to imagine that she spent her time in bed
without washing, wearing the same clothes since she had no point of reference for night or day...
TODAY
1
THIS MONTH
...clearly at sea.
Our intrusion into her little apartment must have felt like an act of violence to her...
And sometimes she reacted very aggressively.
TODAY
TODAY
TODAY
TODAY

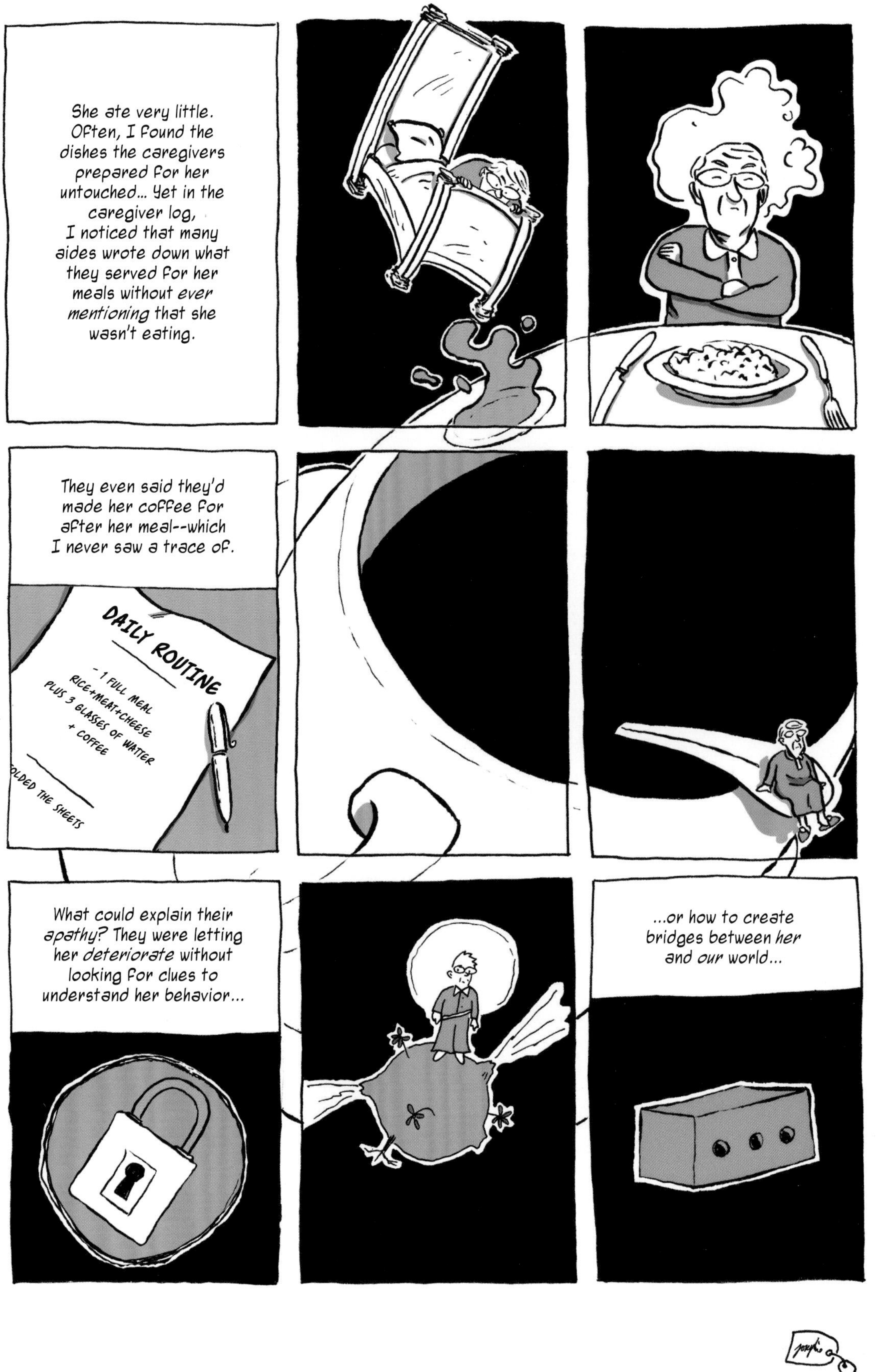

She ate very little. Often, I found the dishes the caregivers prepared for her untouched... Yet in the caregiver log, I noticed that many aides wrote down what they served for her meals without *ever mentioning* that she wasn't eating.
They even said they'd made her coffee for after her meal--which I never saw a trace of.
DAILY ROUTINE
- 1 FULL MEAL
RICE+MEAT+CHEESE
PLUS 3 GLASSES OF WATER
+ COFFEE
FOLDED THE SHEETS
What could explain their *apathy*? They were letting her *deteriorate* without looking for clues to understand her behavior...
...or how to create bridges between *her* and *our* world...

First Contact

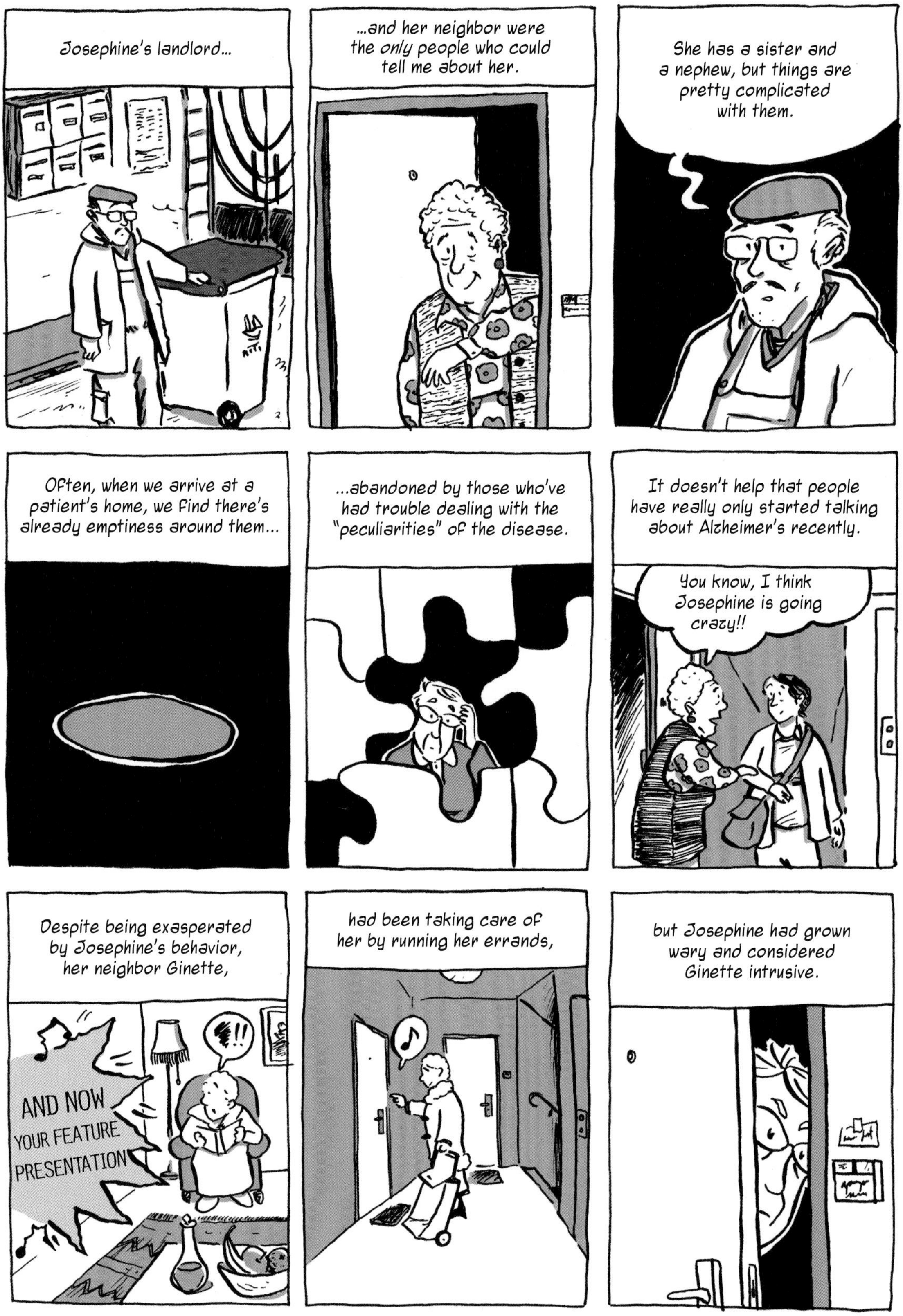
Josephine's landlord...
...and her neighbor were the *only* people who could tell me about her.
She has a sister and a nephew, but things are pretty complicated with them.
Often, when we arrive at a patient's home, we find there's already emptiness around them...
...abandoned by those who've had trouble dealing with the "peculiarities" of the disease.
It doesn't help that people have really only started talking about Alzheimer's recently.
You know, I think Josephine is going crazy!!
Despite being exasperated by Josephine's behavior, her neighbor Ginette,
AND NOW YOUR FEATURE PRESENTATION
!!
had been taking care of her by running her errands,
but Josephine had grown wary and considered Ginette intrusive.

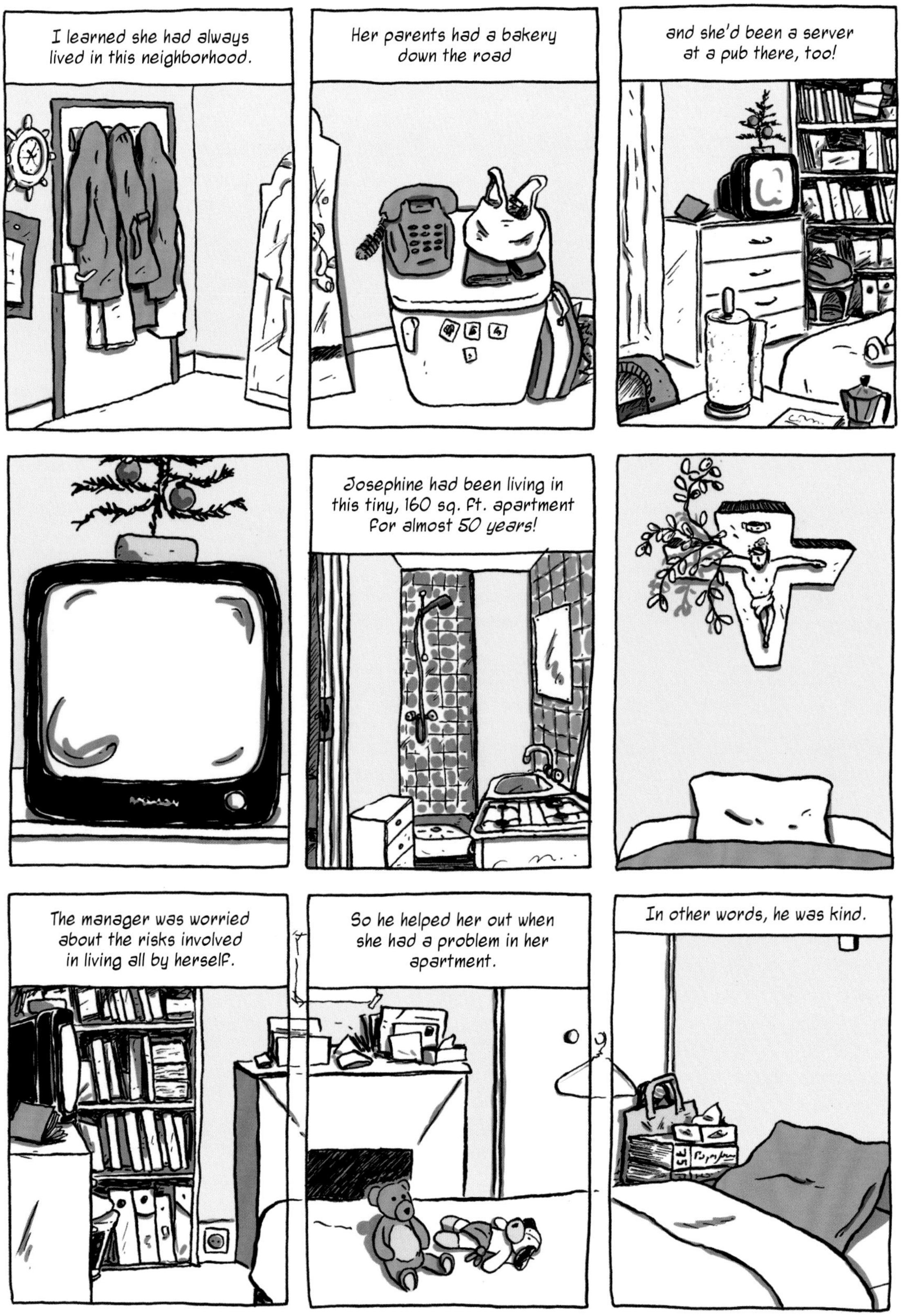
I learned she had always lived in this neighborhood.
Her parents had a bakery down the road
and she'd been a server at a pub there, too!
Josephine had been living in this tiny, 160 sq. ft. apartment for almost 50 years!
The manager was worried about the risks involved in living all by herself.
So he helped her out when she had a problem in her apartment.
In other words, he was kind.

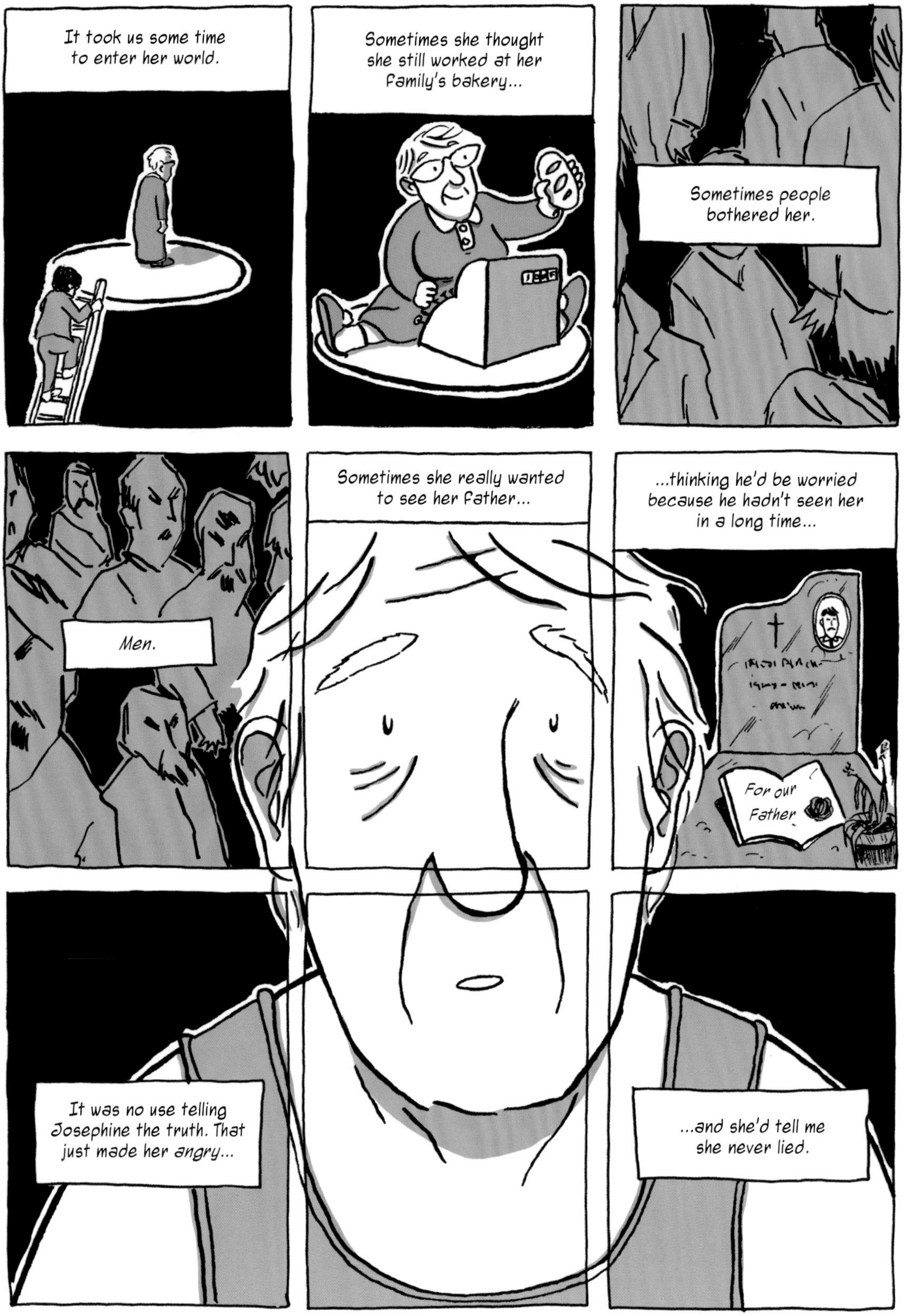
It took us some time to enter her world.
Sometimes she thought she still worked at her family's bakery...
Sometimes people bothered her.
Men.
Sometimes she really wanted to see her father...
...thinking he'd be worried because he hadn't seen her in a long time...
For our Father
It was no use telling Josephine the truth. That just made her *angry*...
...and she'd tell me she never lied.

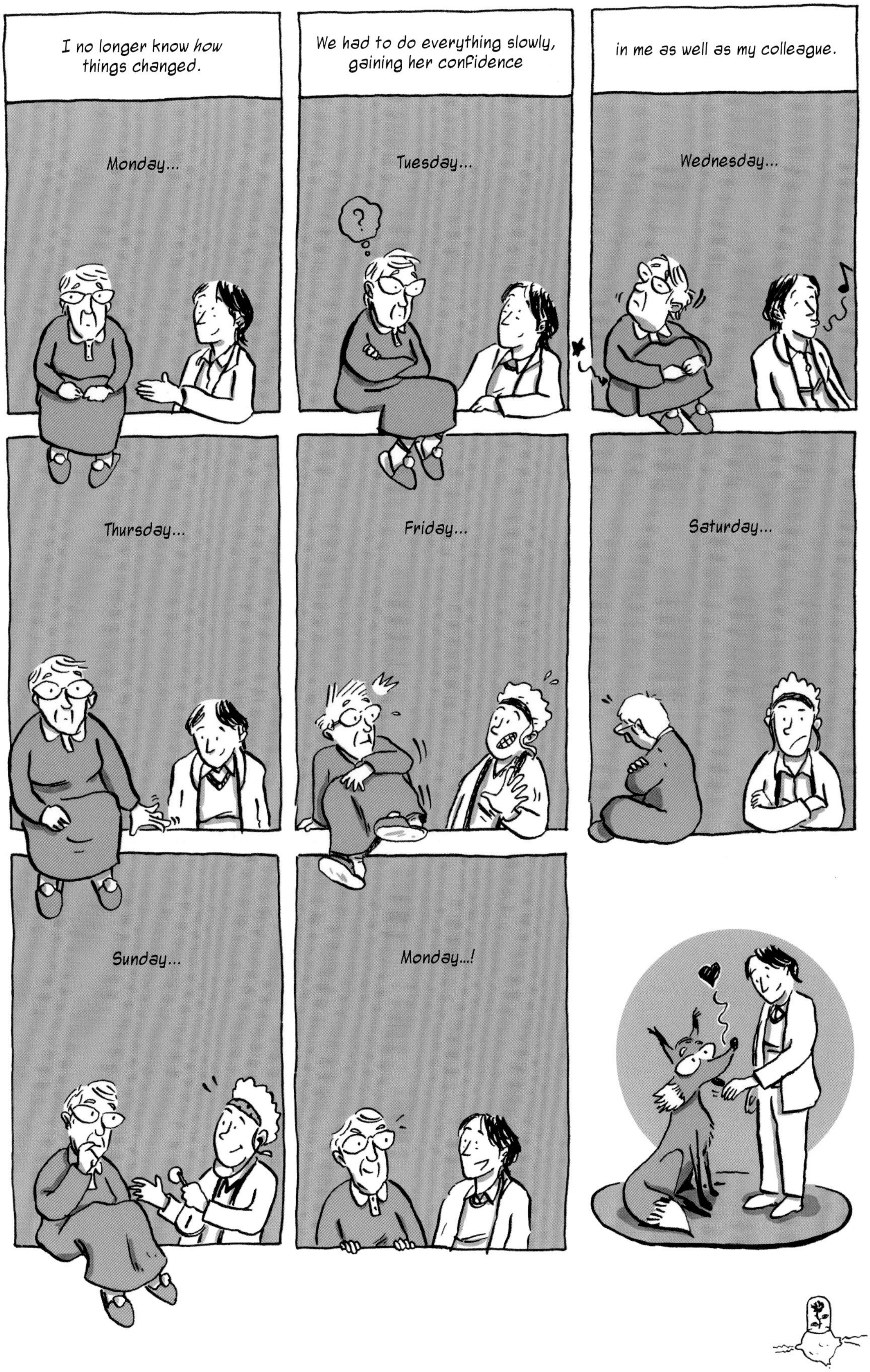
I no longer know *how* things changed.
We had to do everything slowly, gaining her confidence
in me as well as my colleague.
Monday...
Tuesday...
?
Wednesday...
Thursday...
Friday...
Saturday...
Sunday...
Monday...!

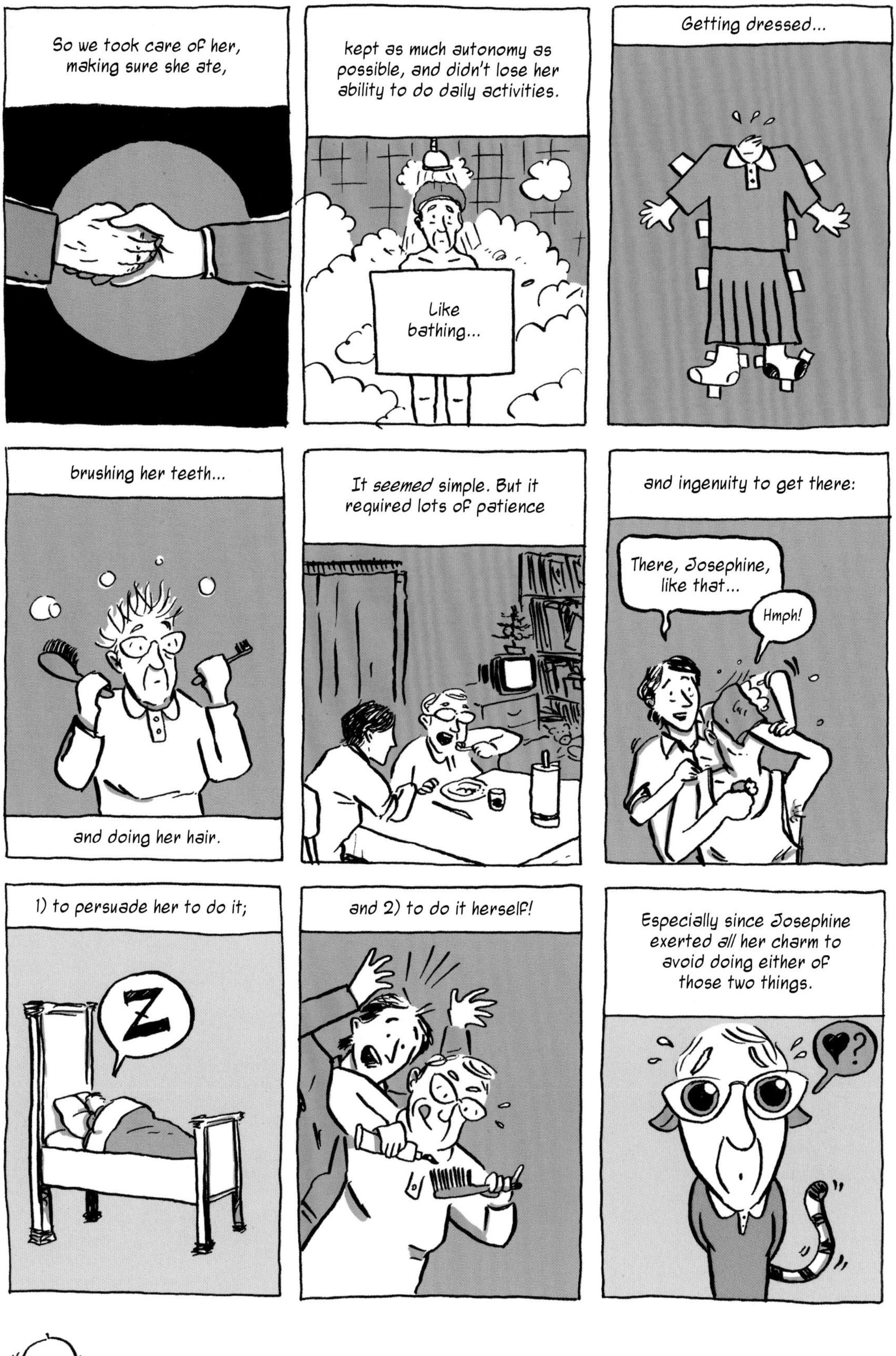
So we took care of her, making sure she ate,
kept as much autonomy as possible, and didn't lose her ability to do daily activities.
Like bathing...
Getting dressed...
brushing her teeth...
and doing her hair.
It *seemed* simple. But it required lots of patience
and ingenuity to get there:
There, Josephine, like that...
Hmph!
1) to persuade her to do it;
Z
and 2) to do it herself!
Especially since Josephine exerted *all* her charm to avoid doing either of those two things.
?

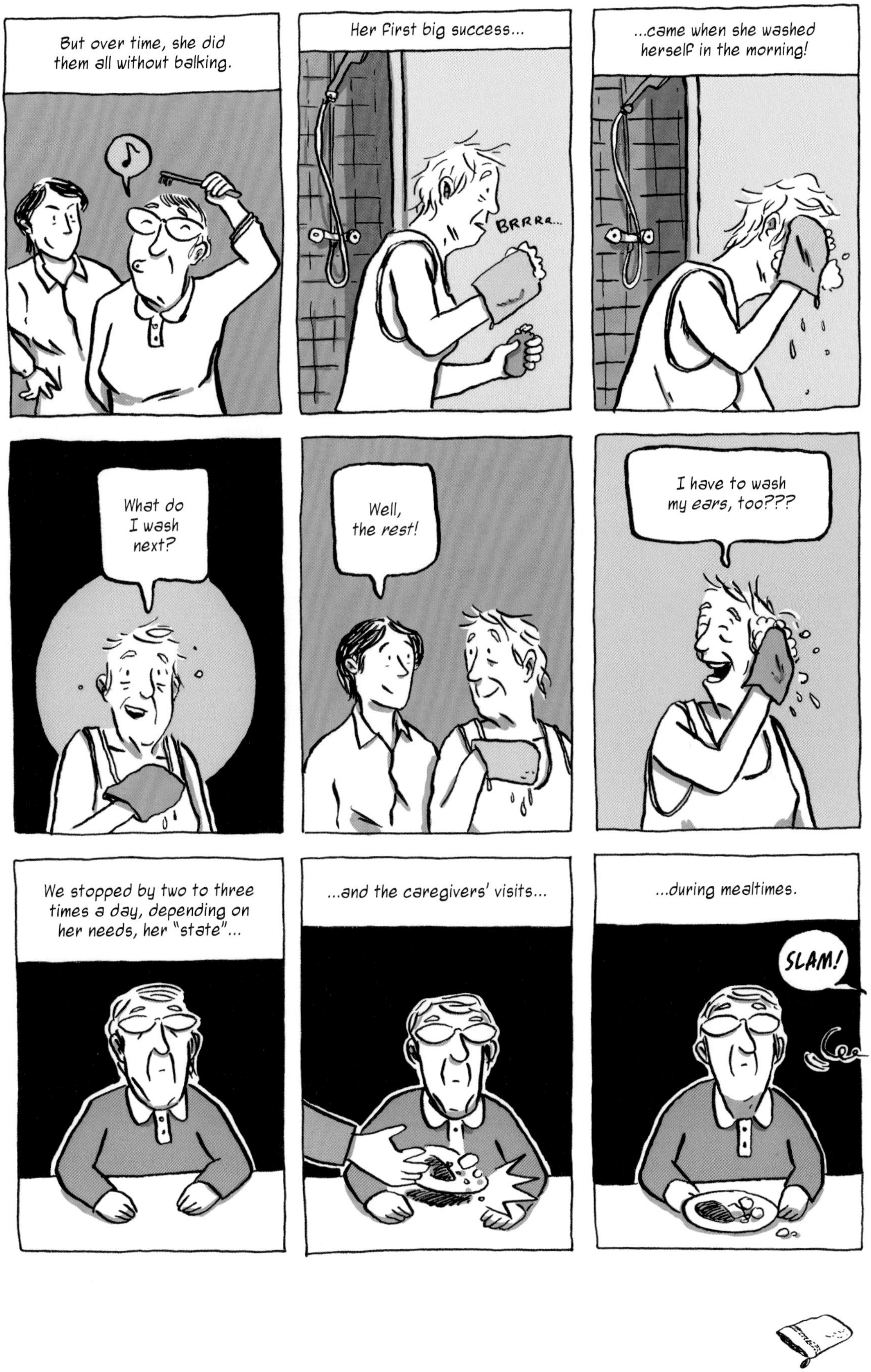

But over time, she did them all without balking.
♪
Her first big success...
BRRRR...
...came when she washed herself in the morning!
What do I wash next?
Well, the *rest*!
I have to wash my *ears*, too???
We stopped by two to three times a day, depending on her needs, her "state"...
...and the caregivers' visits...
...during mealtimes.
SLAM!

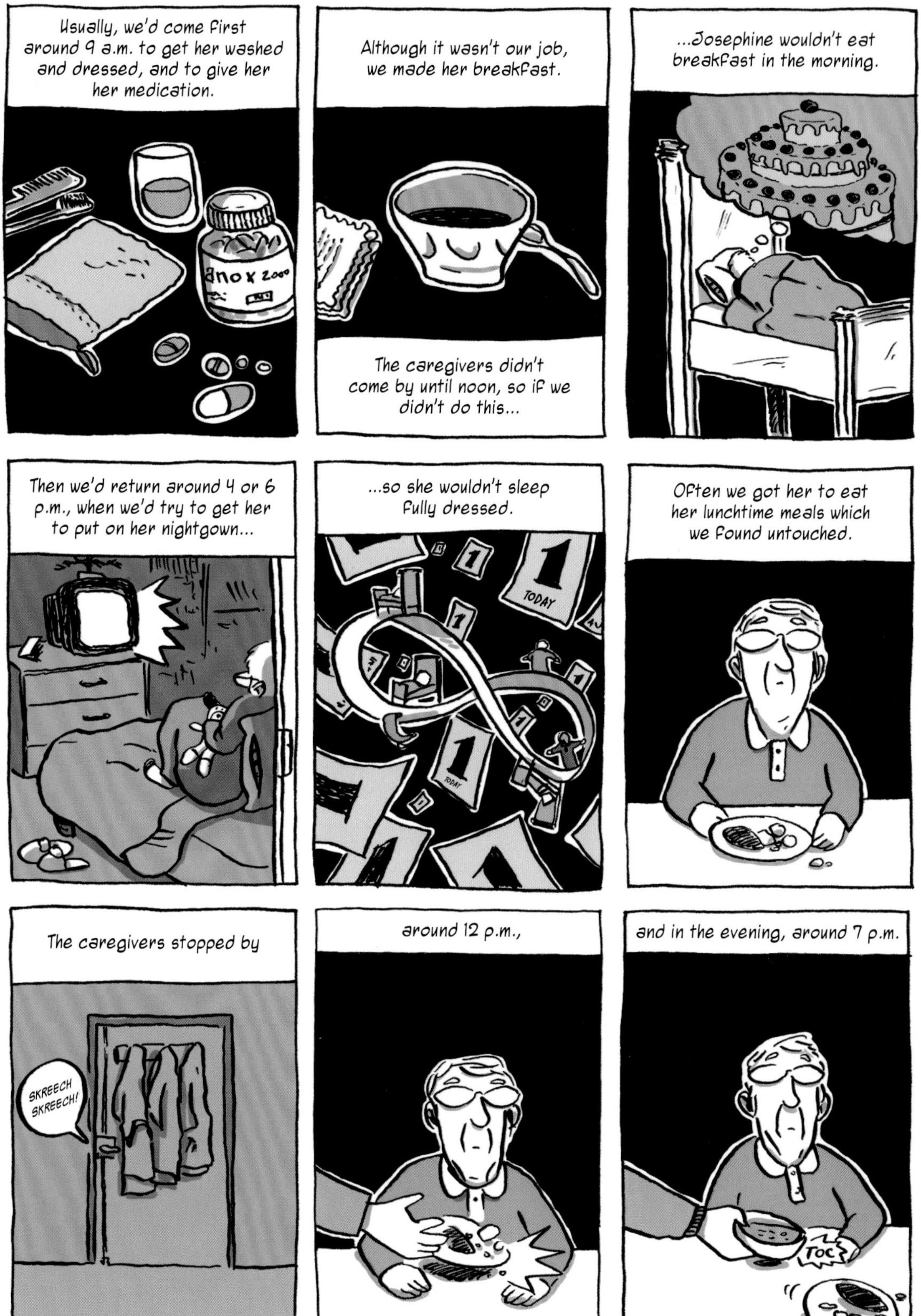
Usually, we'd come first around 9 a.m. to get her washed and dressed, and to give her her medication.
Although it wasn't our job, we made her breakfast.
The caregivers didn't come by until noon, so if we didn't do this...
...Josephine wouldn't eat breakfast in the morning.
Then we'd return around 4 or 6 p.m., when we'd try to get her to put on her nightgown...
...so she wouldn't sleep fully dressed.
TODAY
TODAY
Often we got her to eat her lunchtime meals which we found untouched.
The caregivers stopped by
SKREECH SKREECH!
around 12 p.m.,
and in the evening, around 7 p.m.
TOC

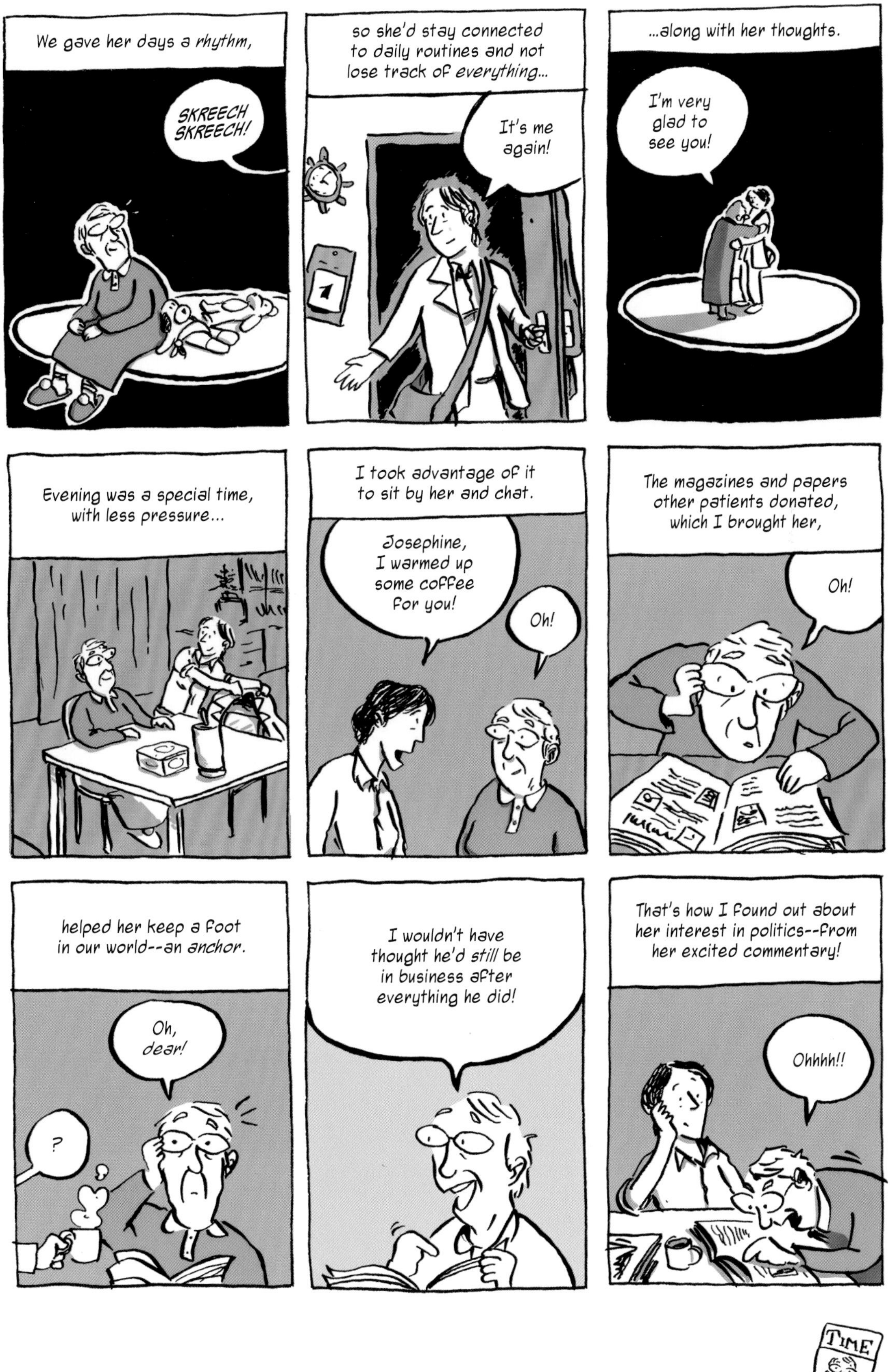
We gave her days a *rhythm,*
SKREECH SKREECH!
so she'd stay connected to daily routines and not lose track of *everything*...
It's me again!
...along with her thoughts.
I'm very glad to see you!
Evening was a special time, with less pressure...
I took advantage of it to sit by her and chat.
Josephine, I warmed up some coffee for you!
Oh!
The magazines and papers other patients donated, which I brought her,
Oh!
helped her keep a foot in our world--an *anchor*.
Oh, dear!
?
I wouldn't have thought he'd *still* be in business after everything he did!
That's how I found out about her interest in politics--from her excited commentary!
Ohhhh!!
TIME

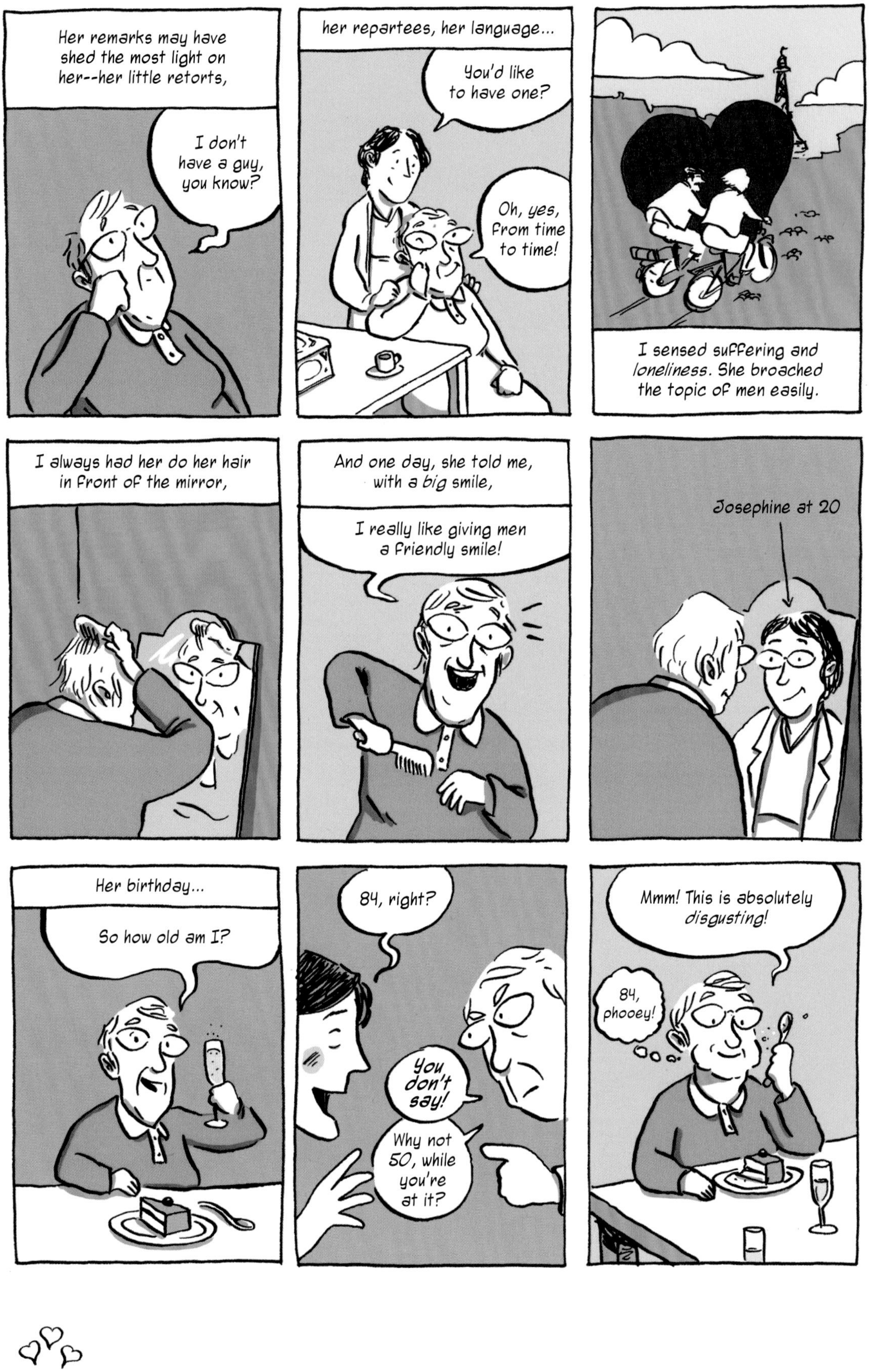
Her remarks may have shed the most light on her--her little retorts,
I don't have a guy, you know?
her repartees, her language...
You'd like to have one?
Oh, yes, from time to time!
I sensed suffering and *loneliness*. She broached the topic of men easily.
I always had her do her hair in front of the mirror,
And one day, she told me, with a *big* smile,
I really like giving men a friendly smile!
Josephine at 20
Her birthday...
So how old am I?
84, right?
You don't say!
Why not 50, while you're at it?
Mmm! This is absolutely *disgusting*!
84, phooey!

It's May 1st today, International Labor day!
1 MAY
Why should I care?
And sometimes we sang:
meow meow
One song kept coming back
It's enough to make me weep...
'Cause I'm fast asleep...*
And another one, too!
'TIS THE FINAL CONFLICT
THE INNNNTERNATIONAL WORKING CLAAAASS SHALL BE THE HUMAN RACE!**
"And do you know any religious songs?" I asked.
Oh, you know, that's faded away...
We talked a lot, about everything and nothing, and I did my best to not put her on the spot...
What makes you happy?
Blah
Blah
Blah
Blah
Blah
Blah
Blah
...by never asking her exact questions about her past.
Being with my family!
I never had words with my mother!
What is happiness?
It's being happy!
Thanks, Josephine!

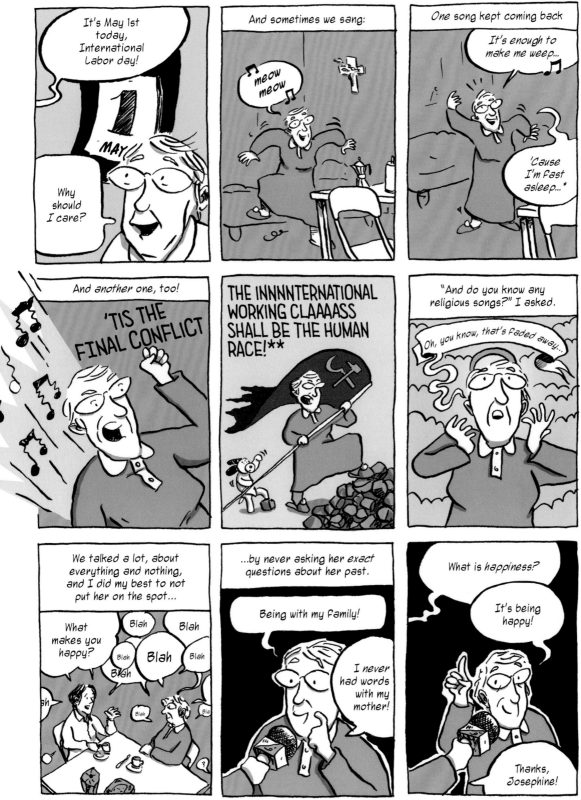

* Adapted from "The General's Fast Asleep", A 1935 military fox-trot originally recorded by Vera Lynn.
** "The International" (1871), a leftist wartime anthem written by Eugene Pottier, adapted in the United States by Charles Hope Kerr.

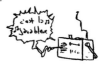

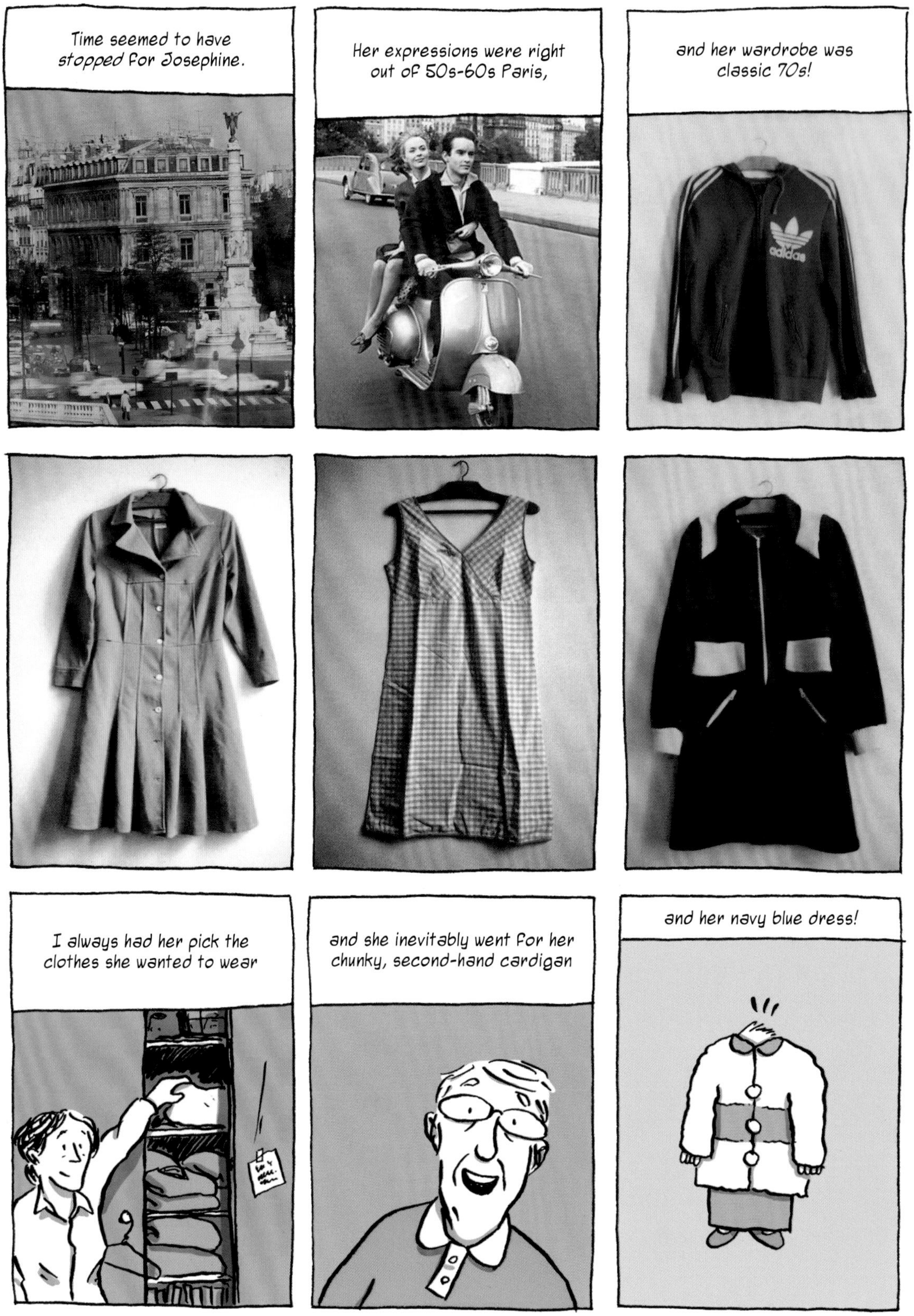
Time seemed to have stopped for Josephine.
Her expressions were right out of 50s-60s Paris,
and her wardrobe was classic 70s!
adidas
I always had her pick the clothes she wanted to wear
and she inevitably went for her chunky, second-hand cardigan
and her navy blue dress!

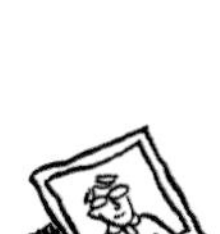

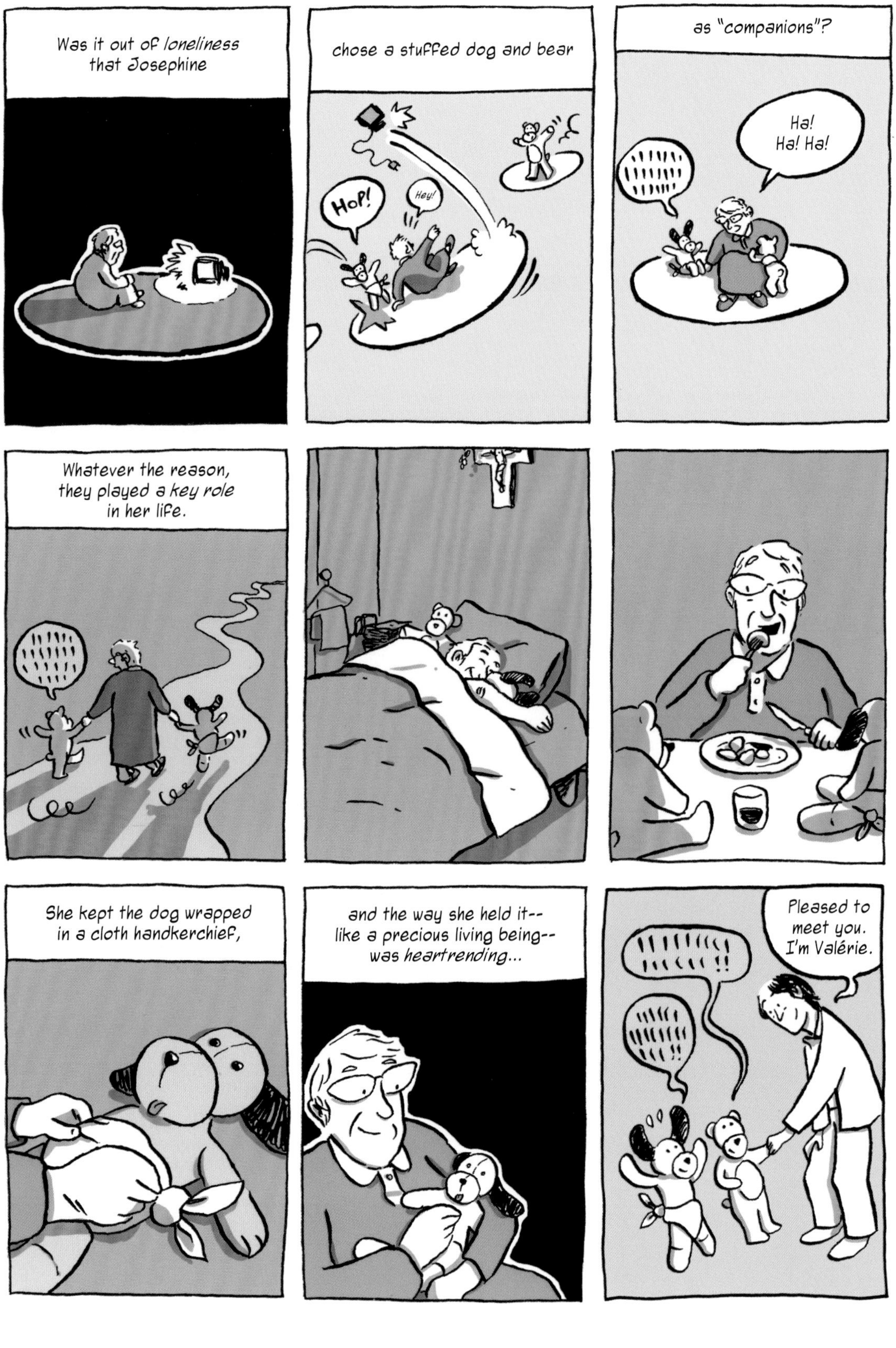
Was it out of *loneliness* that Josephine
chose a stuffed dog and bear
HOP!
Hey!
as "companions"?
!!!!!!!
Ha! Ha! Ha!
Whatever the reason, they played a *key role* in her life.
She kept the dog wrapped in a cloth handkerchief,
and the way she held it-- like a precious living being-- was *heartrending*...
Pleased to meet you. I'm Valérie.

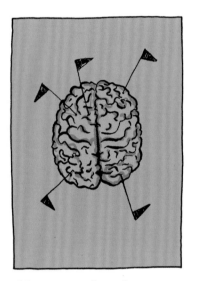

Memory is strange.

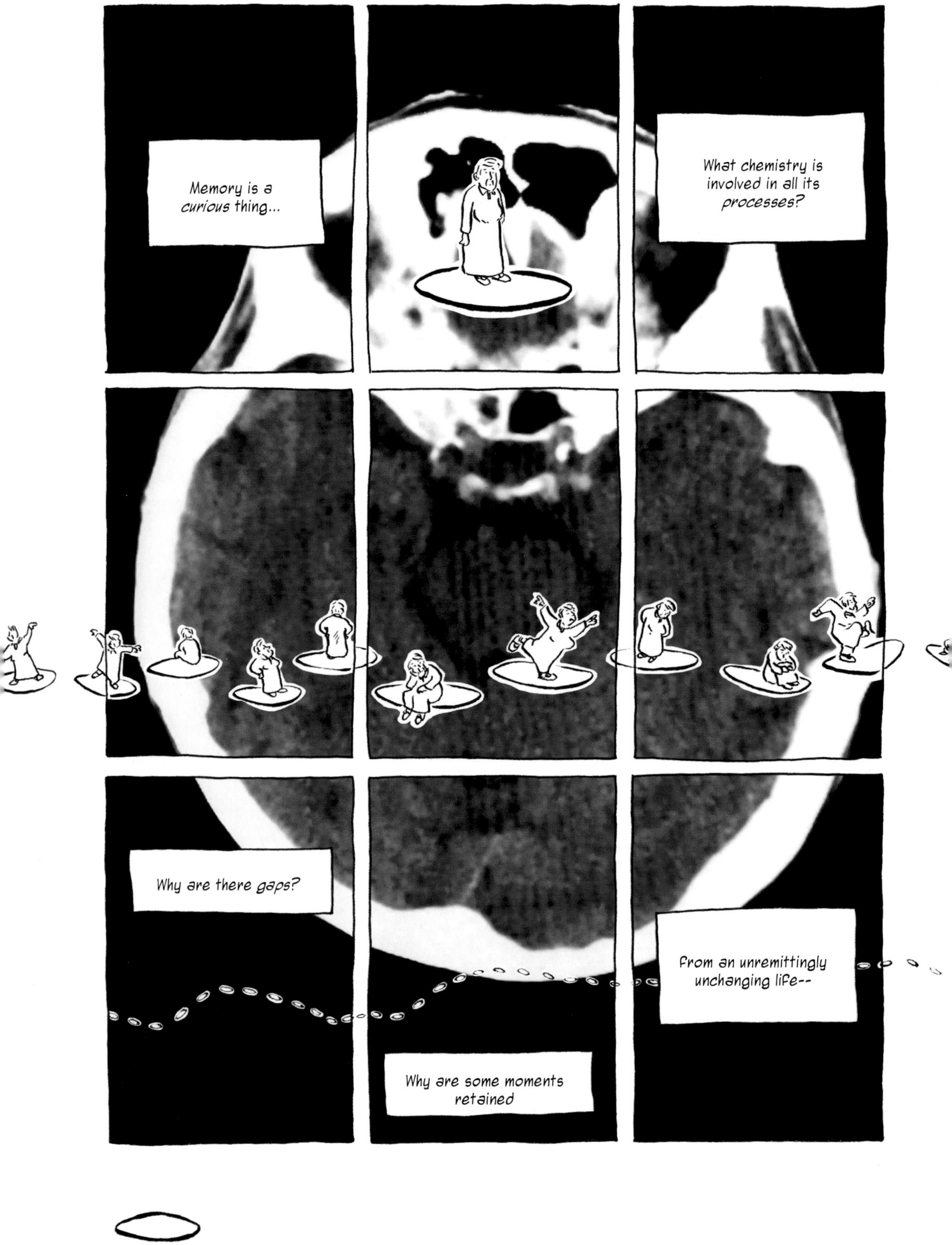

Memory is a curious thing...
What chemistry is involved in all its processes?
Why are there gaps?
Why are some moments retained
from an unremittingly unchanging life--

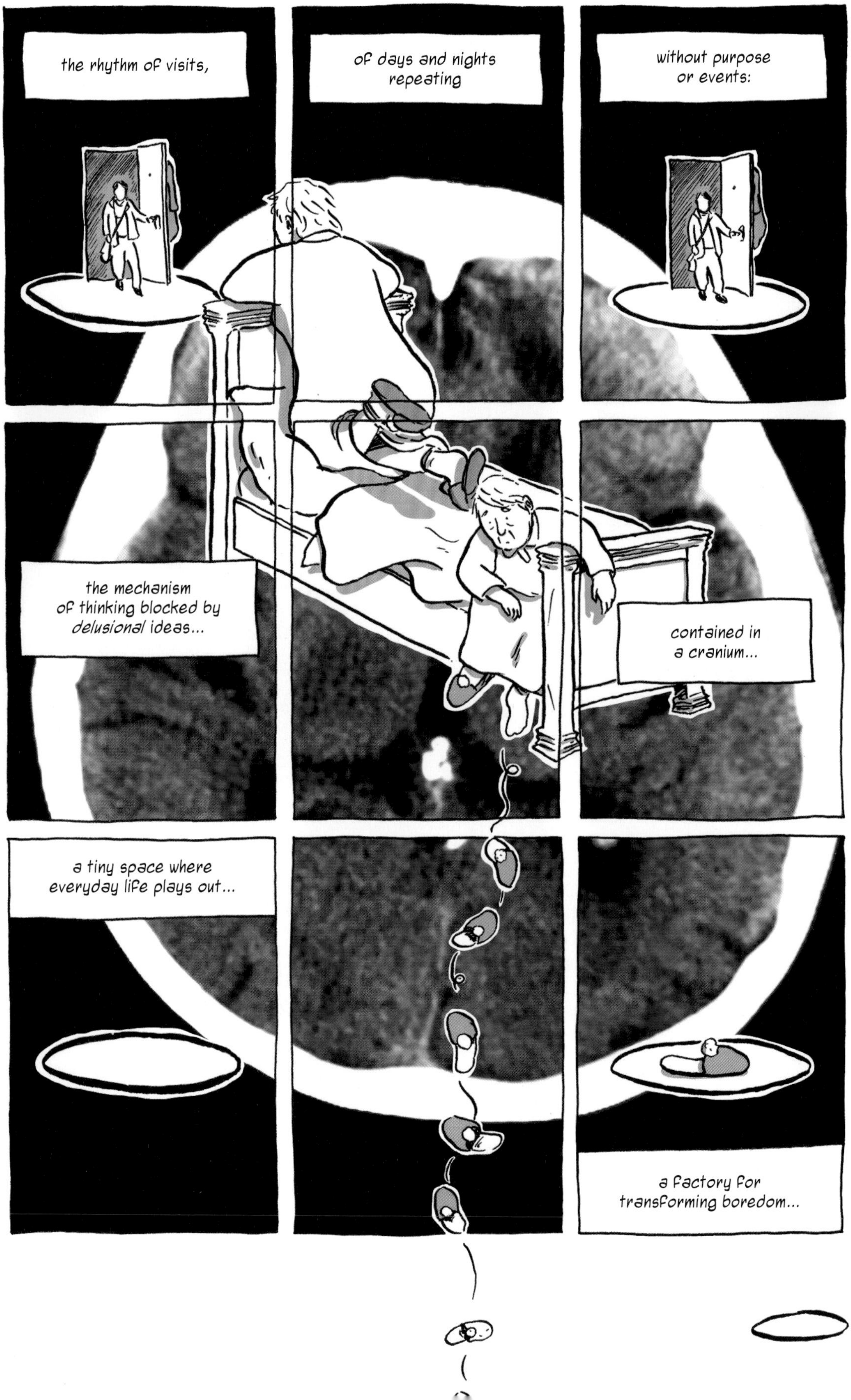

the rhythm of visits,
of days and nights repeating
without purpose or events:
the mechanism of thinking blocked by *delusional* ideas...
contained in a cranium...
a tiny space where everyday life plays out...
a factory for transforming boredom...

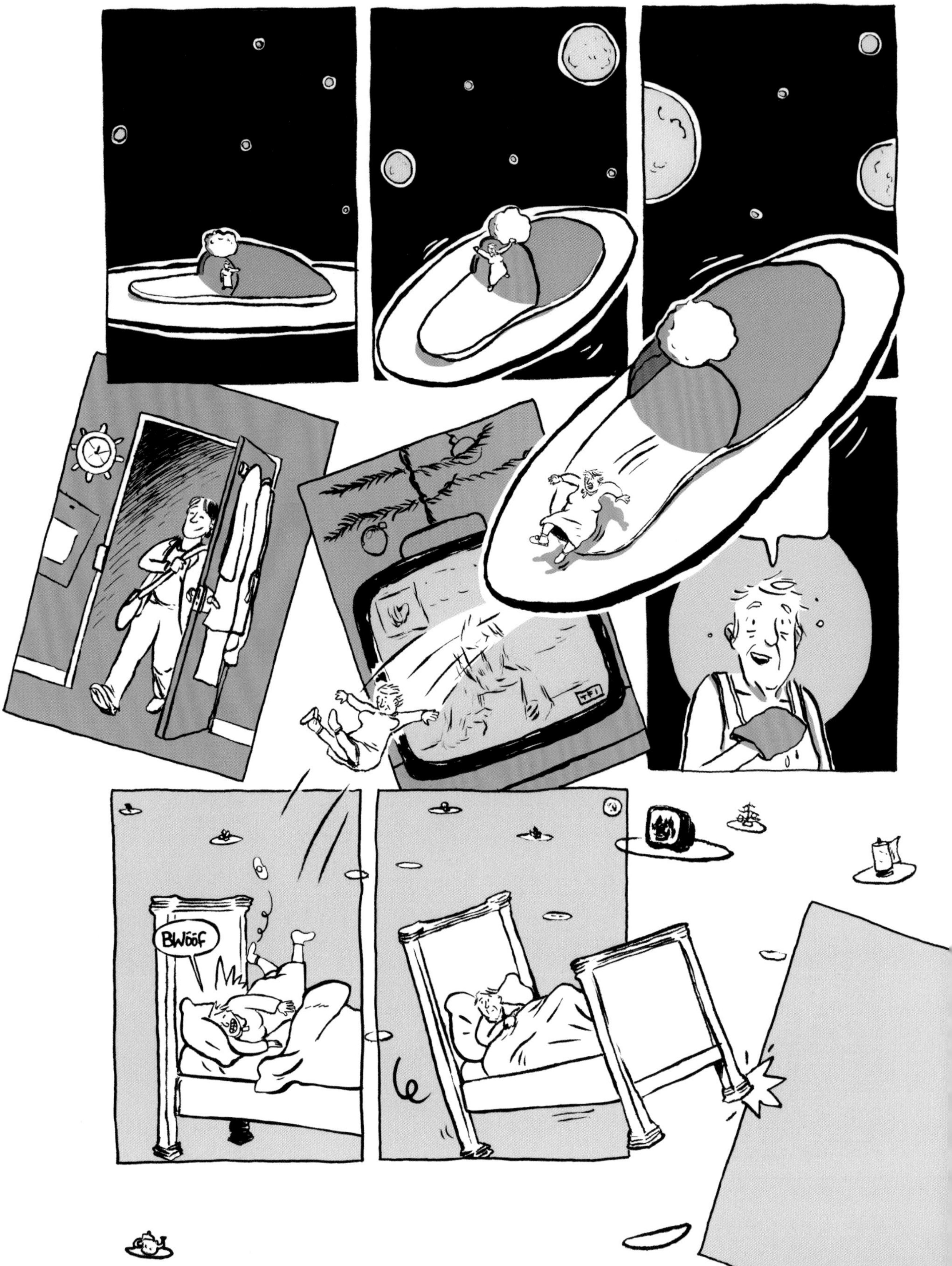
TF1
BWóóf

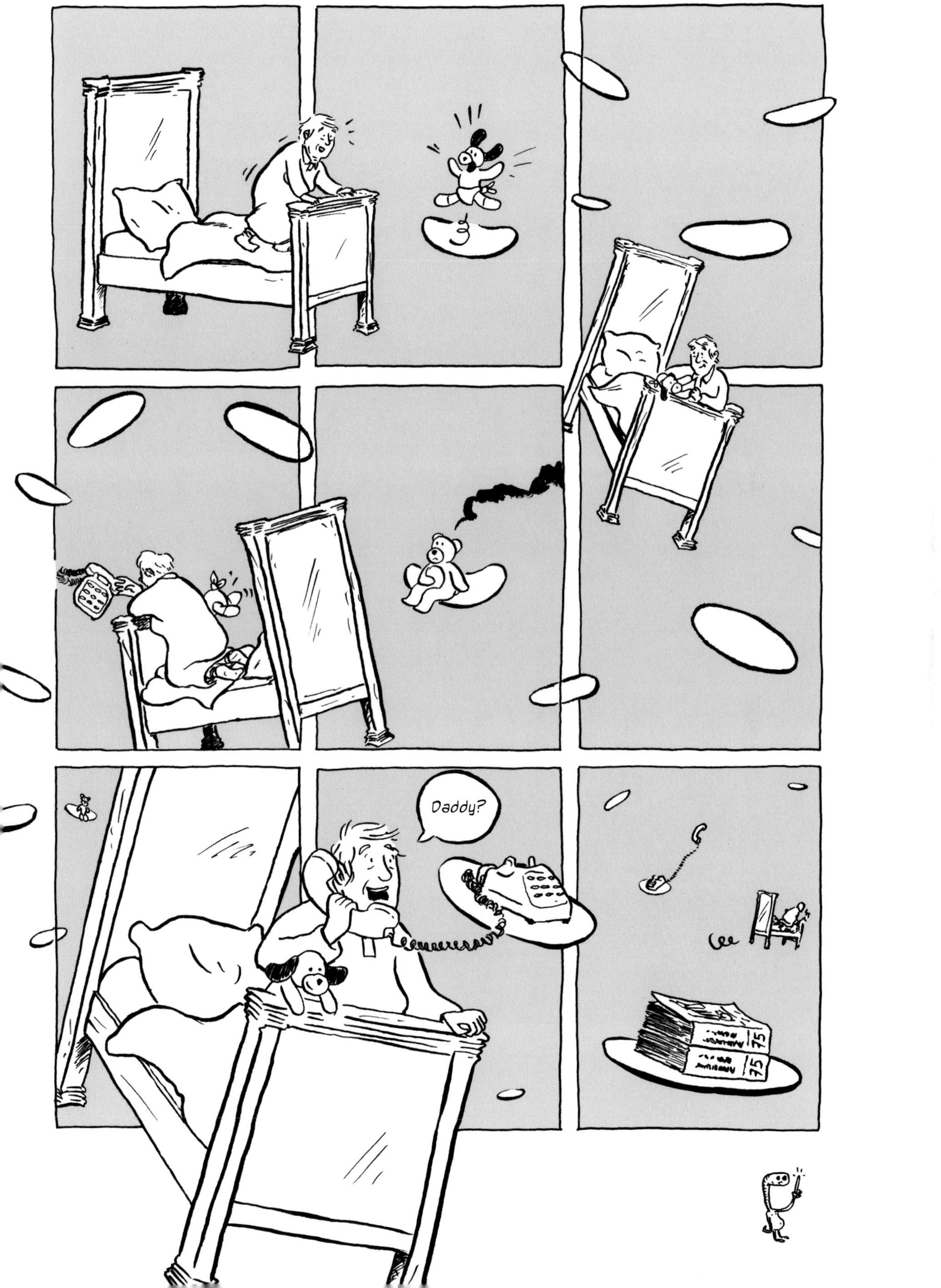
Daddy?

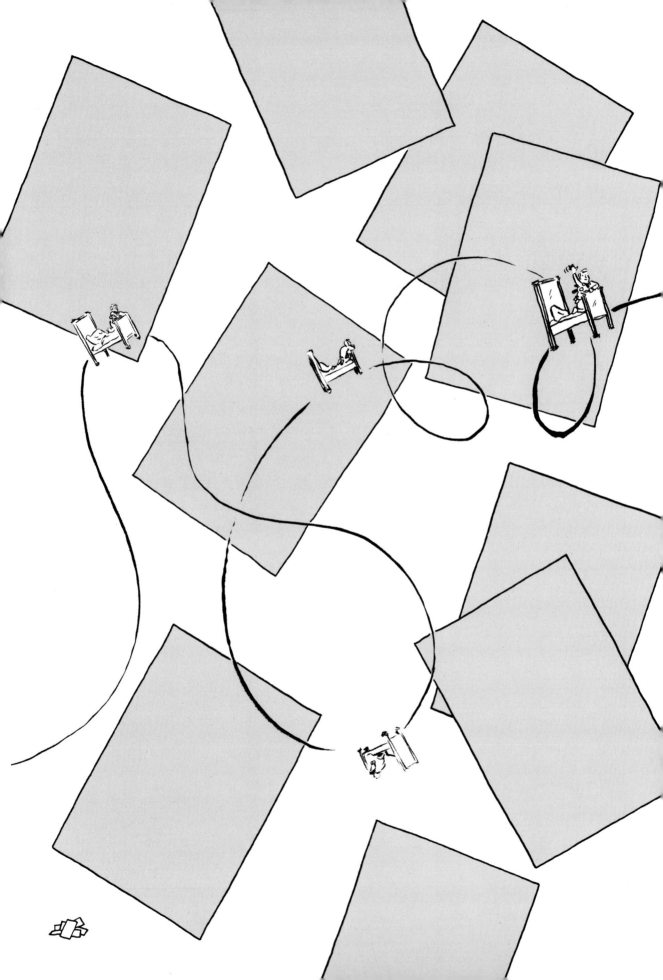

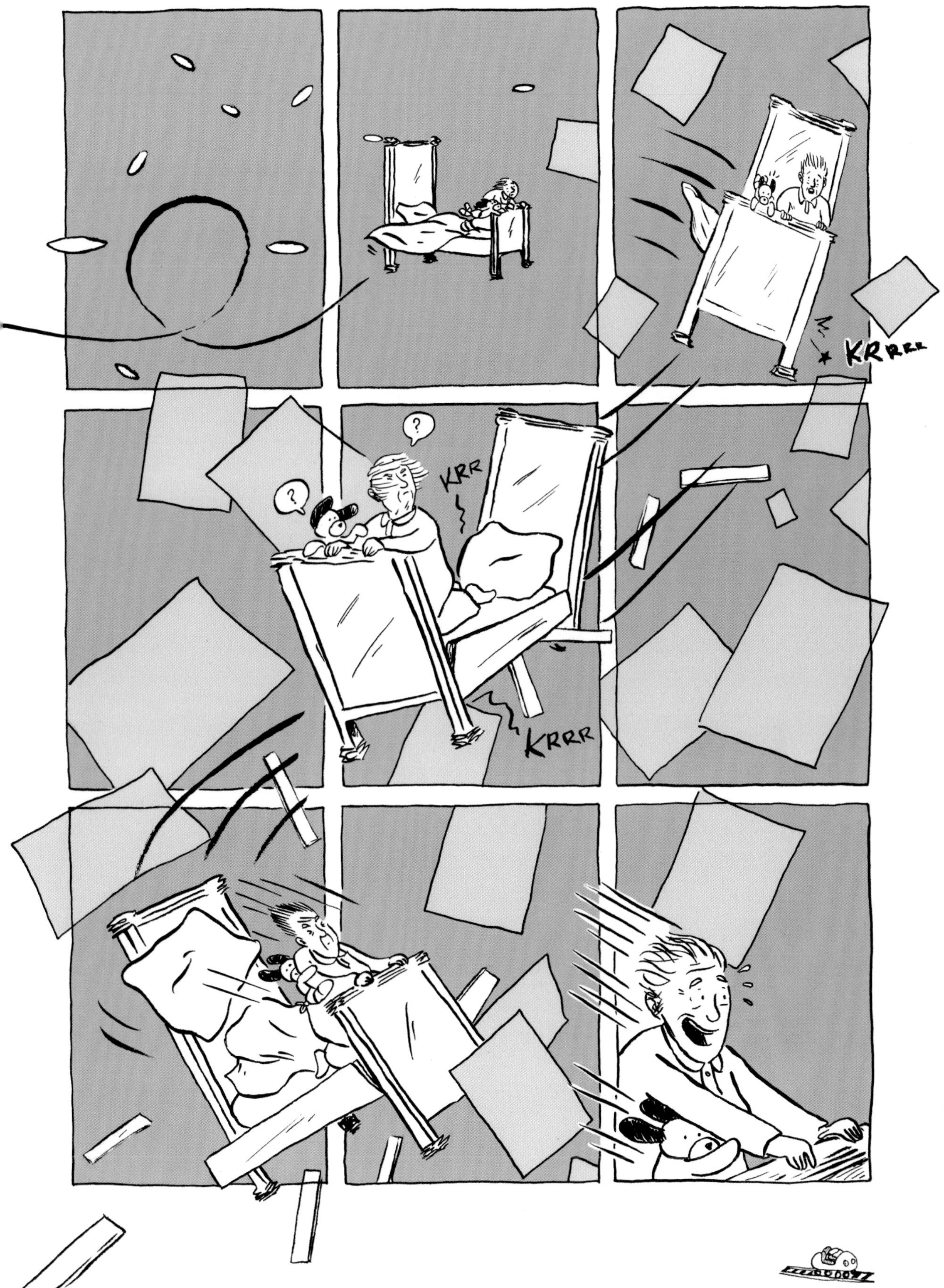
KRRRR
?
?
KRR
KRRR

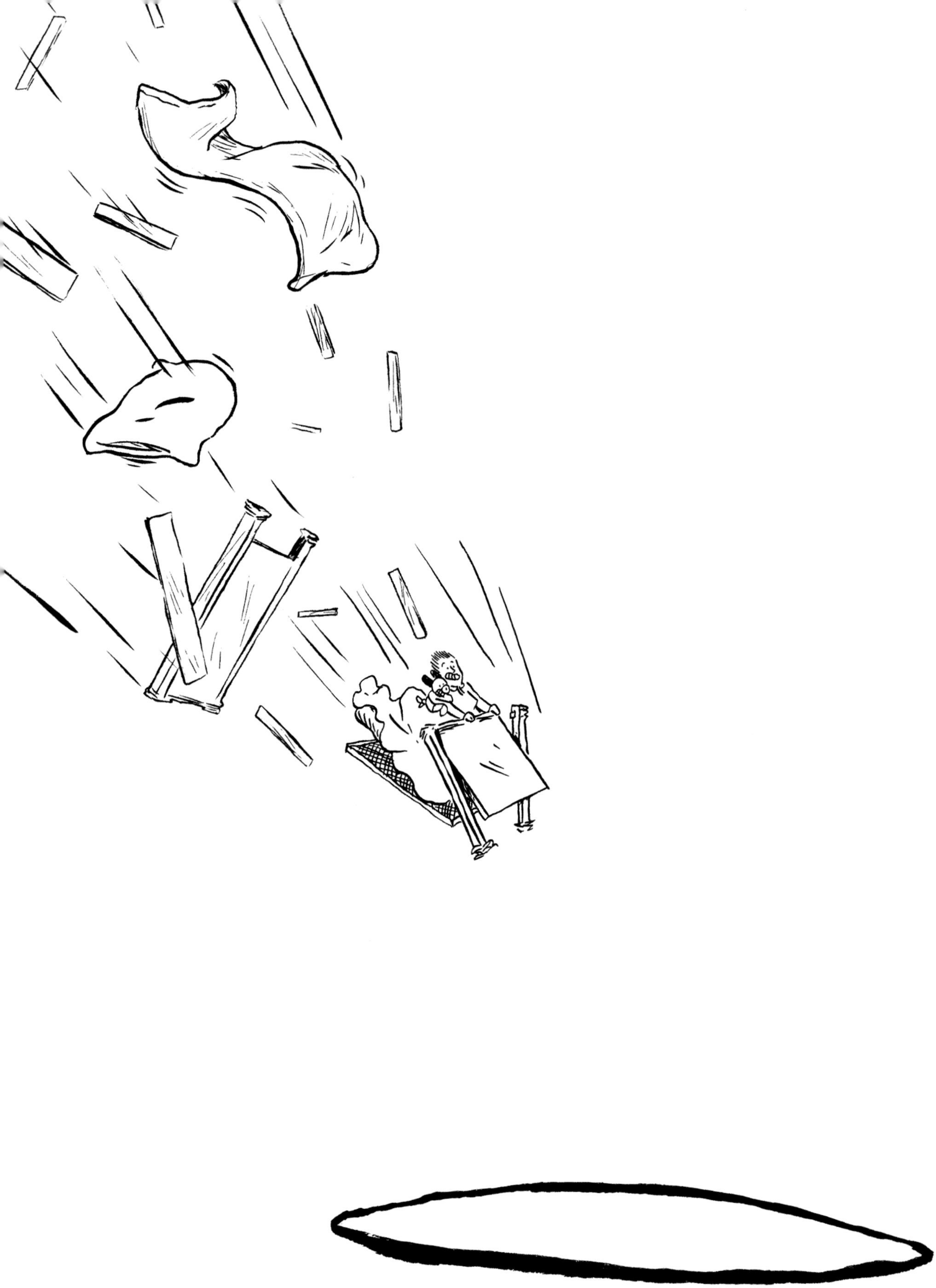

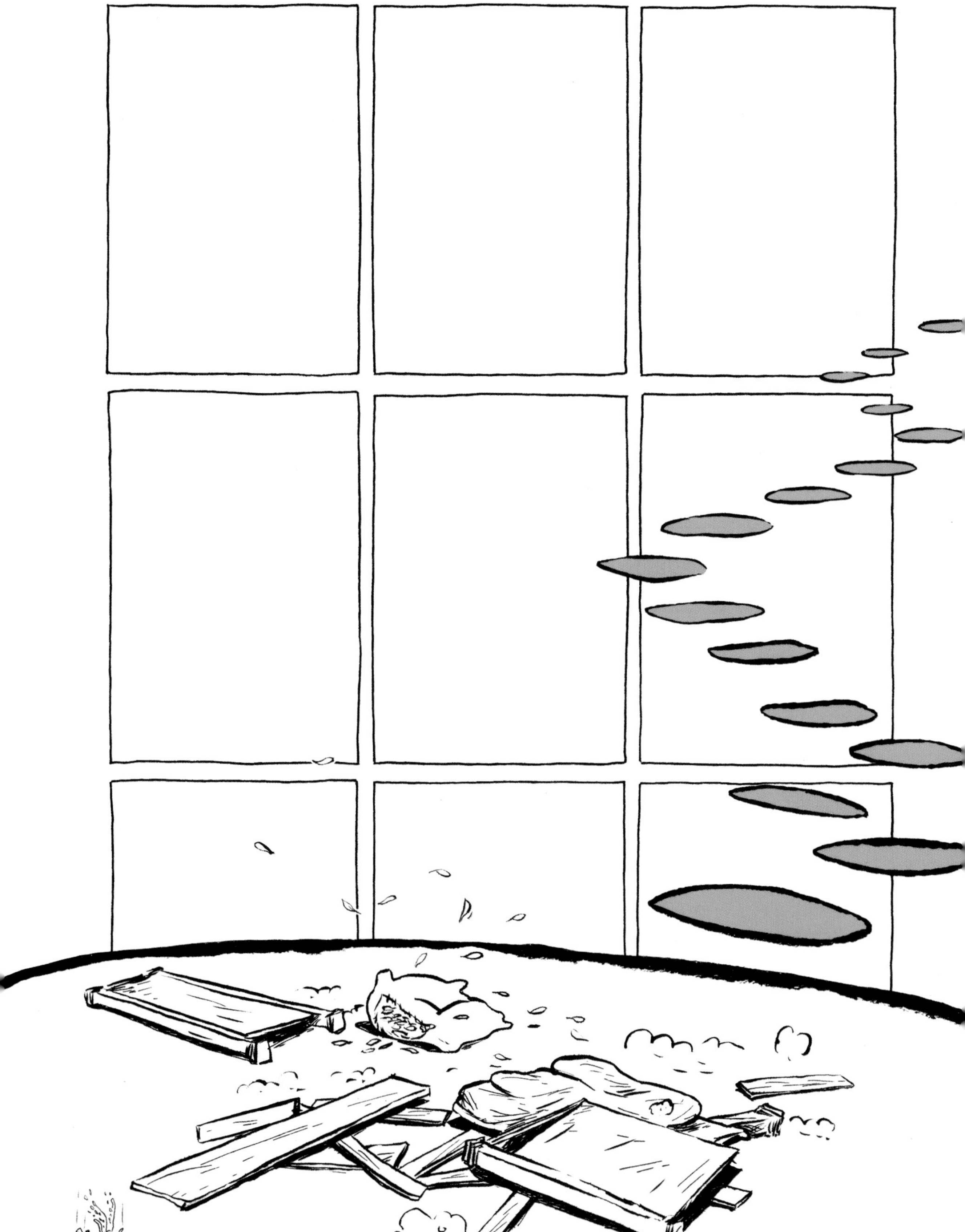

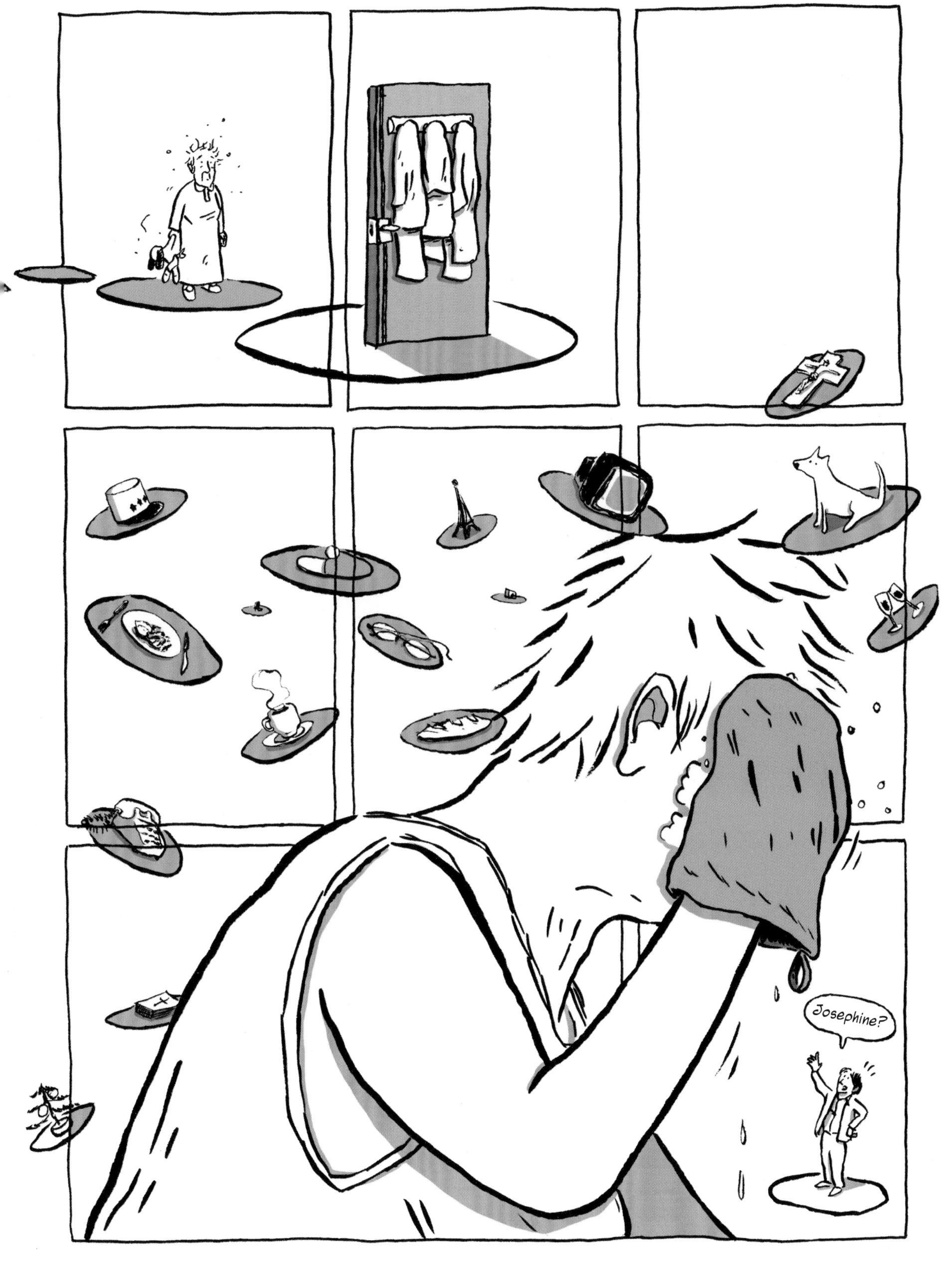
Josephine?

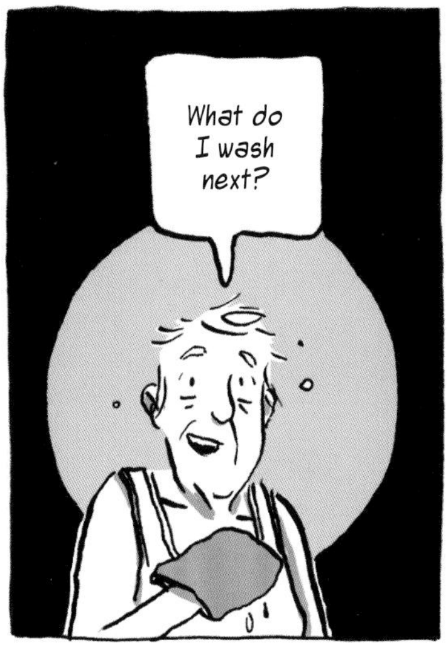
What do I wash next?

Caregivers?

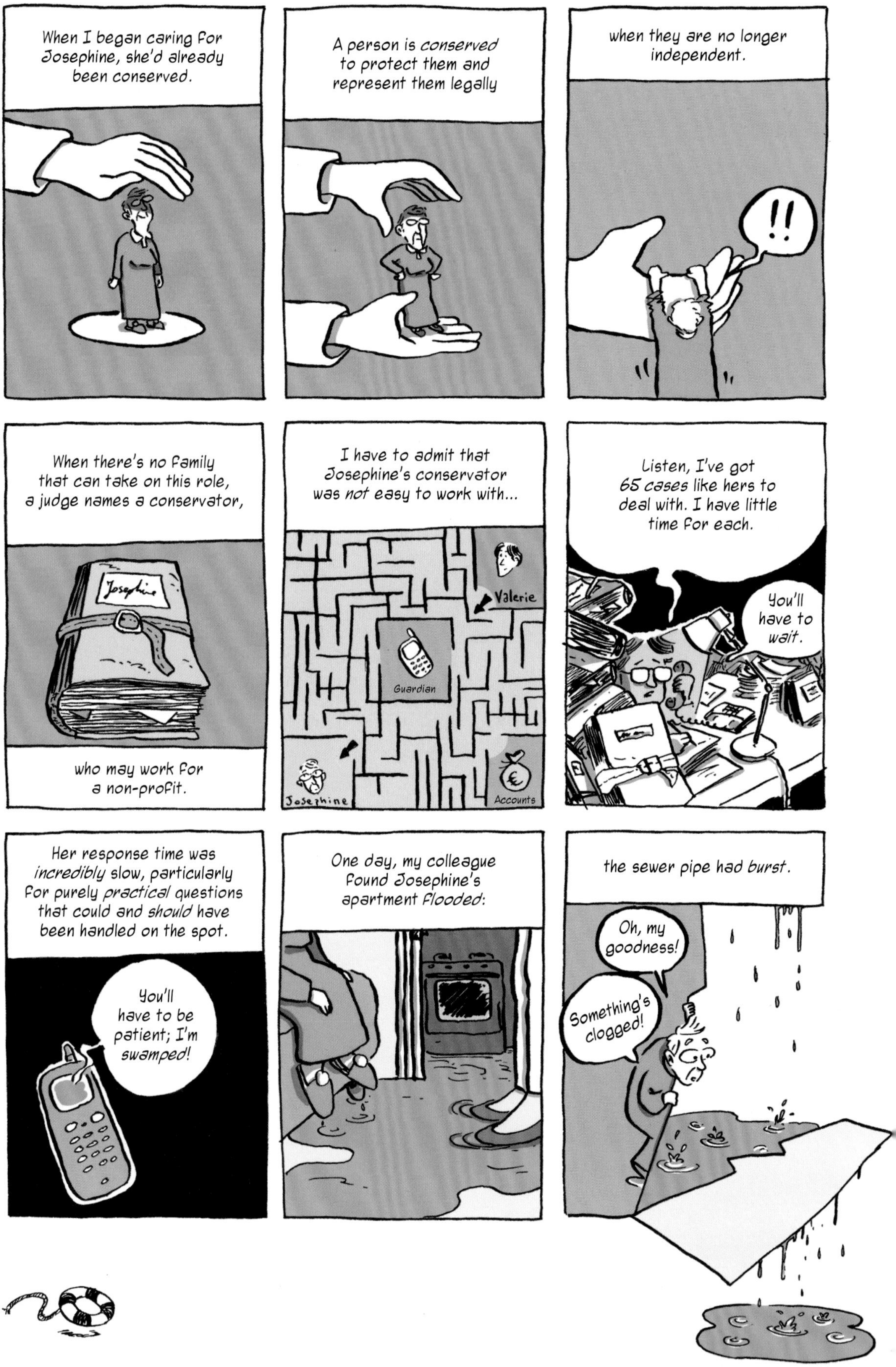
When I began caring for Josephine, she'd already been conserved.
A person is *conserved* to protect them and represent them legally
when they are no longer independent.
!!
When there's no family that can take on this role, a judge names a conservator,
Josephine
who may work for a non-profit.
I have to admit that Josephine's conservator was *not* easy to work with...
Valerie
Guardian
Josephine
Accounts
Listen, I've got *65 cases* like hers to deal with. I have little time for each.
You'll have to *wait*.
Her response time was *incredibly* slow, particularly for purely *practical* questions that could and *should* have been handled on the spot.
You'll have to be patient; I'm *swamped*!
One day, my colleague found Josephine's apartment *flooded*:
the sewer pipe had *burst*.
Oh, my goodness!
Something's clogged!

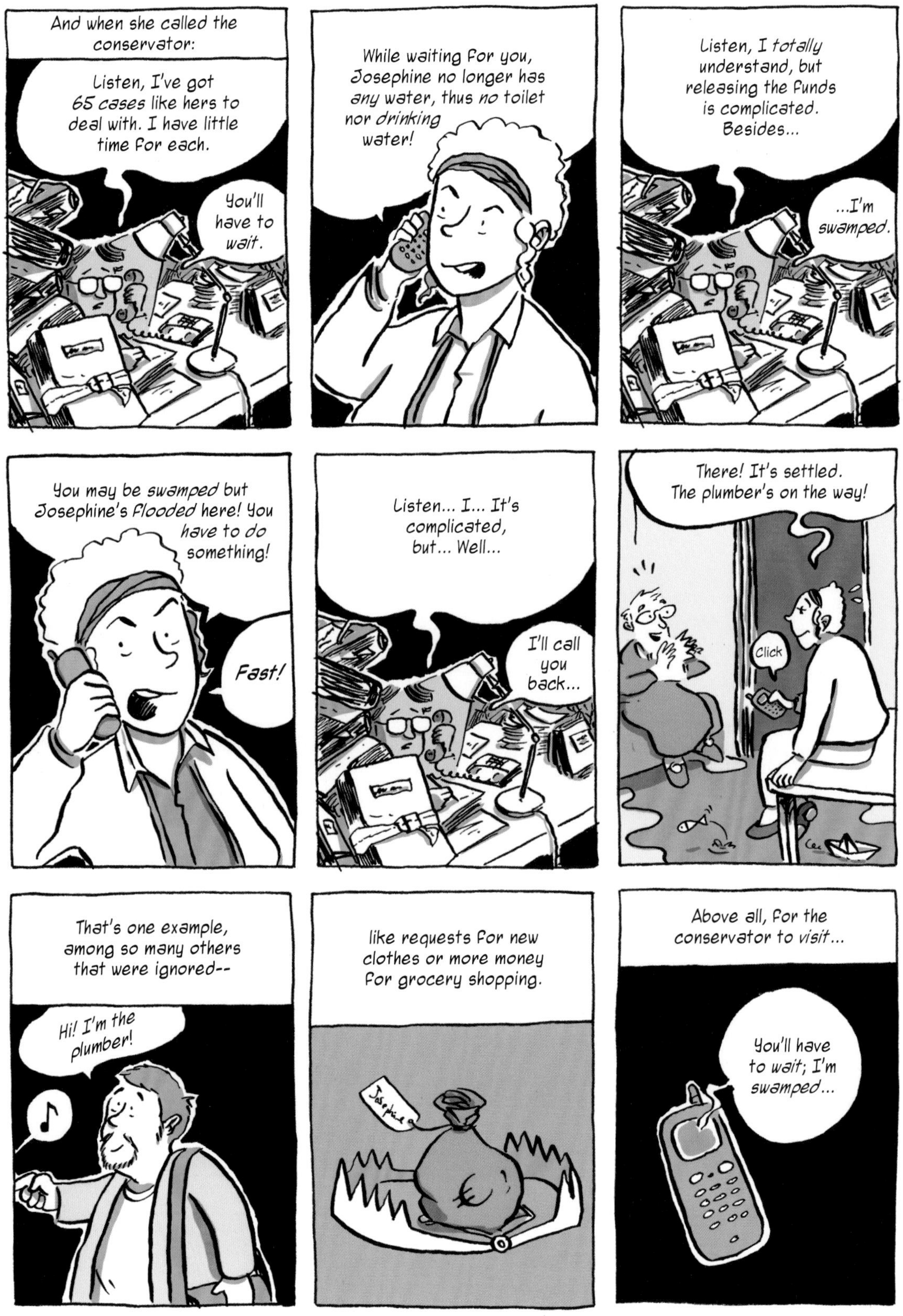
And when she called the conservator:
Listen, I've got 65 cases like hers to deal with. I have little time for each.
You'll have to wait.
While waiting for you, Josephine no longer has any water, thus no toilet nor drinking water!
Listen, I totally understand, but releasing the funds is complicated. Besides...
...I'm swamped.
You may be swamped but Josephine's flooded here! You have to do something!
Fast!
Listen... I... It's complicated, but... Well...
I'll call you back...
There! It's settled. The plumber's on the way!
Click
That's one example, among so many others that were ignored--
Hi! I'm the plumber!
like requests for new clothes or more money for grocery shopping.
Josephine
Above all, for the conservator to visit...
You'll have to wait; I'm swamped...

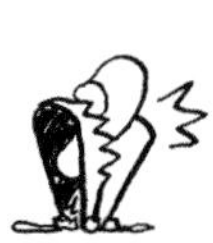

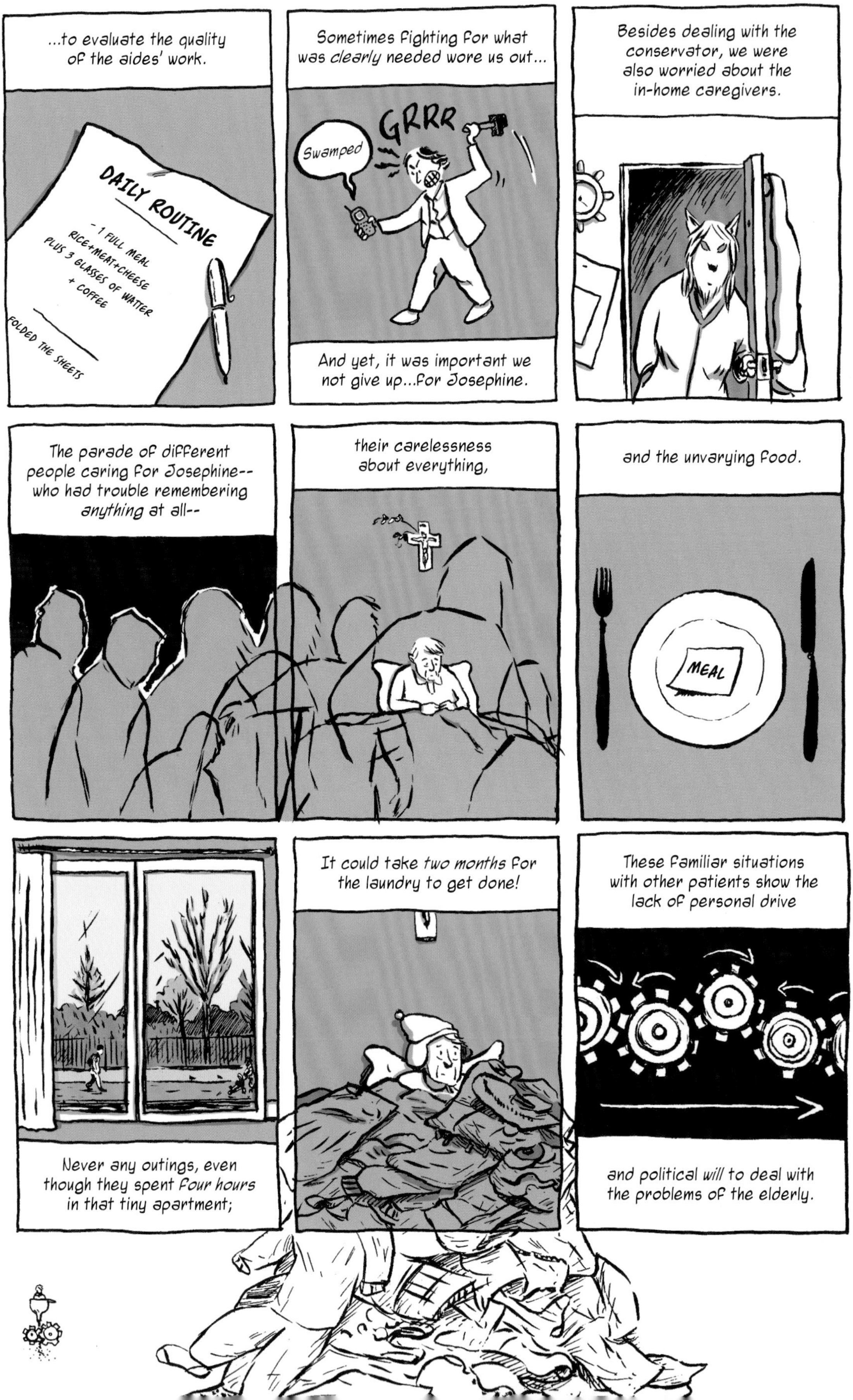
...to evaluate the quality of the aides' work.
DAILY ROUTINE
- 1 FULL MEAL
RICE+MEAT+CHEESE
PLUS 3 GLASSES OF WATER
+ COFFEE
FOLDED THE SHEETS
Sometimes fighting for what was *clearly* needed wore us out...
Swamped
GRRR
And yet, it was important we not give up...for Josephine.
Besides dealing with the conservator, we were also worried about the in-home caregivers.
The parade of different people caring for Josephine--who had trouble remembering *anything* at all--
their carelessness about everything,
and the unvarying food.
MEAL
Never any outings, even though they spent *four hours* in that tiny apartment;
It could take *two months* for the laundry to get done!
These familiar situations with other patients show the lack of personal drive
and political *will* to deal with the problems of the elderly.

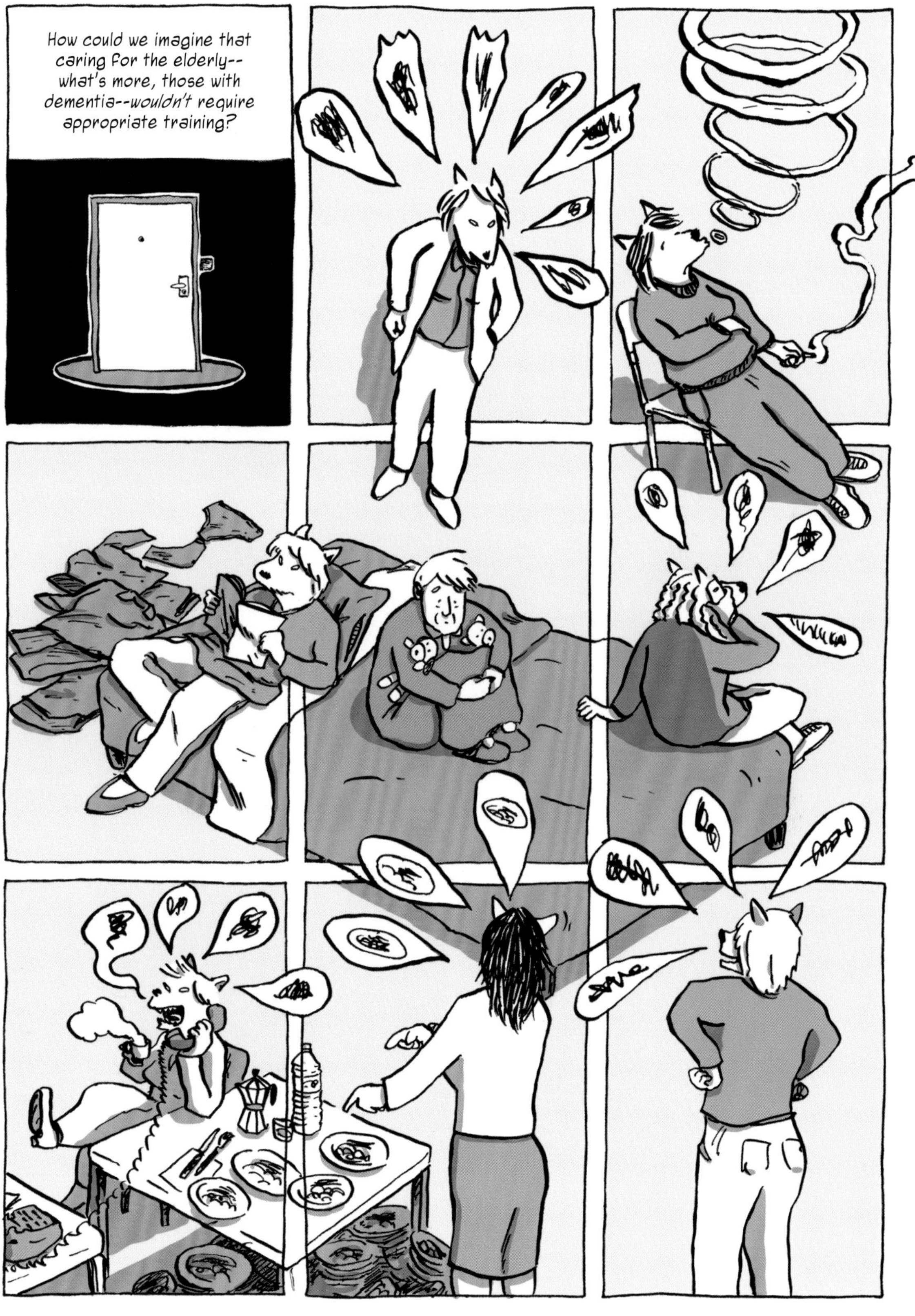
How could we imagine that caring for the elderly--what's more, those with dementia--*wouldn't* require appropriate training?

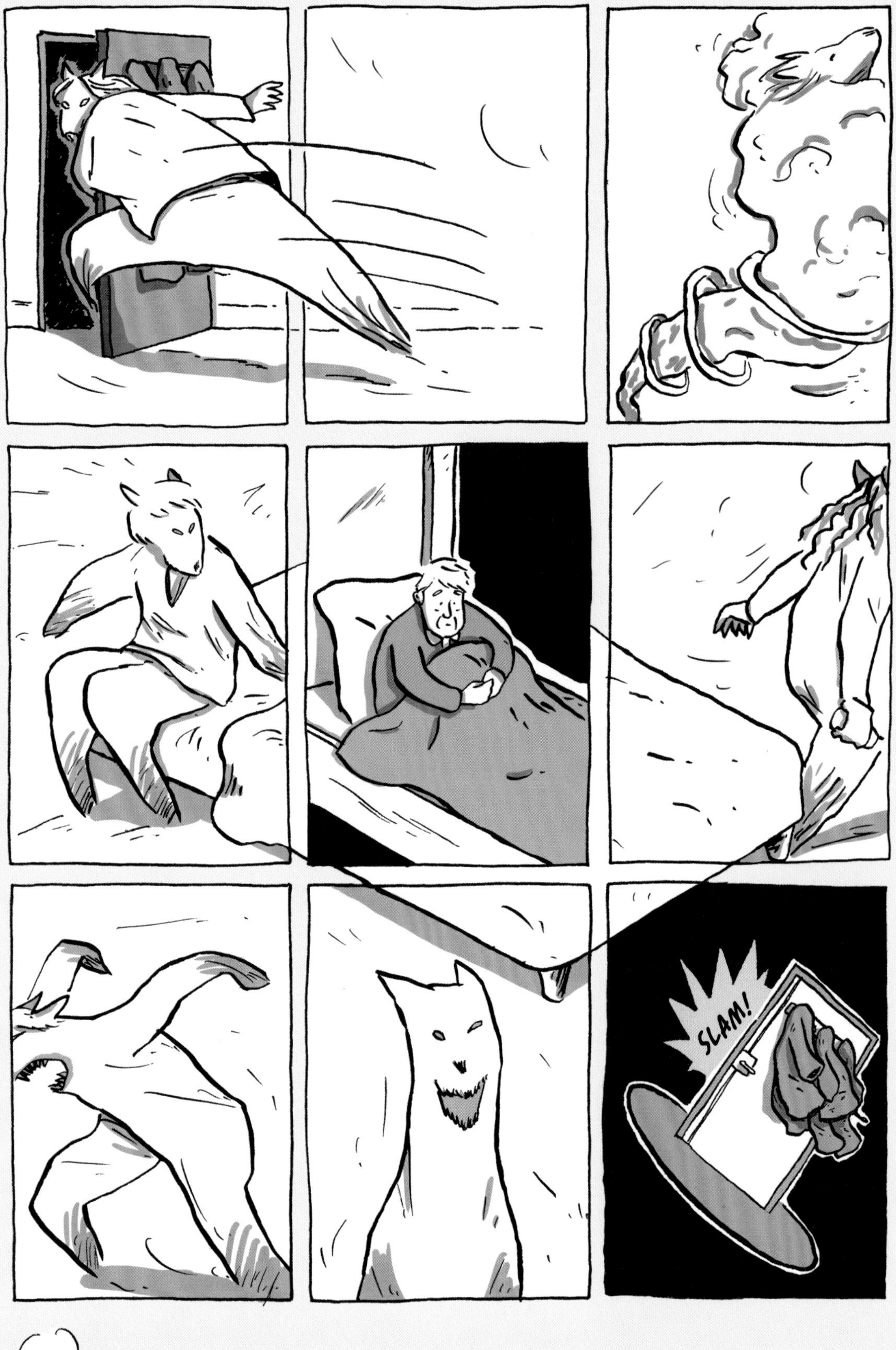
SLAM!

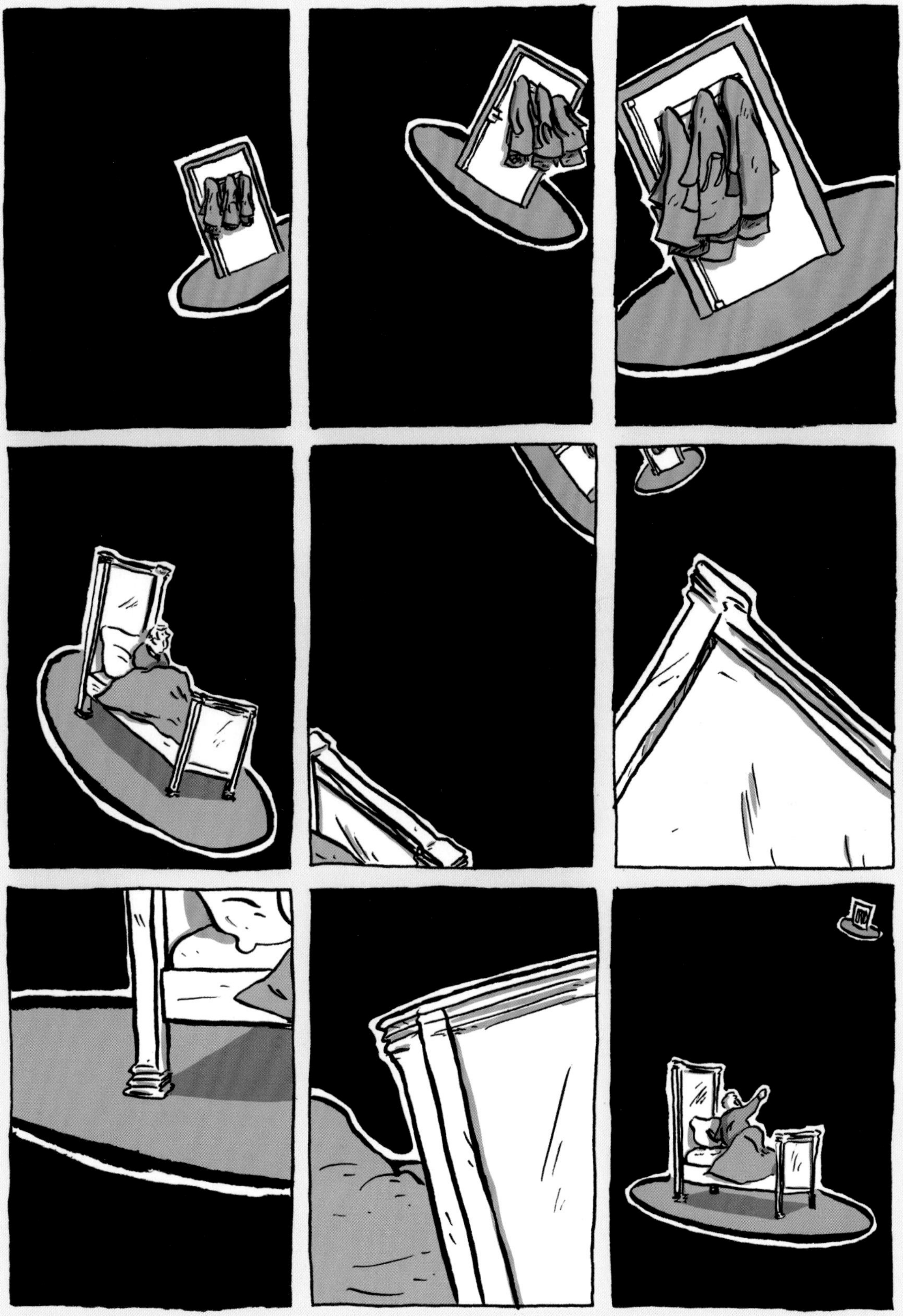

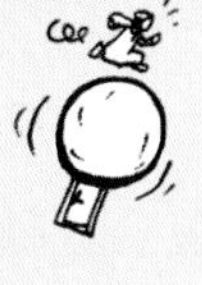

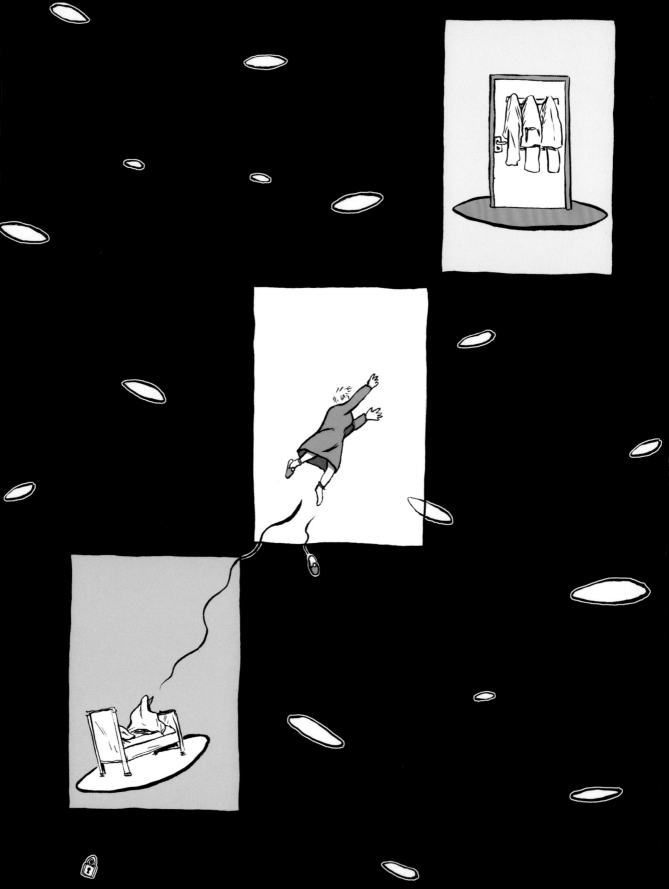

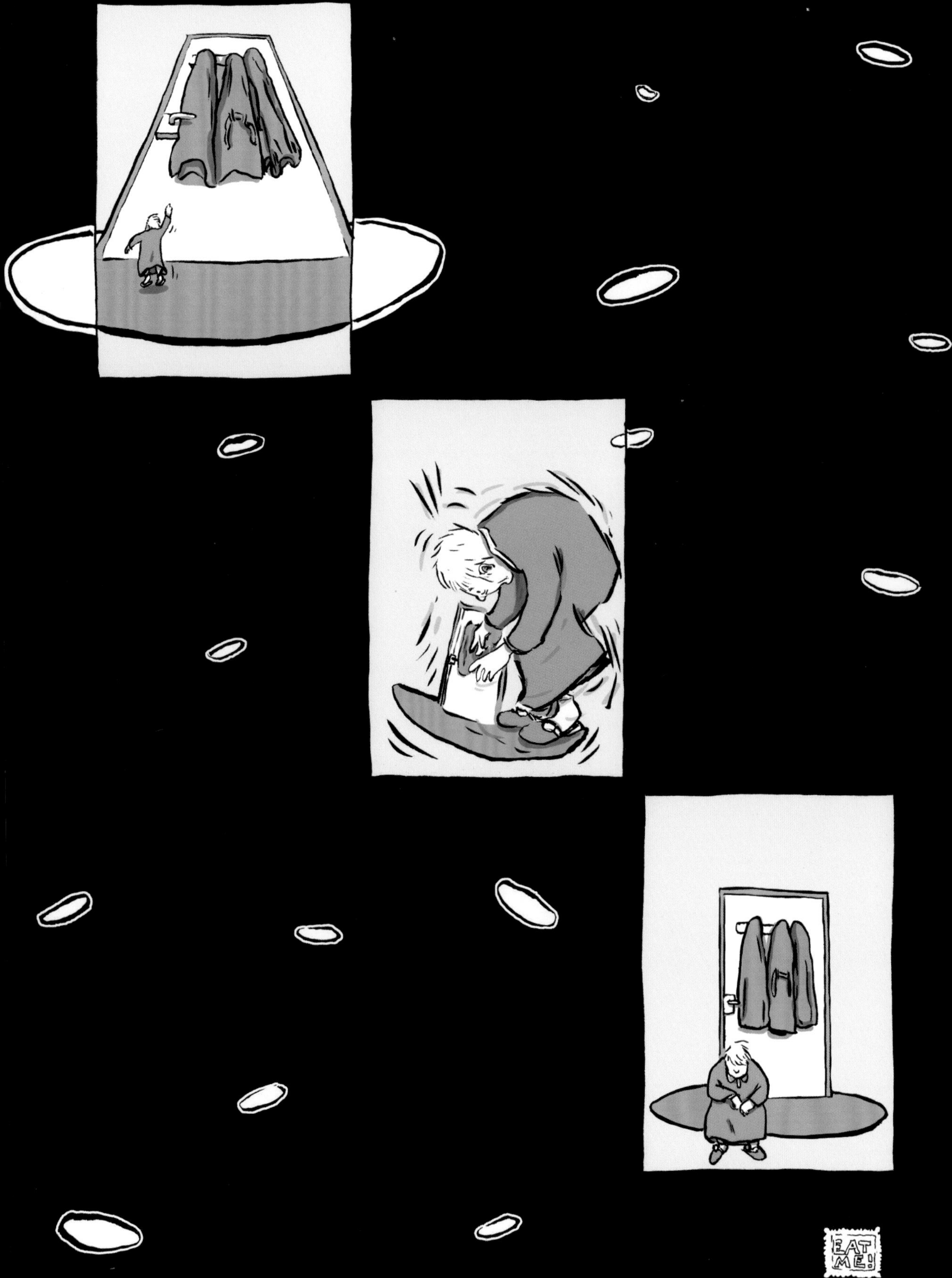
EAT ME!

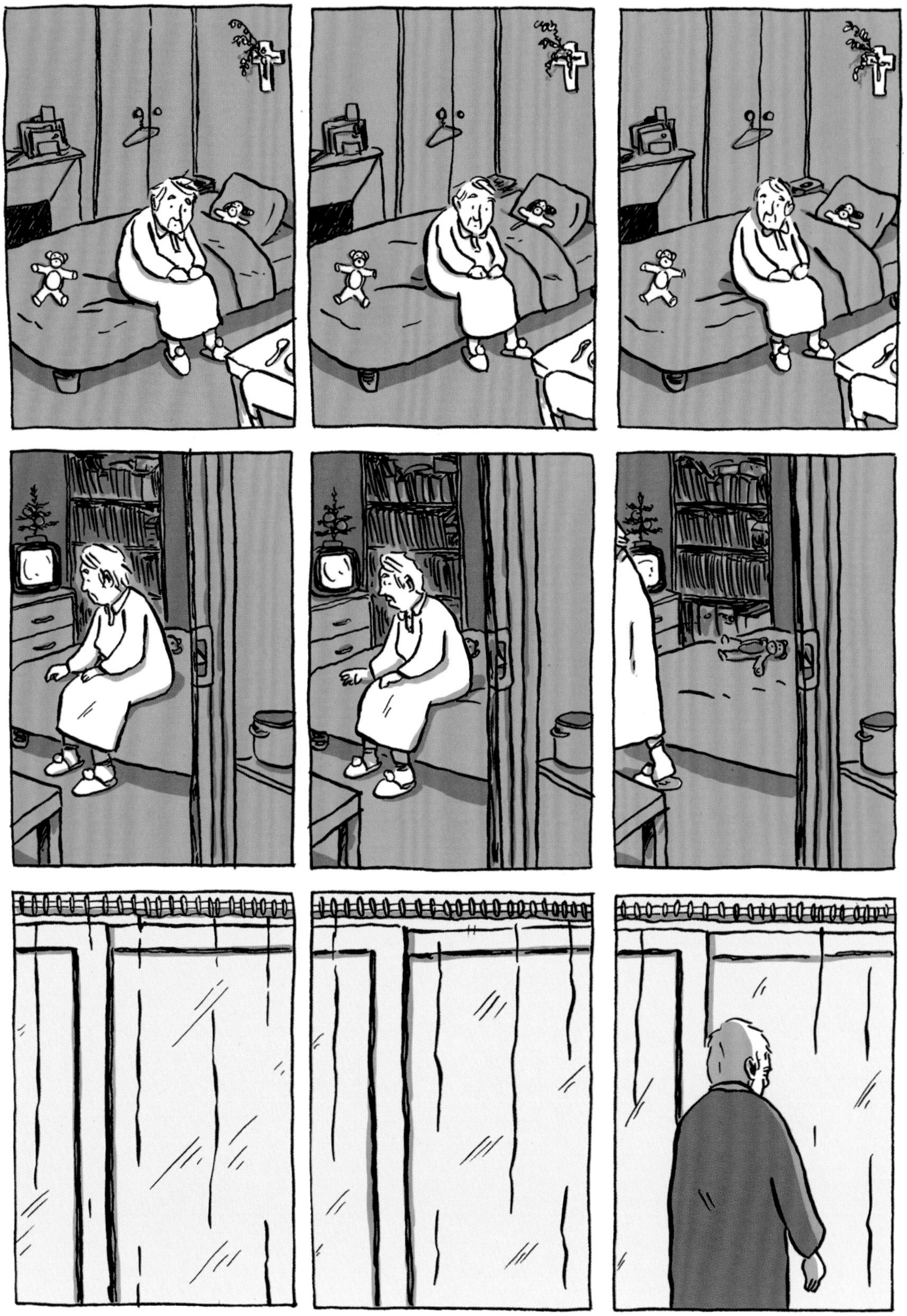

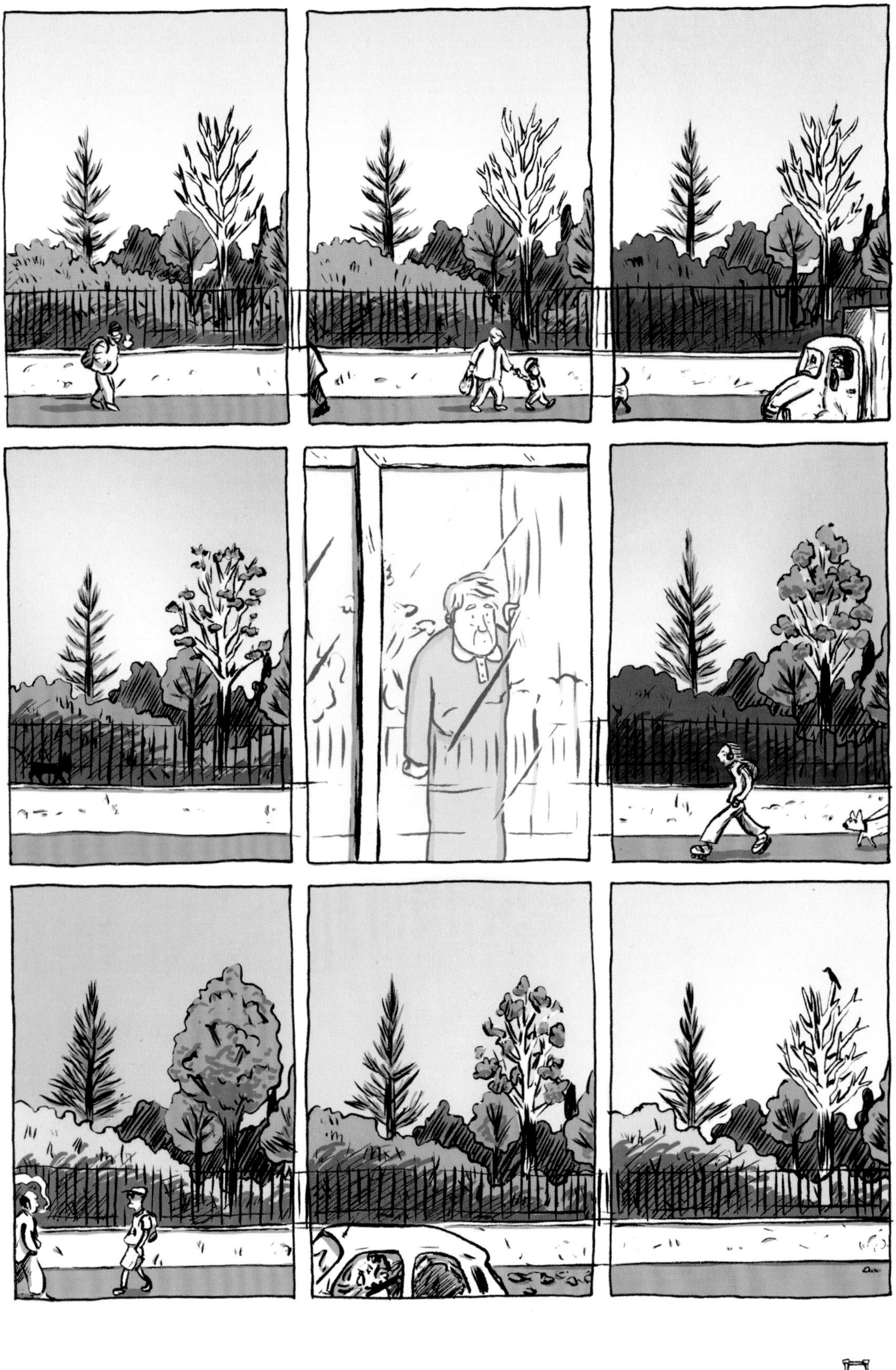

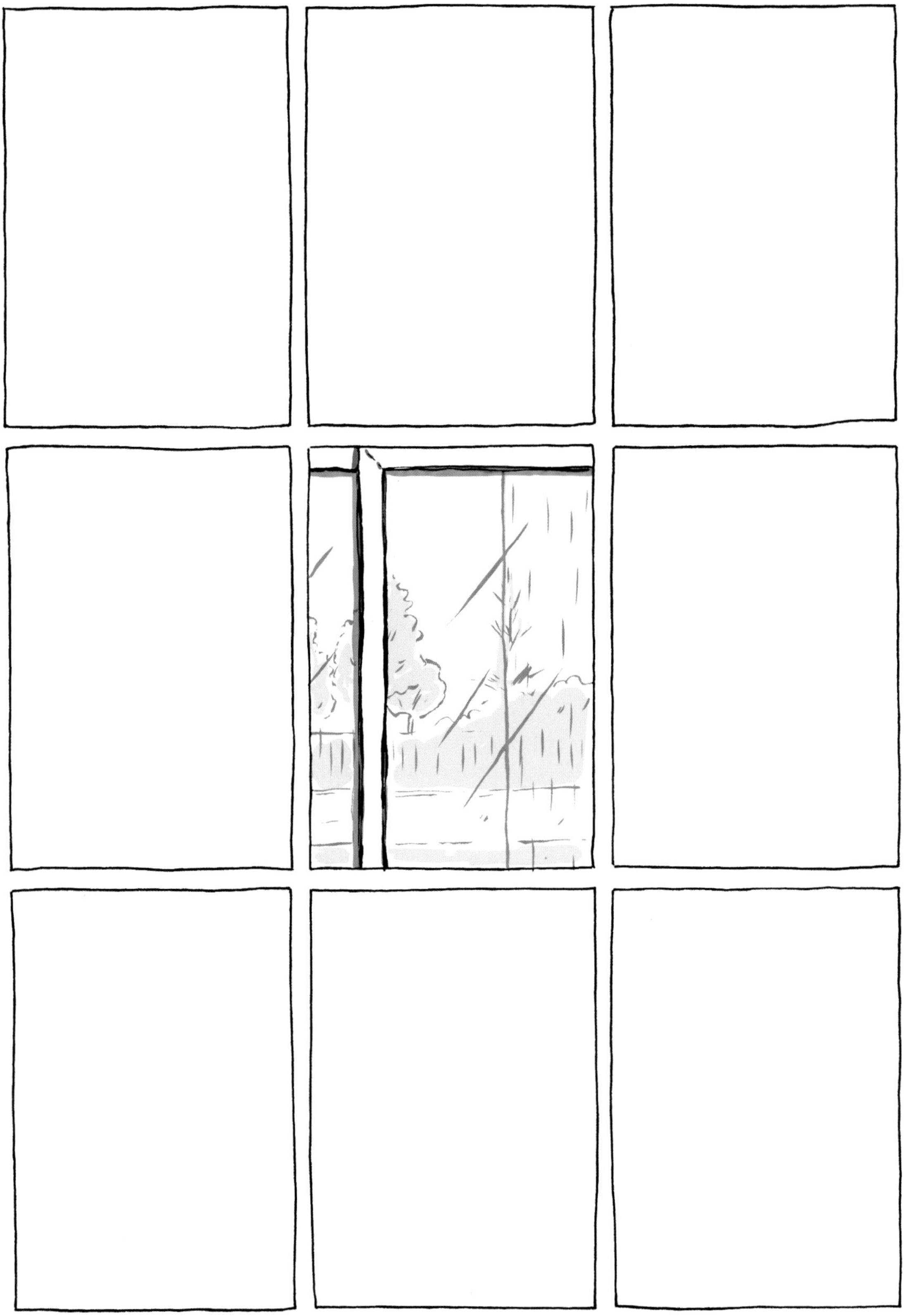

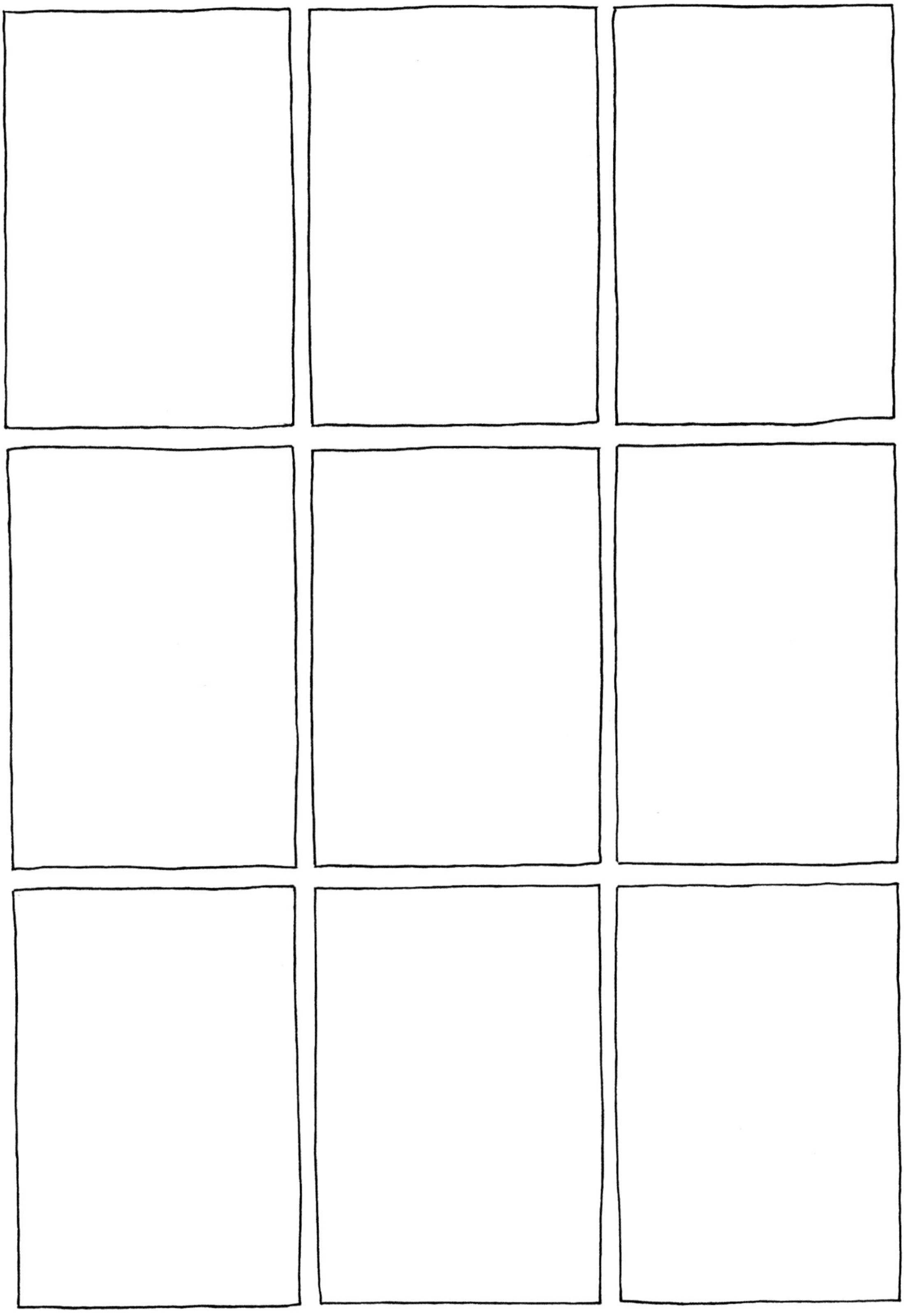

Caregiver!

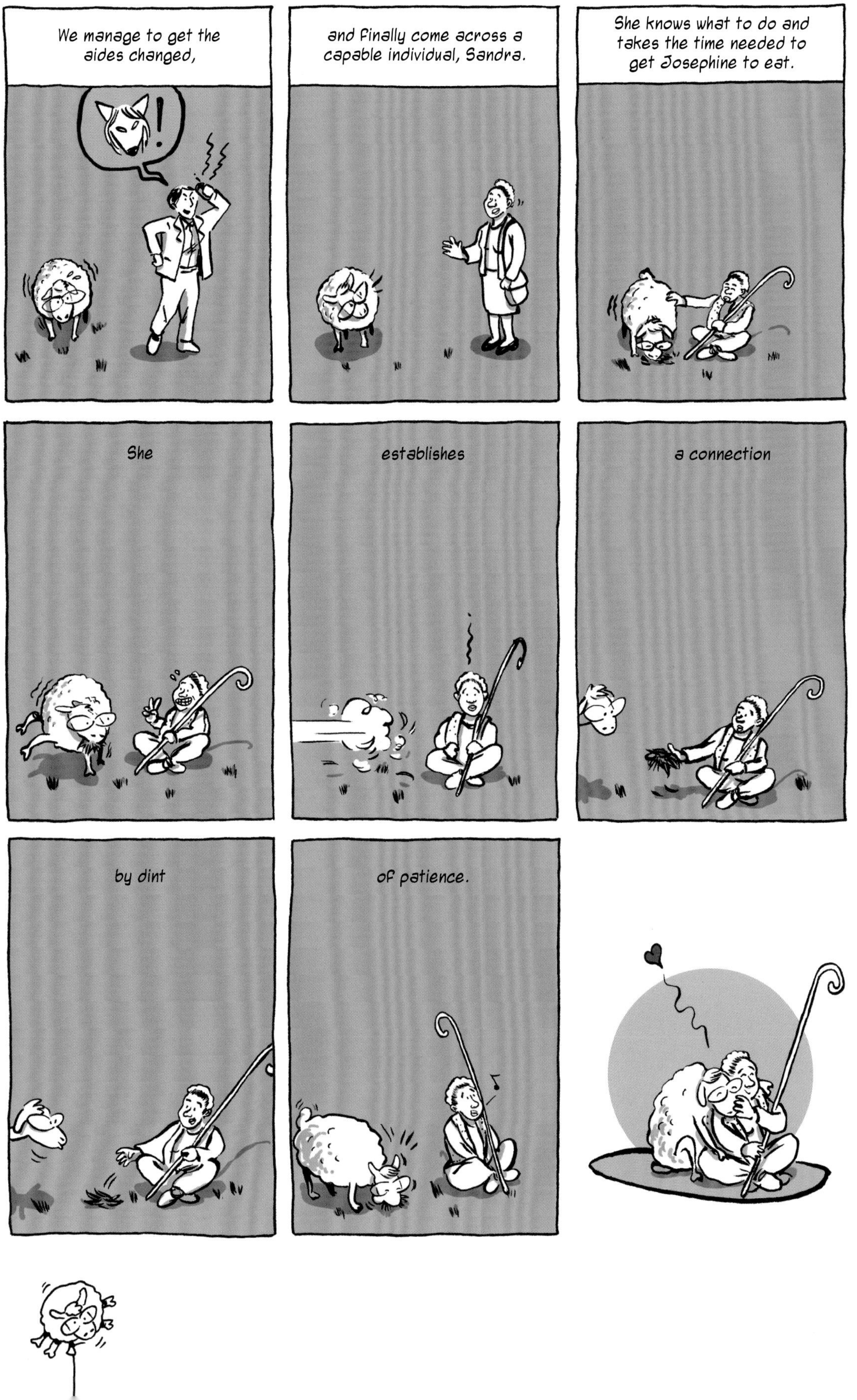
We manage to get the aides changed,
!
and finally come across a capable individual, Sandra.
She knows what to do and takes the time needed to get Josephine to eat.
She
establishes
a connection
by dint
of patience.

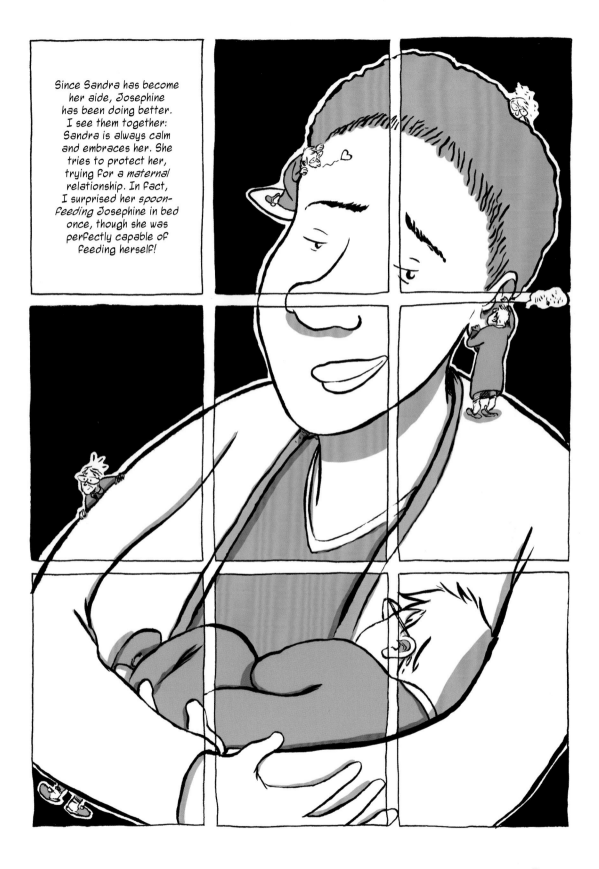

Since Sandra has become her aide, Josephine has been doing better. I see them together: Sandra is always calm and embraces her. She tries to protect her, trying for a maternal relationship. In fact, I surprised her spoon-feeding Josephine in bed once, though she was perfectly capable of feeding herself!

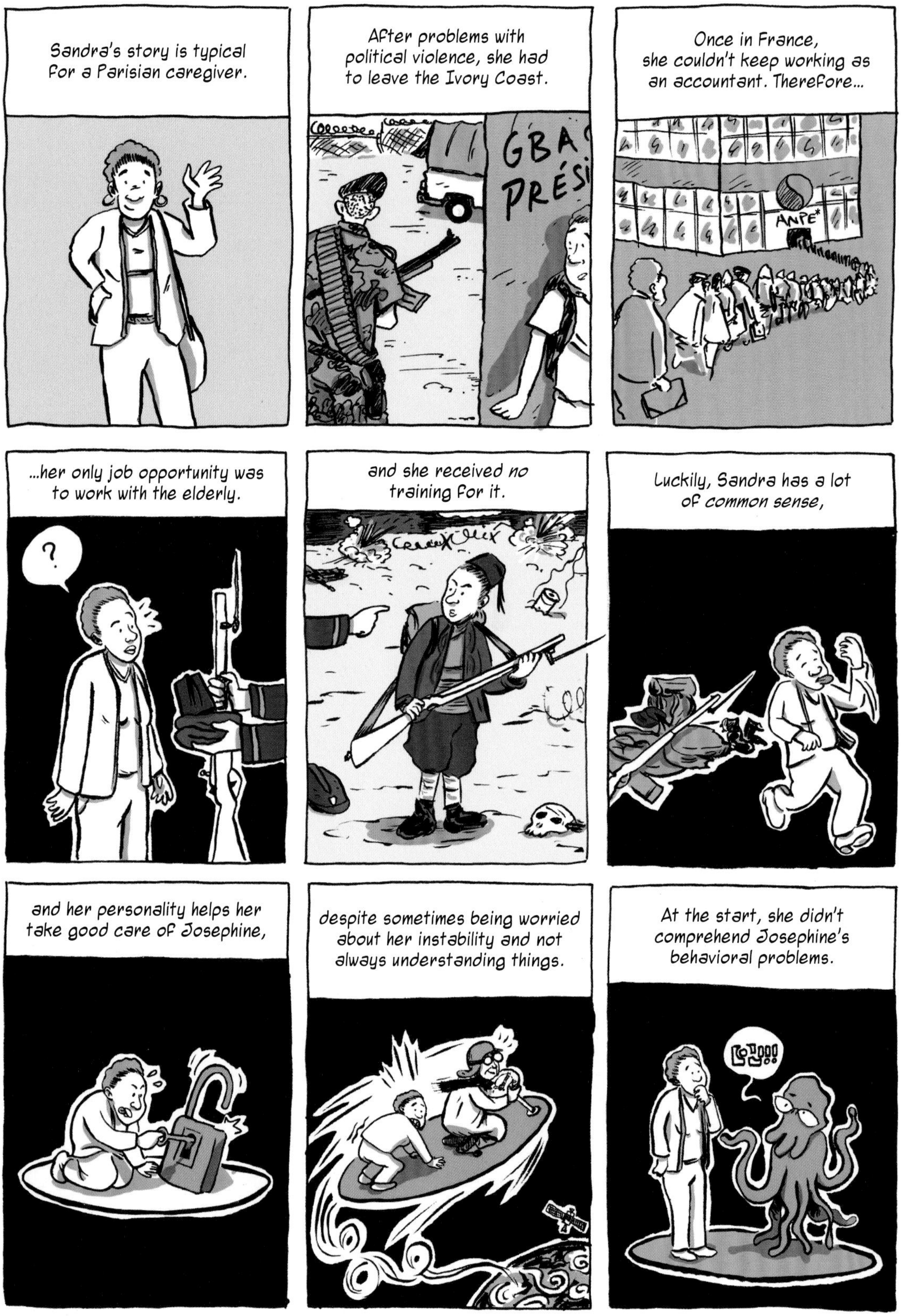
Sandra's story is typical for a Parisian caregiver.
After problems with political violence, she had to leave the Ivory Coast.
GBA
PRÉSI
Once in France, she couldn't keep working as an accountant. Therefore...
ANPE*
...her only job opportunity was to work with the elderly.
?
and she received no training for it.
Luckily, Sandra has a lot of common sense,
and her personality helps her take good care of Josephine,
despite sometimes being worried about her instability and not always understanding things.
At the start, she didn't comprehend Josephine's behavioral problems.

*National Employment Agency

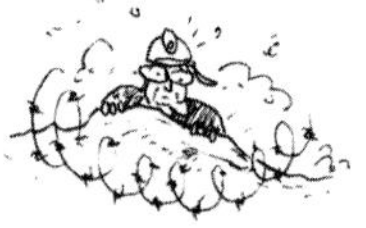

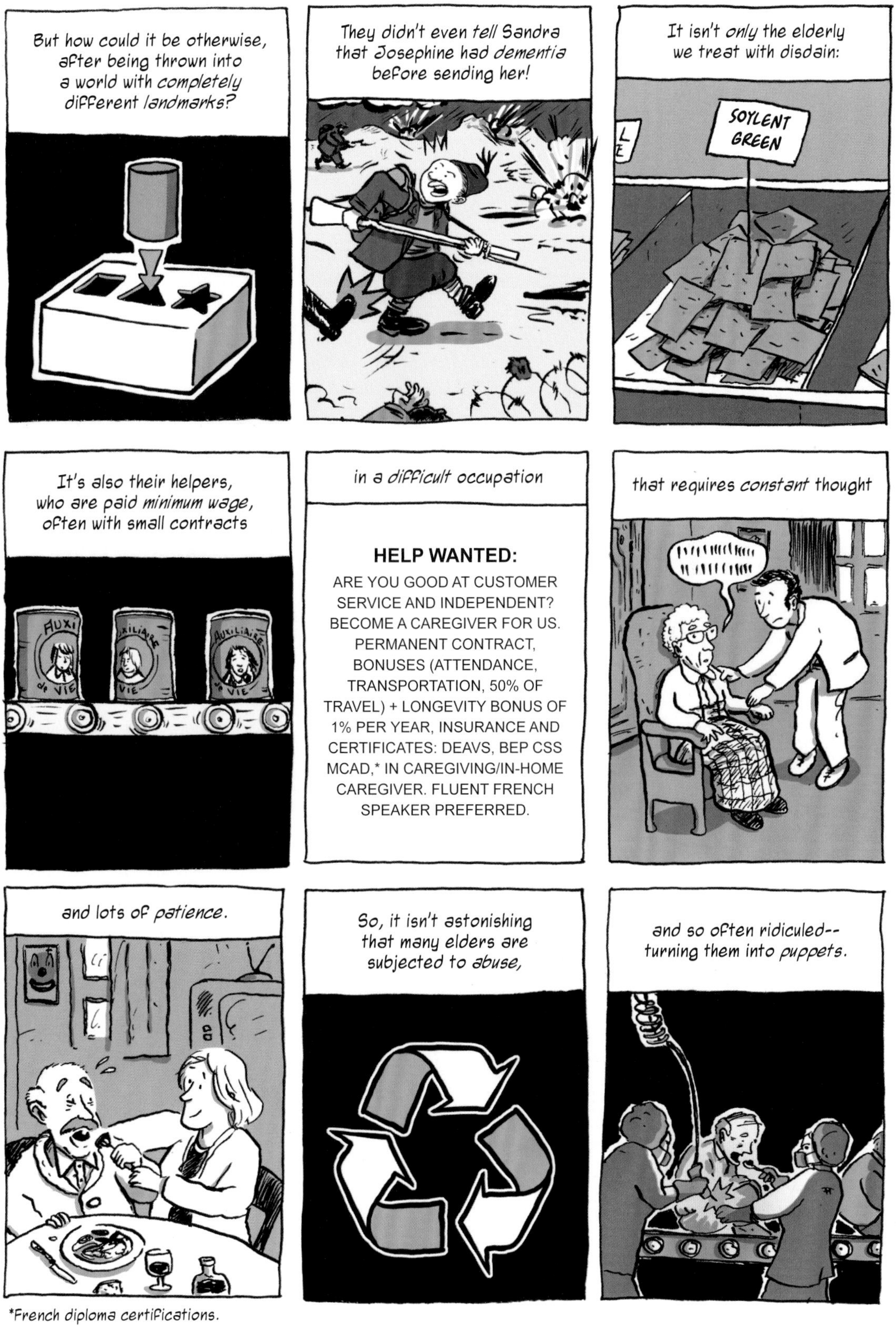
But how could it be otherwise, after being thrown into a world with completely different landmarks?
They didn't even tell Sandra that Josephine had dementia before sending her!
It isn't only the elderly we treat with disdain:
SOYLENT GREEN
It's also their helpers, who are paid minimum wage, often with small contracts
AUXI
AUXILIAIRE
VIE
in a difficult occupation
HELP WANTED:
ARE YOU GOOD AT CUSTOMER SERVICE AND INDEPENDENT? BECOME A CAREGIVER FOR US. PERMANENT CONTRACT, BONUSES (ATTENDANCE, TRANSPORTATION, 50% OF TRAVEL) + LONGEVITY BONUS OF 1% PER YEAR, INSURANCE AND CERTIFICATES: DEAVS, BEP CSS MCAD,* IN CAREGIVING/IN-HOME CAREGIVER. FLUENT FRENCH SPEAKER PREFERRED.
that requires constant thought
and lots of patience.
So, it isn't astonishing that many elders are subjected to abuse,
and so often ridiculed-- turning them into puppets.

*French diploma certifications.

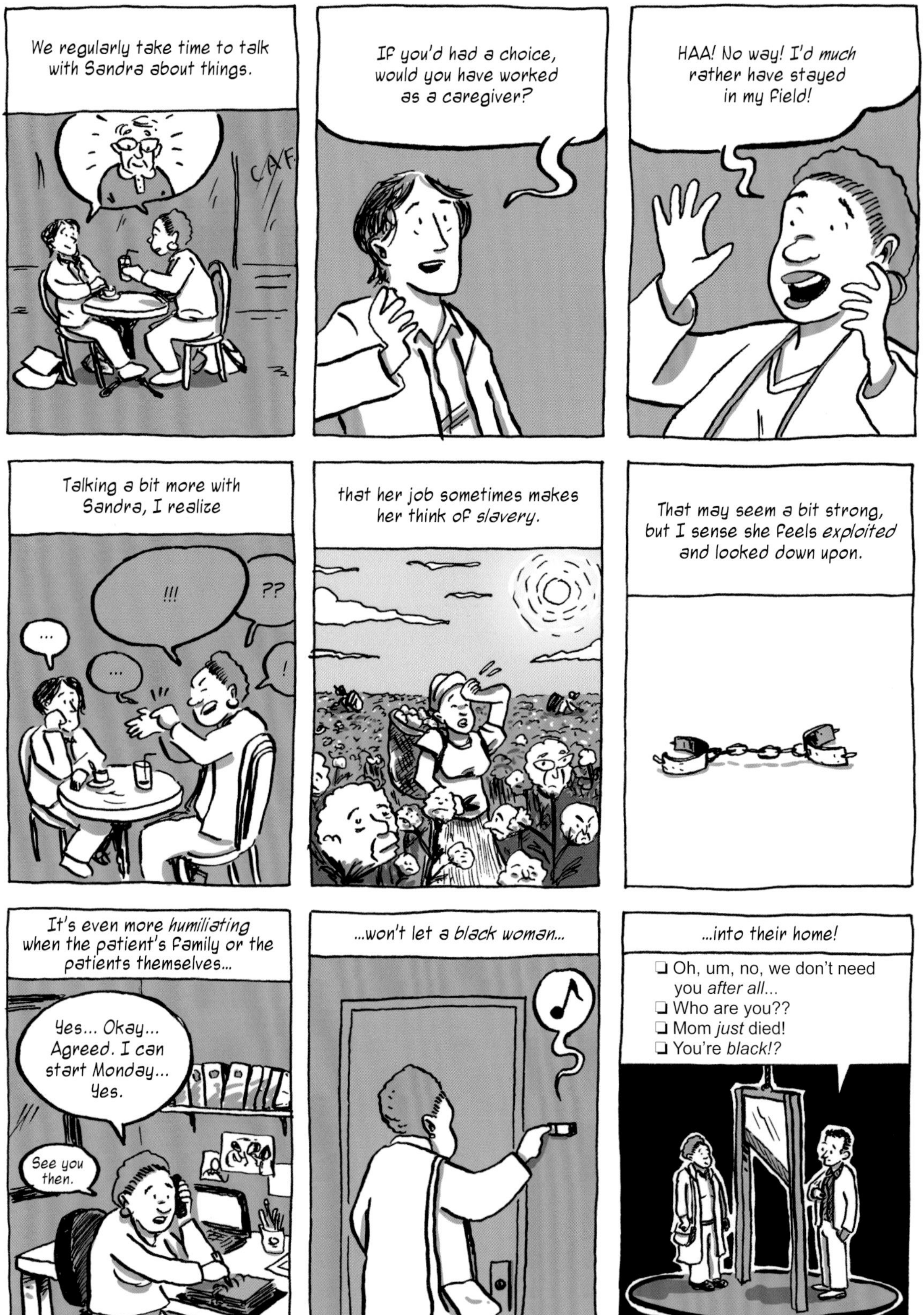

We regularly take time to talk with Sandra about things.
CAF
If you'd had a choice, would you have worked as a caregiver?
HAA! No way! I'd *much* rather have stayed in my field!
Talking a bit more with Sandra, I realize
!!!
??
...
...
!
that her job sometimes makes her think of *slavery*.
That may seem a bit strong, but I sense she feels *exploited* and looked down upon.
It's even more *humiliating* when the patient's family or the patients themselves...
Yes... Okay... Agreed. I can start Monday... Yes.
See you then.
...won't let a *black woman*...
...into their home!
❏ Oh, um, no, we don't need you *after all*...
❏ Who are you??
❏ Mom *just* died!
❏ You're *black!?*

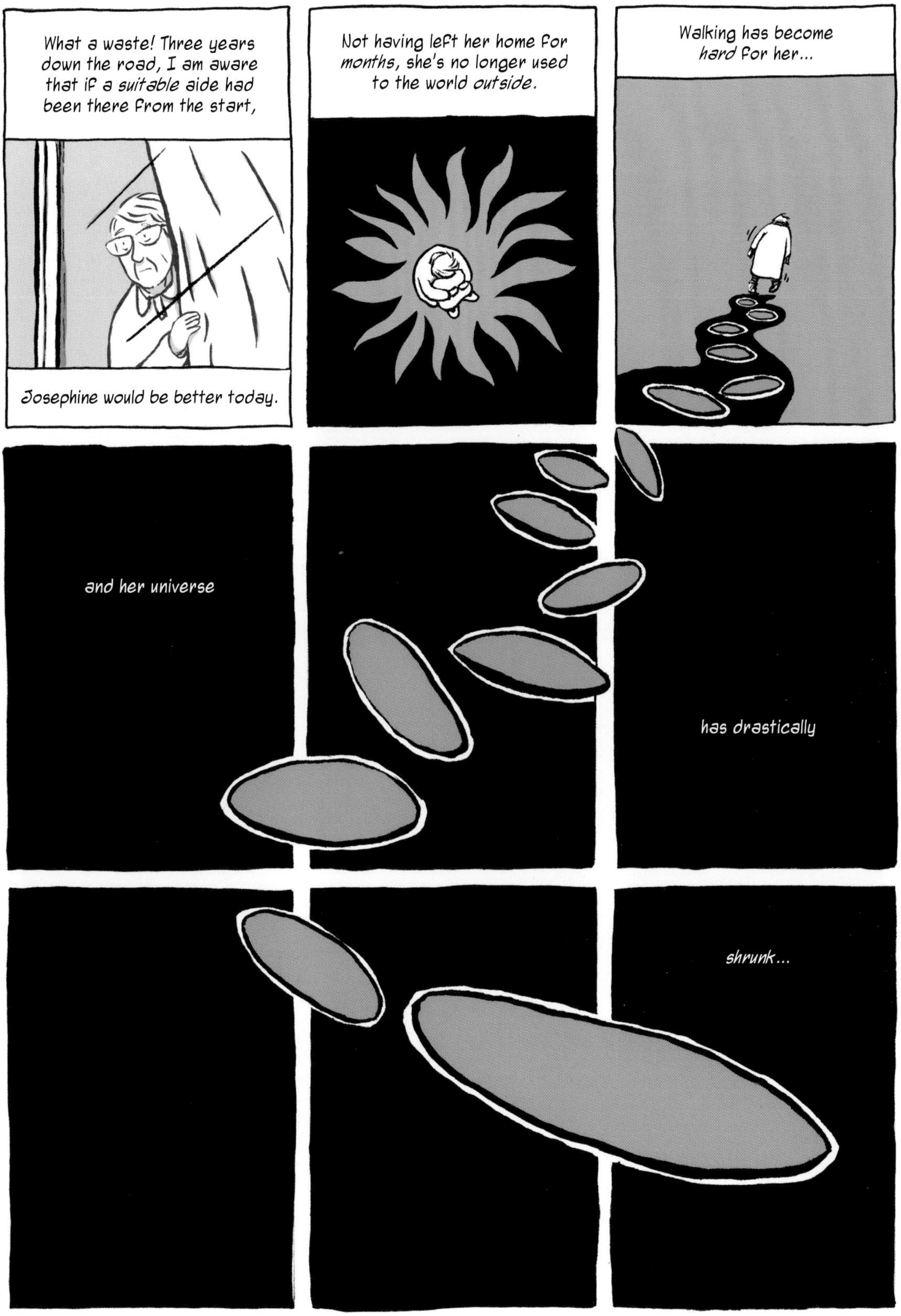
What a waste! Three years down the road, I am aware that if a *suitable* aide had been there from the start,
Josephine would be better today.
Not having left her home for *months*, she's no longer used to the world *outside*.
Walking has become *hard* for her...
and her universe
has drastically
shrunk...

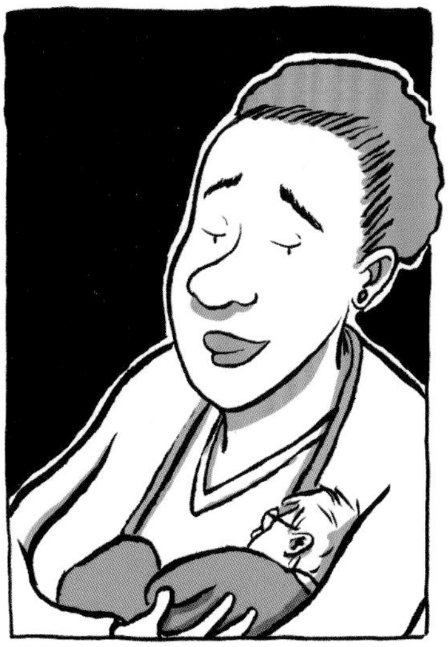

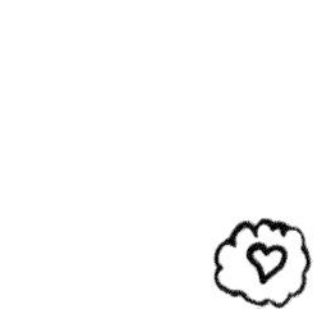

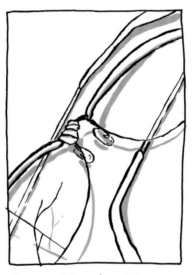

Josephine's Glasses

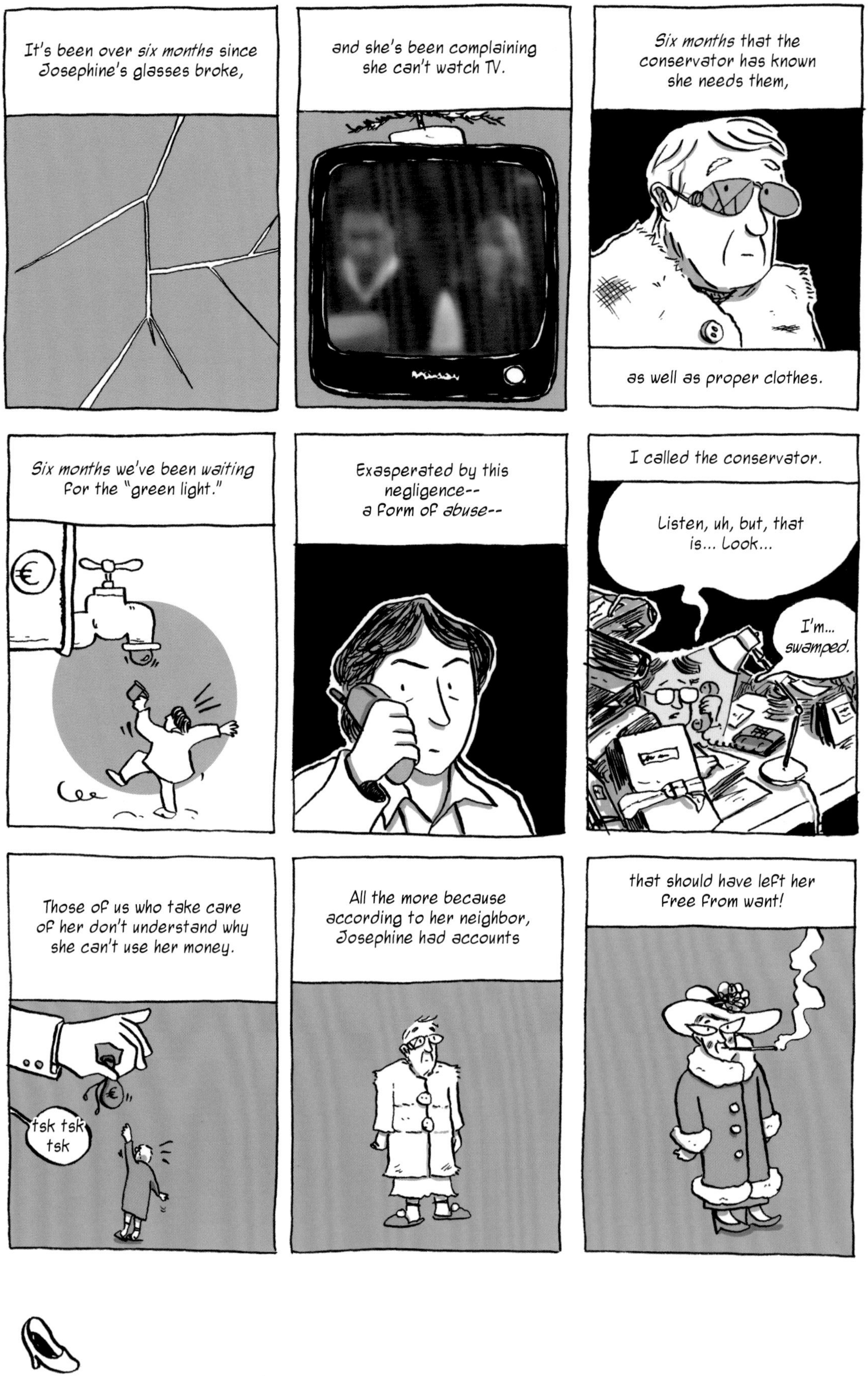
It's been over *six months* since Josephine's glasses broke,
and she's been complaining she can't watch TV.
Six months that the conservator has known she needs them,
as well as proper clothes.
Six months we've been *waiting* for the "green light."
Exasperated by this negligence-- a form of *abuse*--
I called the conservator.
Listen, uh, but, that is... Look...
I'm... *swamped.*
Those of us who take care of her don't understand why she can't use her money.
tsk tsk tsk
All the more because according to her neighbor, Josephine had accounts
that should have left her free from want!

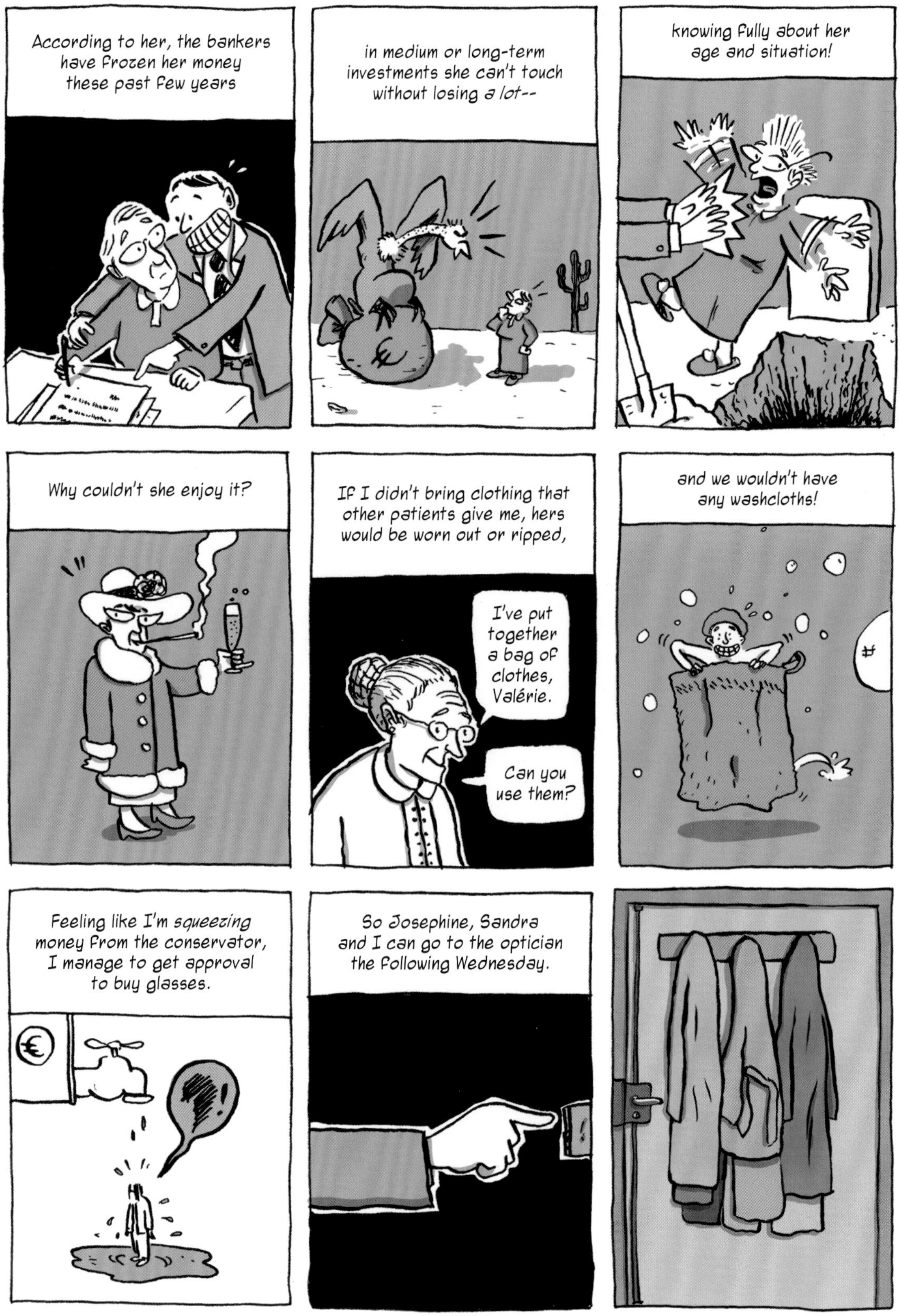
According to her, the bankers have frozen her money these past few years
in medium or long-term investments she can't touch without losing a *lot*--
knowing fully about her age and situation!
Why couldn't she enjoy it?
If I didn't bring clothing that other patients give me, hers would be worn out or ripped,
I've put together a bag of clothes, Valérie.
Can you use them?
and we wouldn't have any washcloths!
Feeling like I'm *squeezing* money from the conservator, I manage to get approval to buy glasses.
So Josephine, Sandra and I can go to the optician the following Wednesday.

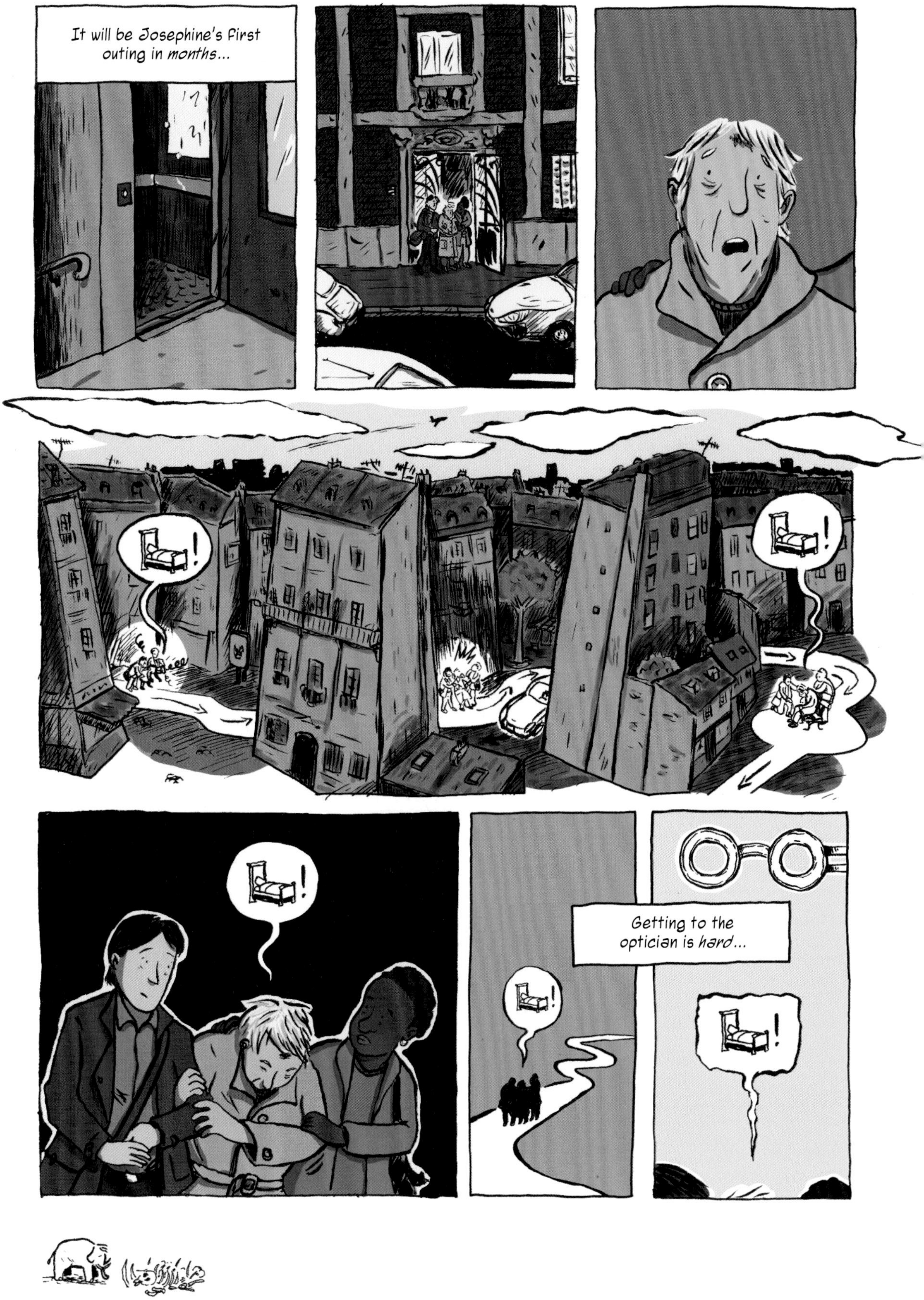
It will be Josephine's first outing in *months*...
Getting to the optician is *hard*...

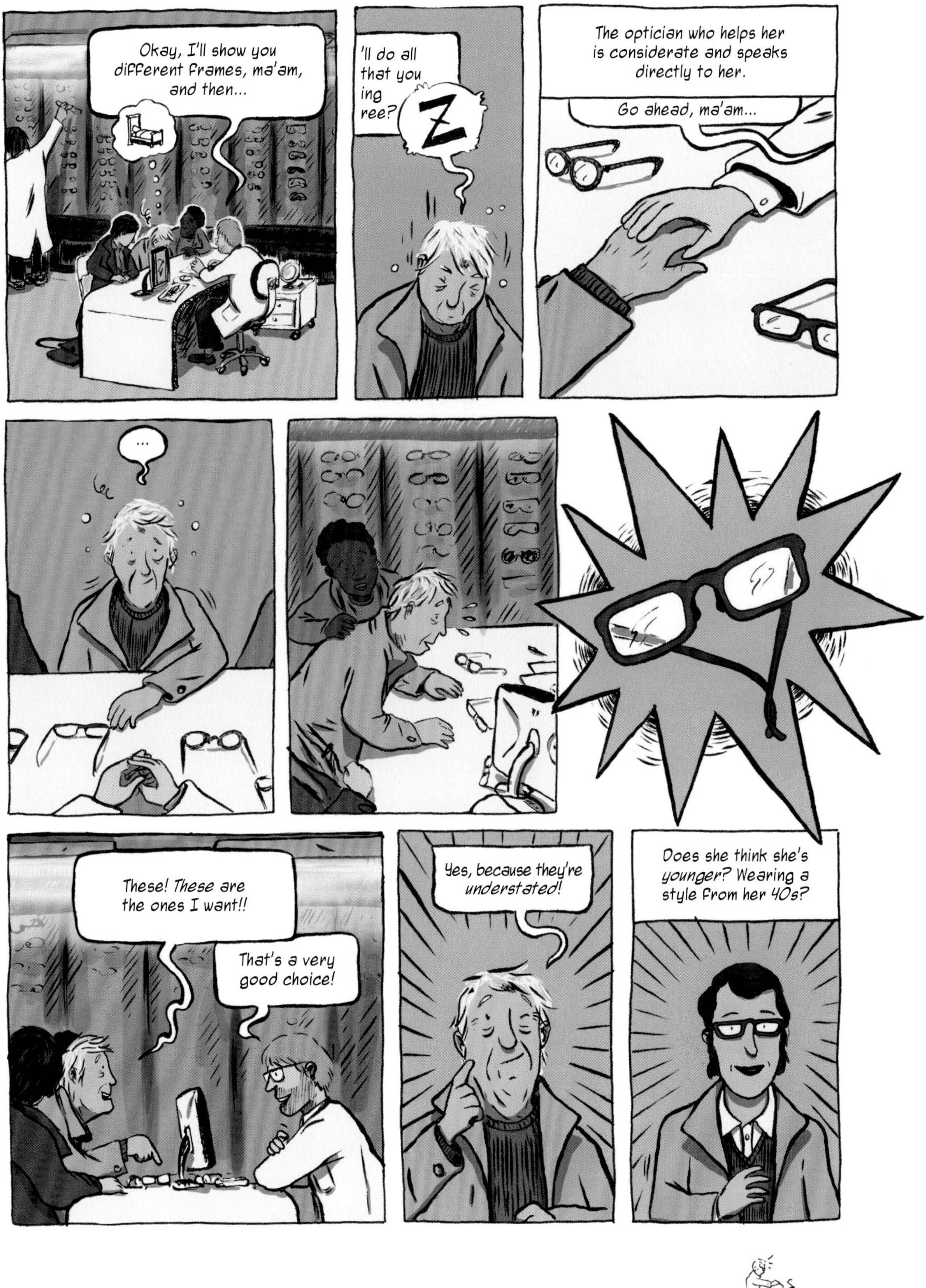
Okay, I'll show you different frames, ma'am, and then...
'll do all that you ing ree?
Z
The optician who helps her is considerate and speaks directly to her.
Go ahead, ma'am...
...
These! *These* are the ones I want!!
That's a very good choice!
Yes, because they're *understated*!
Does she think she's *younger*? Wearing a style from her 40s?

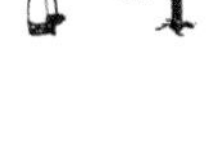

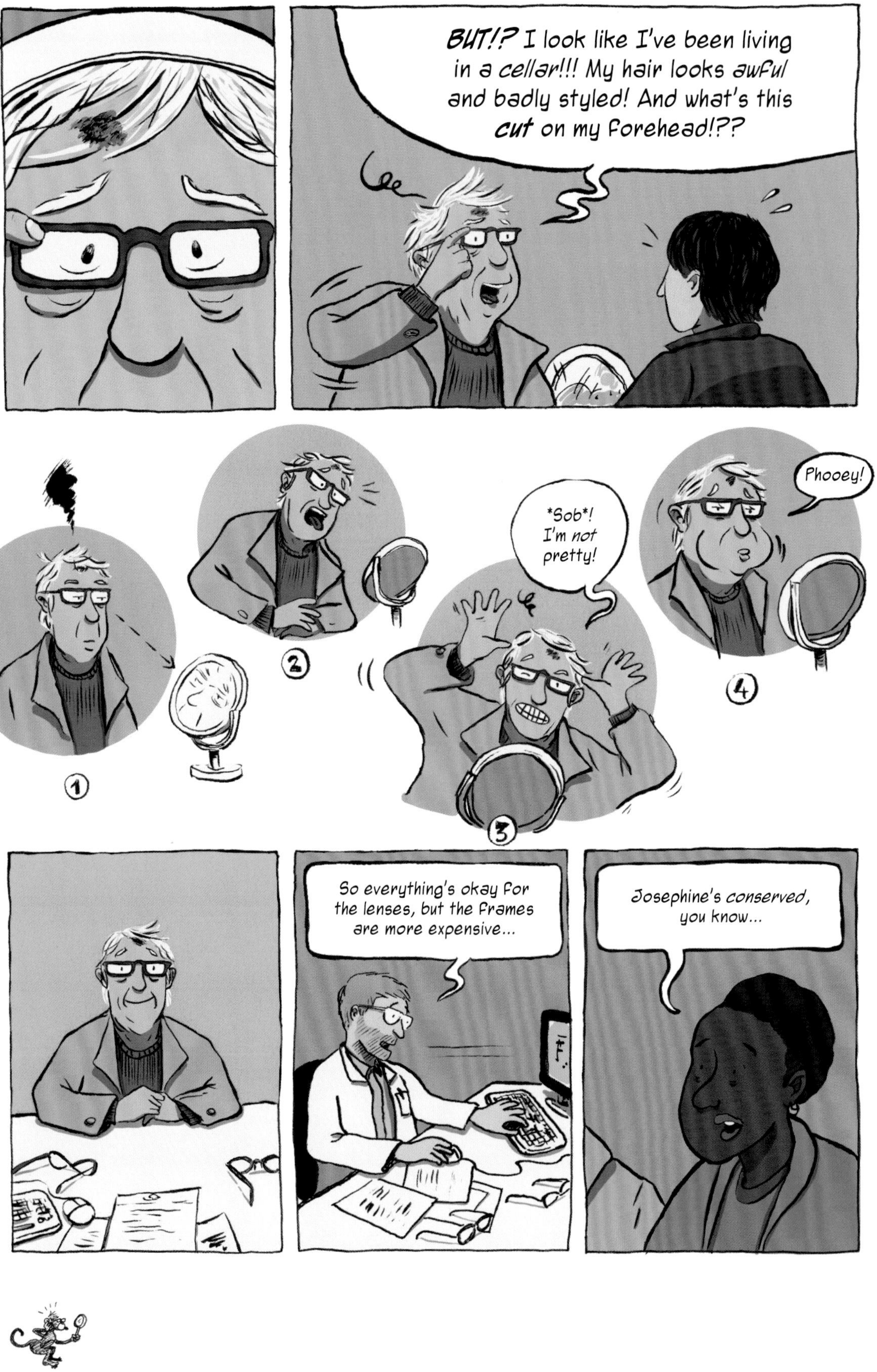
BUT!? I look like I've been living in a cellar!!! My hair looks awful and badly styled! And what's this cut on my forehead!??
1
2
Sob! I'm not pretty!
3
Phooey!
4
So everything's okay for the lenses, but the frames are more expensive...
Josephine's conserved, you know...

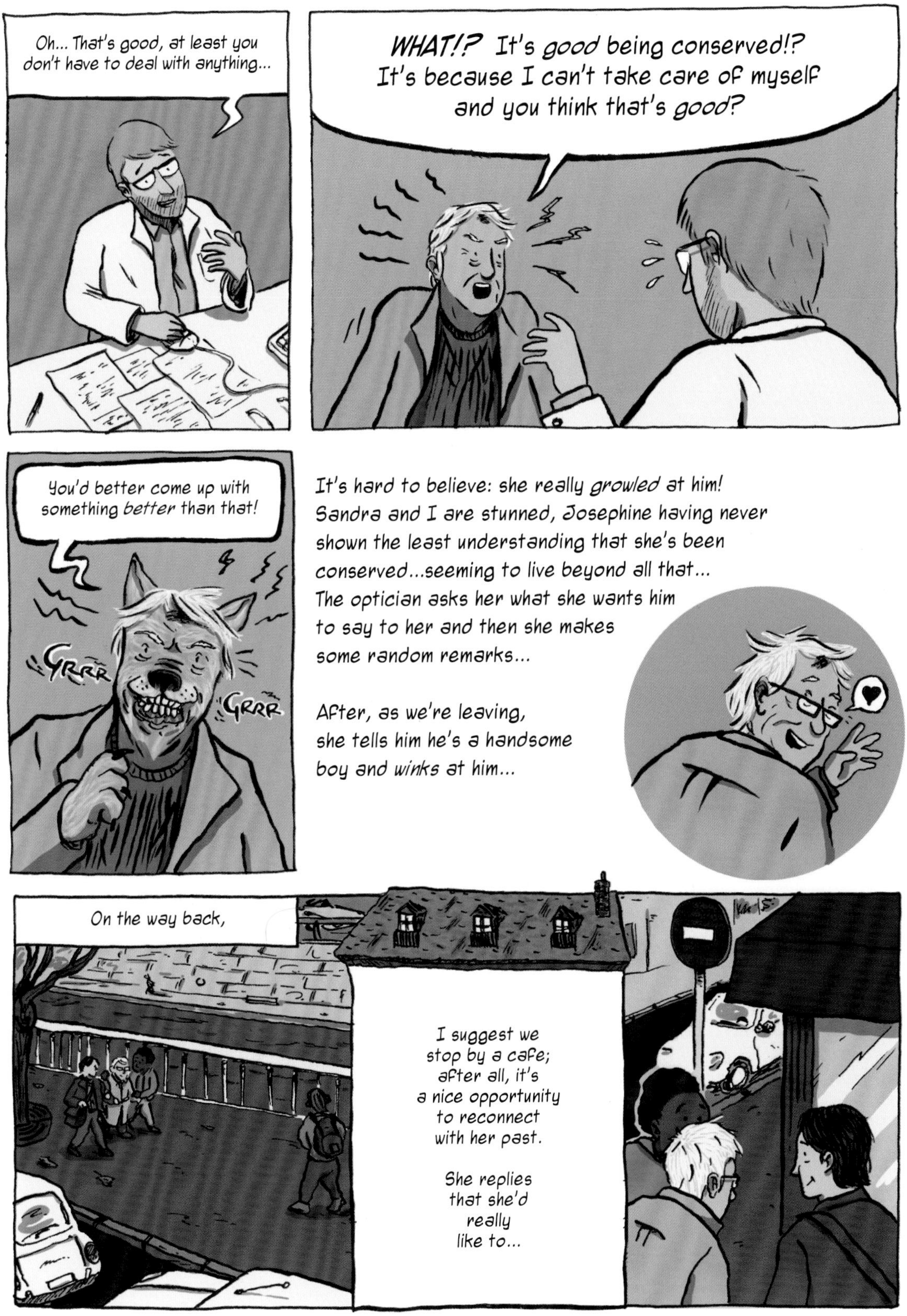
Oh... That's good, at least you don't have to deal with anything...
WHAT!? It's good being conserved!? It's because I can't take care of myself and you think that's good?
You'd better come up with something better than that!
GRRR
GRRR
It's hard to believe: she really growled at him! Sandra and I are stunned, Josephine having never shown the least understanding that she's been conserved...seeming to live beyond all that... The optician asks her what she wants him to say to her and then she makes some random remarks...
After, as we're leaving, she tells him he's a handsome boy and winks at him...
On the way back,
I suggest we stop by a cafe; after all, it's a nice opportunity to reconnect with her past.
She replies that she'd really like to...

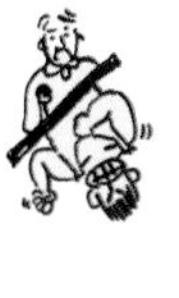

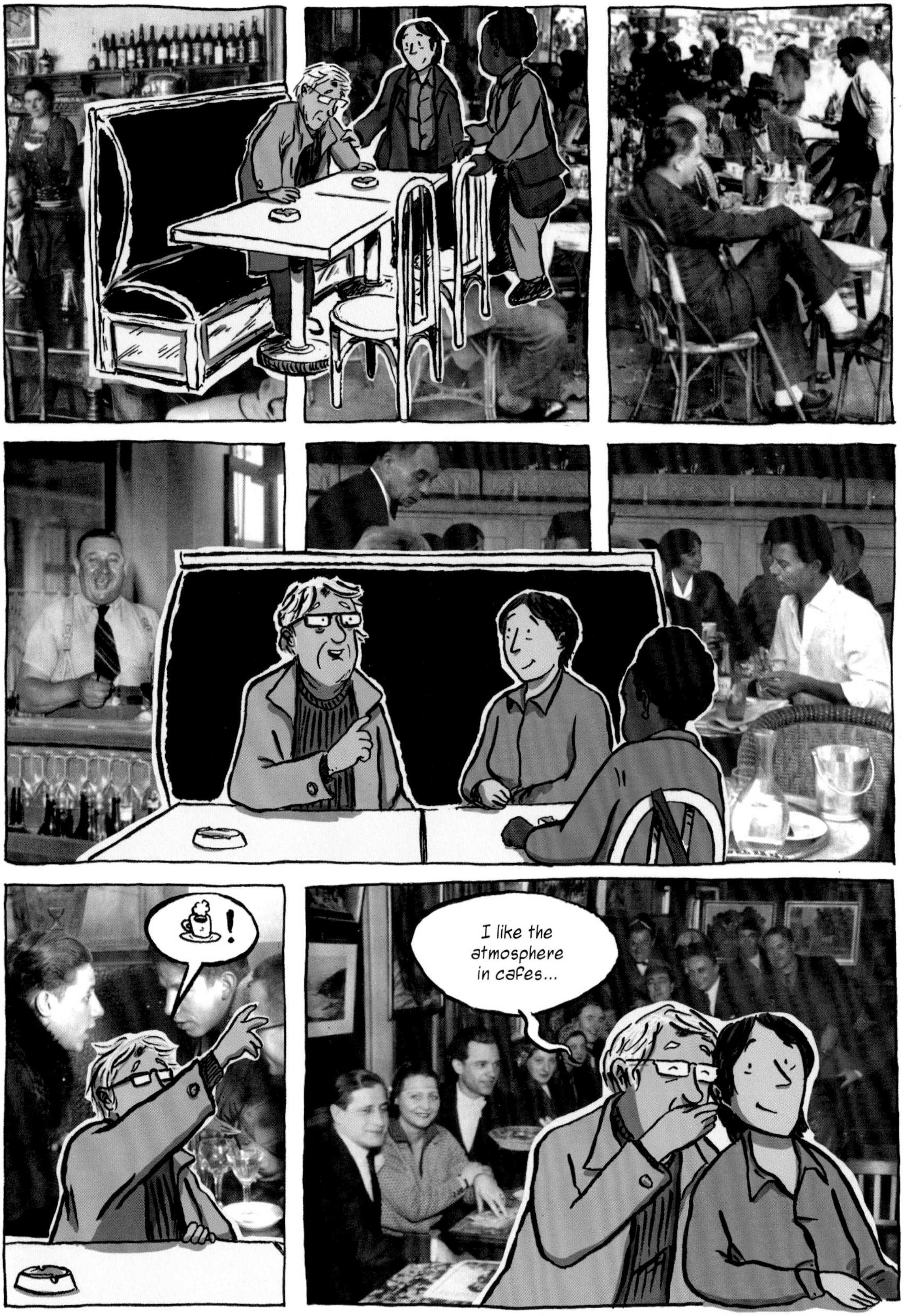
!
I like the atmosphere in cafes...

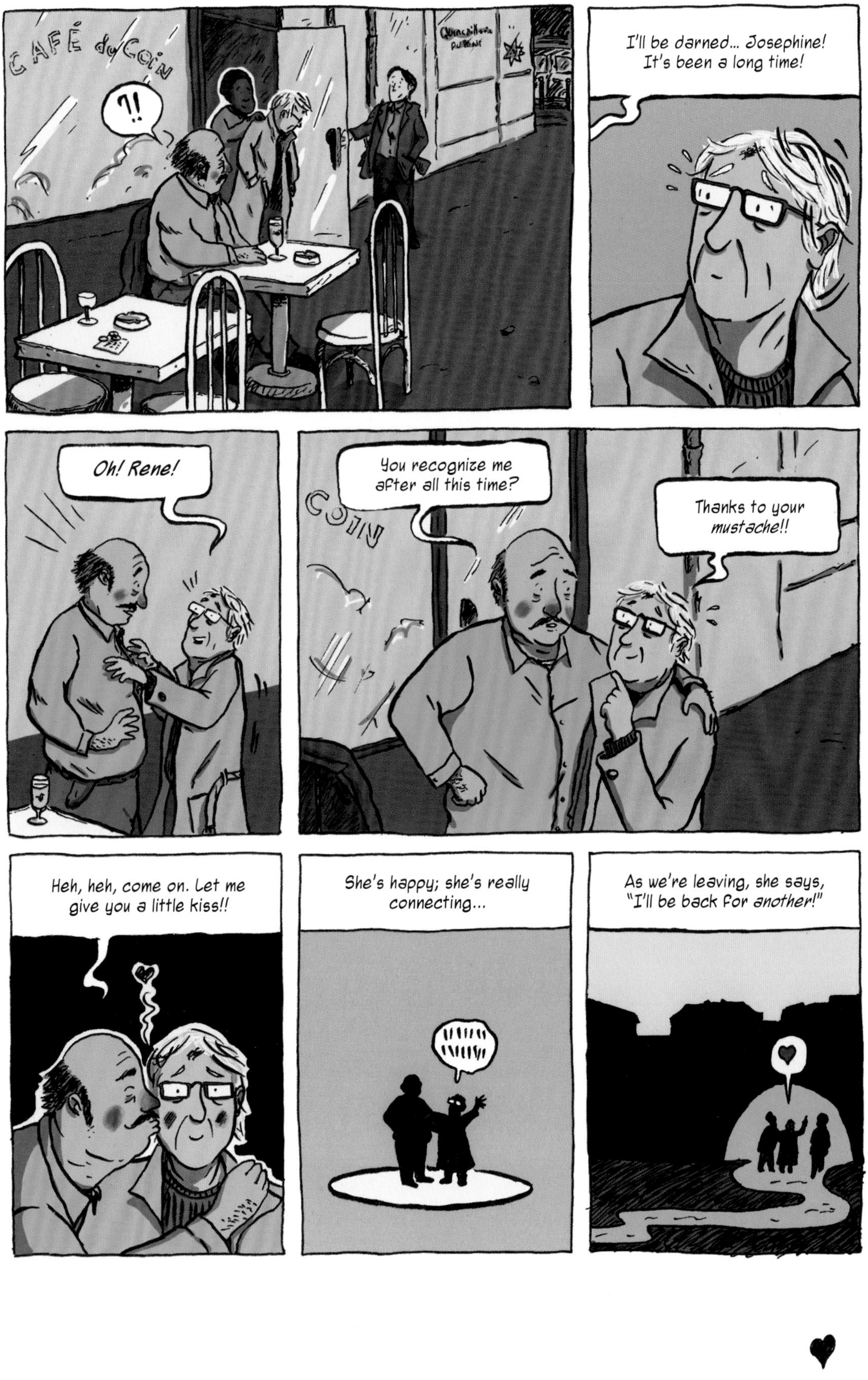
CAFÉ du Coin
?!
I'll be darned... Josephine! It's been a long time!
Oh! Rene!
You recognize me after all this time?
Thanks to your *mustache*!!
Heh, heh, come on. Let me give you a little kiss!!
She's happy; she's really connecting...
As we're leaving, she says, "I'll be back for *another*!"

Little Josephine,
wearing her new glasses,
finally enjoys reading
The Touch of Aphrodite...

Days of Paranoia

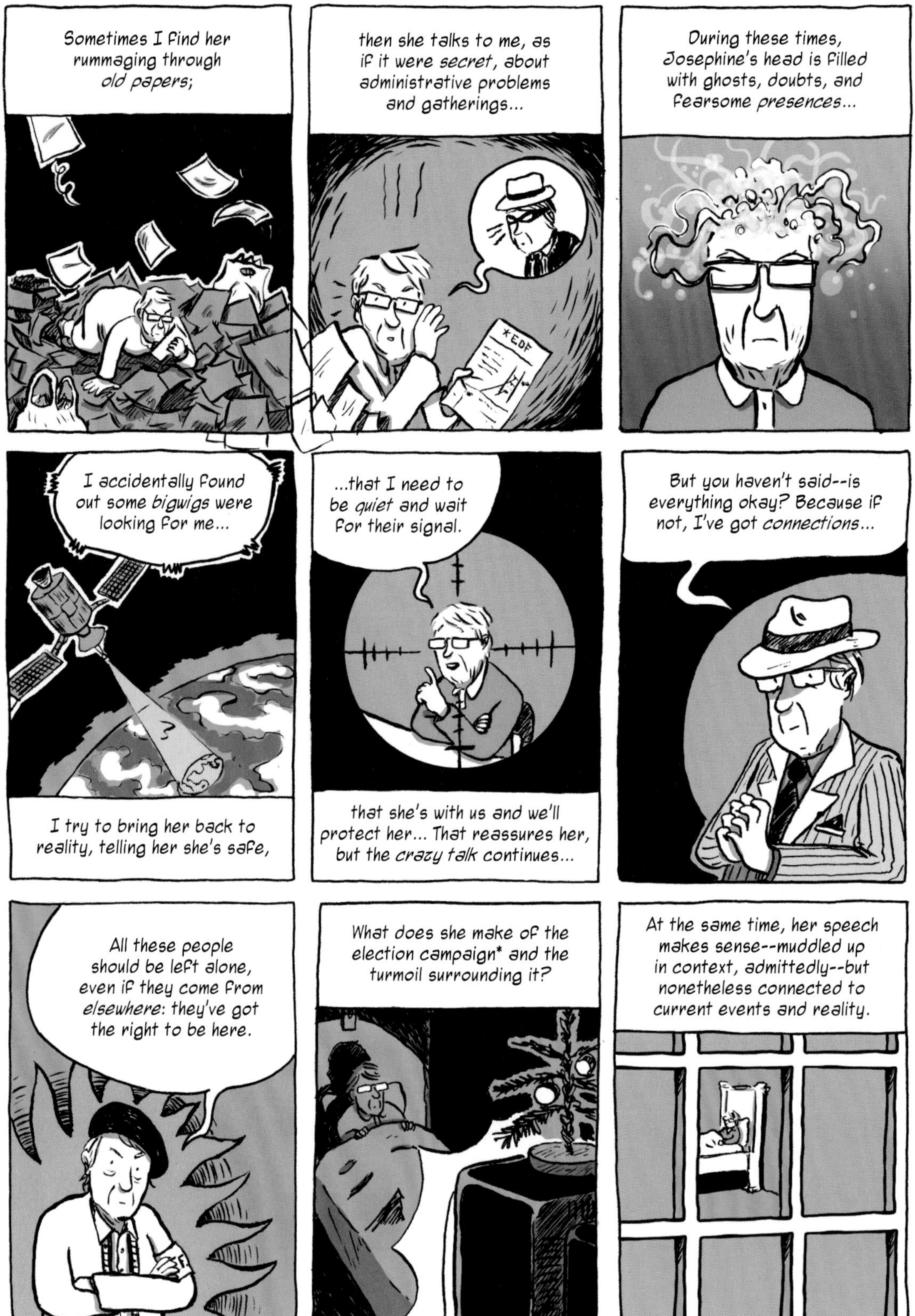
Sometimes I find her rummaging through old papers;
then she talks to me, as if it were secret, about administrative problems and gatherings...
EDF
During these times, Josephine's head is filled with ghosts, doubts, and fearsome presences...
I accidentally found out some bigwigs were looking for me...
I try to bring her back to reality, telling her she's safe,
...that I need to be quiet and wait for their signal.
that she's with us and we'll protect her... That reassures her, but the crazy talk continues...
But you haven't said--is everything okay? Because if not, I've got connections...
All these people should be left alone, even if they come from elsewhere: they've got the right to be here.
What does she make of the election campaign* and the turmoil surrounding it?
At the same time, her speech makes sense--muddled up in context, admittedly--but nonetheless connected to current events and reality.

*For the 2007 French presidential election.

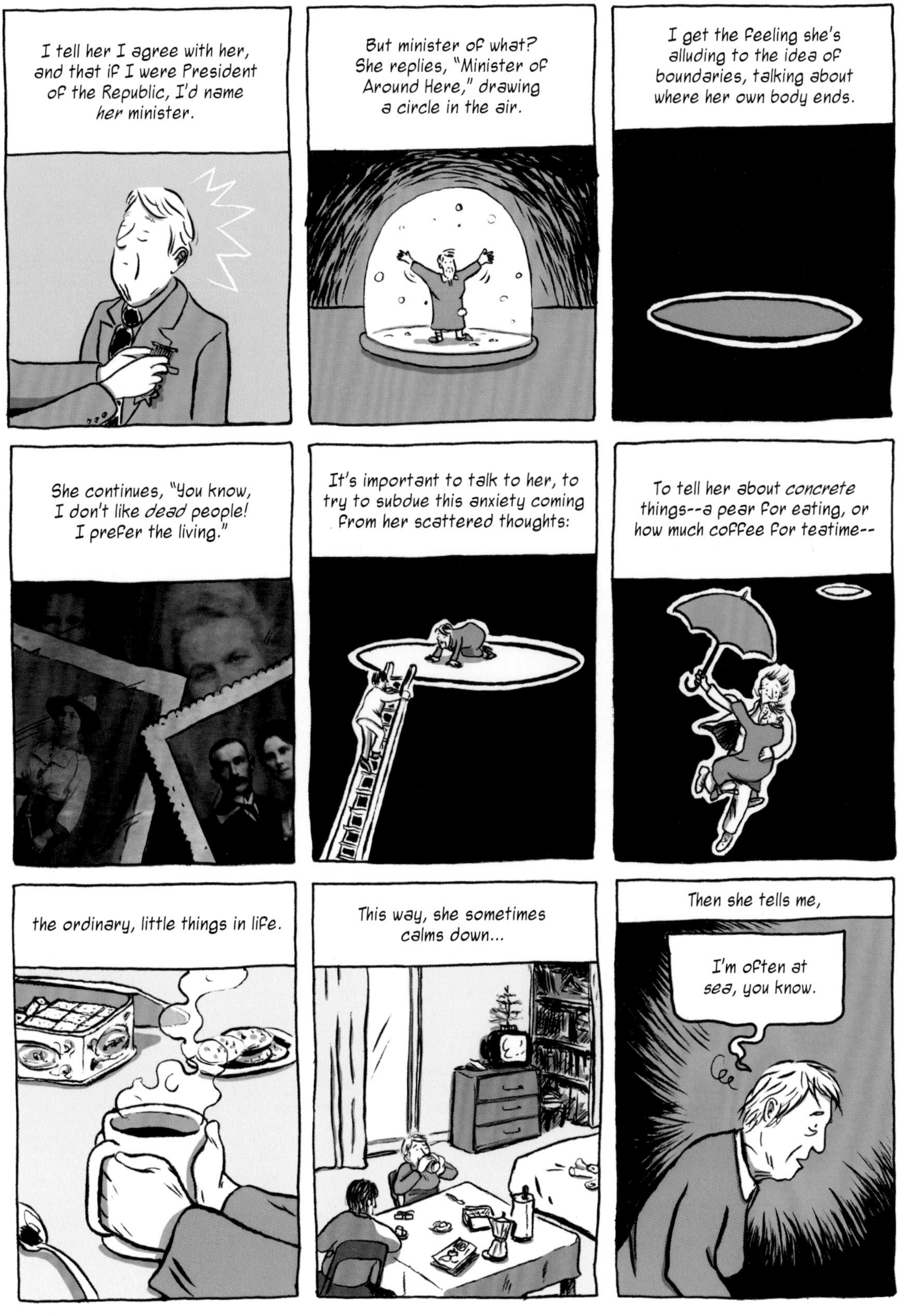

I tell her I agree with her, and that if I were President of the Republic, I'd name *her* minister.
But minister of what? She replies, "Minister of Around Here," drawing a circle in the air.
I get the feeling she's alluding to the idea of boundaries, talking about where her own body ends.
She continues, "You know, I don't like *dead* people! I prefer the living."
It's important to talk to her, to try to subdue this anxiety coming from her scattered thoughts:
To tell her about *concrete* things--a pear for eating, or how much coffee for teatime--
the ordinary, little things in life.
This way, she sometimes calms down...
Then she tells me,
I'm often at sea, you know.

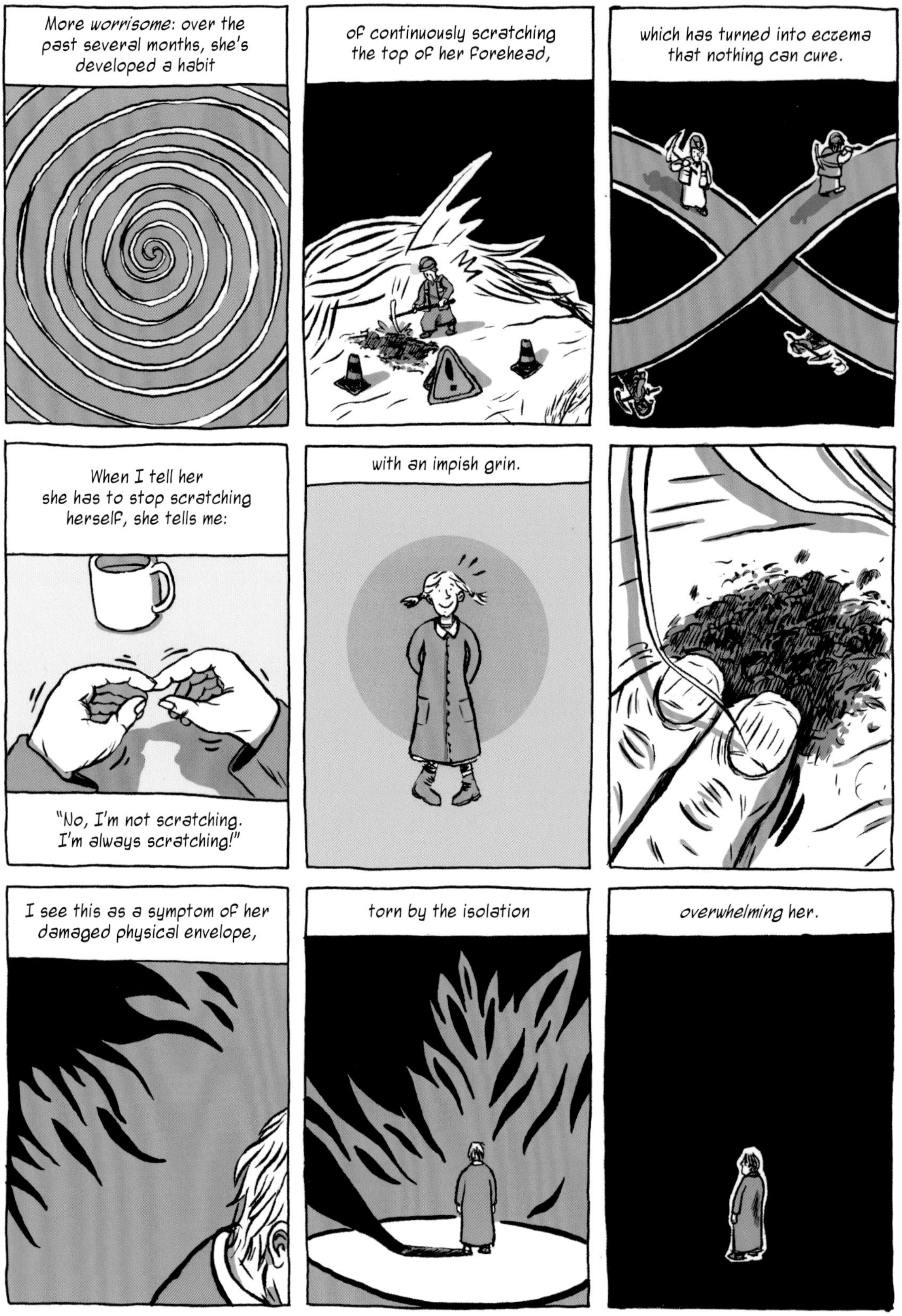
More worrisome: over the past several months, she's developed a habit
of continuously scratching the top of her forehead,
which has turned into eczema that nothing can cure.
When I tell her she has to stop scratching herself, she tells me:
"No, I'm not scratching. I'm always scratching!"
with an impish grin.
I see this as a symptom of her damaged physical envelope,
torn by the isolation
overwhelming her.

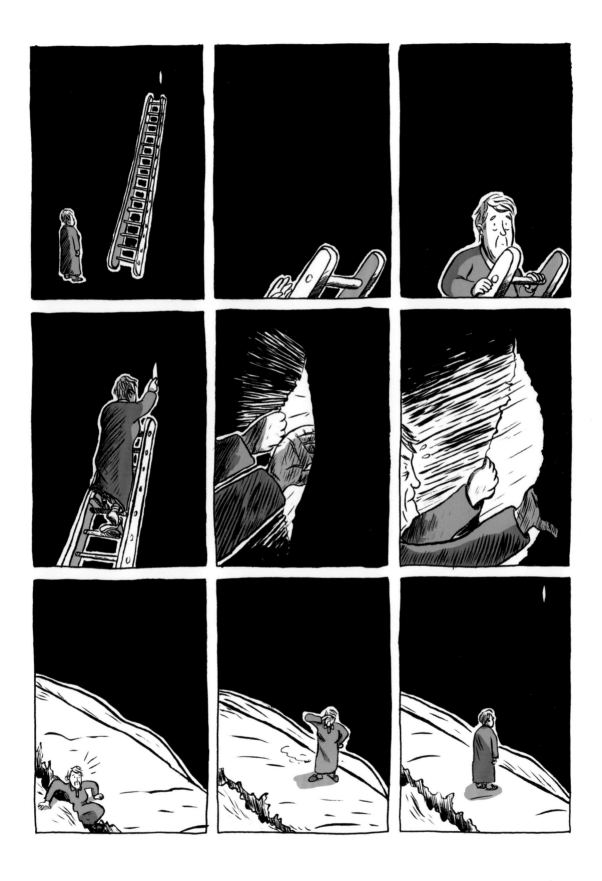

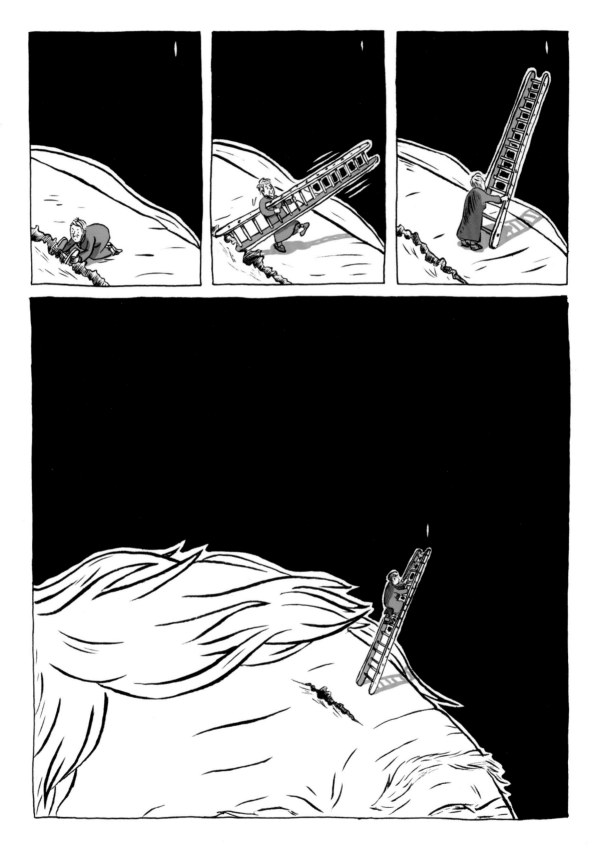

And the emptiness
returns...

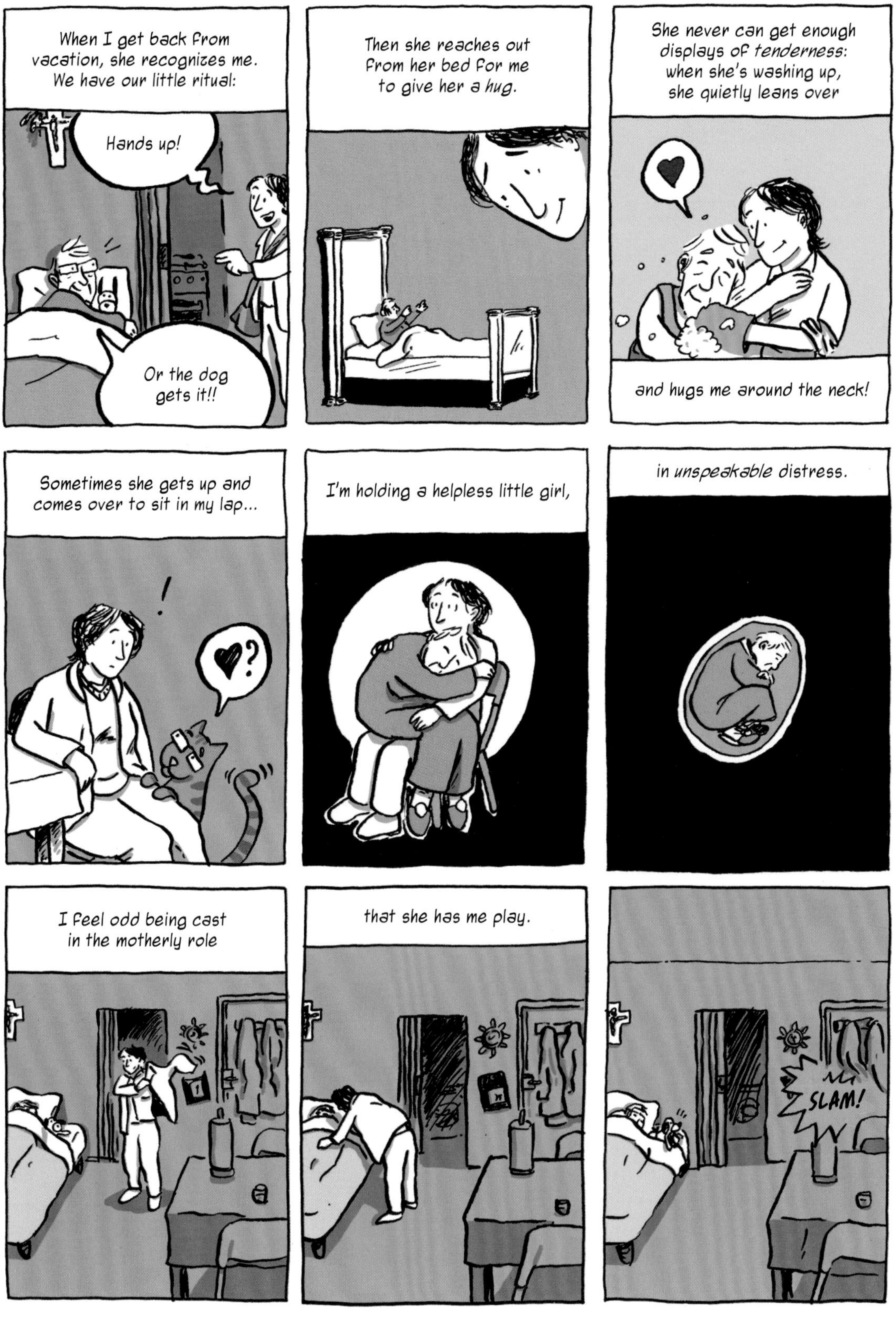
When I get back from vacation, she recognizes me. We have our little ritual:
Hands up!
Or the dog gets it!!
Then she reaches out from her bed for me to give her a *hug*.
She never can get enough displays of *tenderness*: when she's washing up, she quietly leans over
and hugs me around the neck!
Sometimes she gets up and comes over to sit in my lap...
!
?
I'm holding a helpless little girl,
in *unspeakable* distress.
I feel odd being cast in the motherly role
that she has me play.
SLAM!

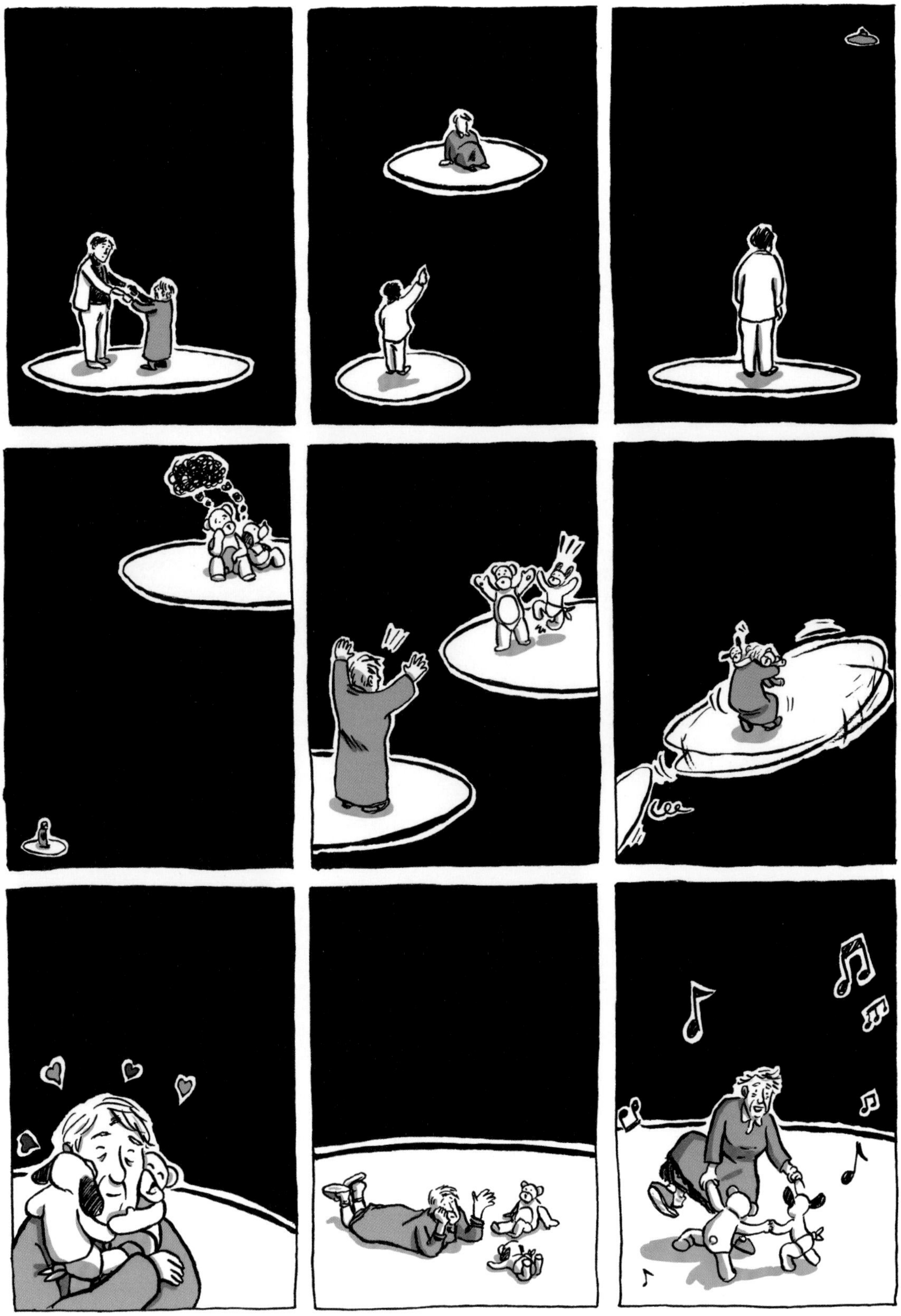

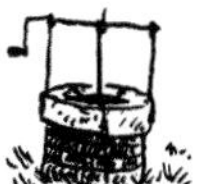

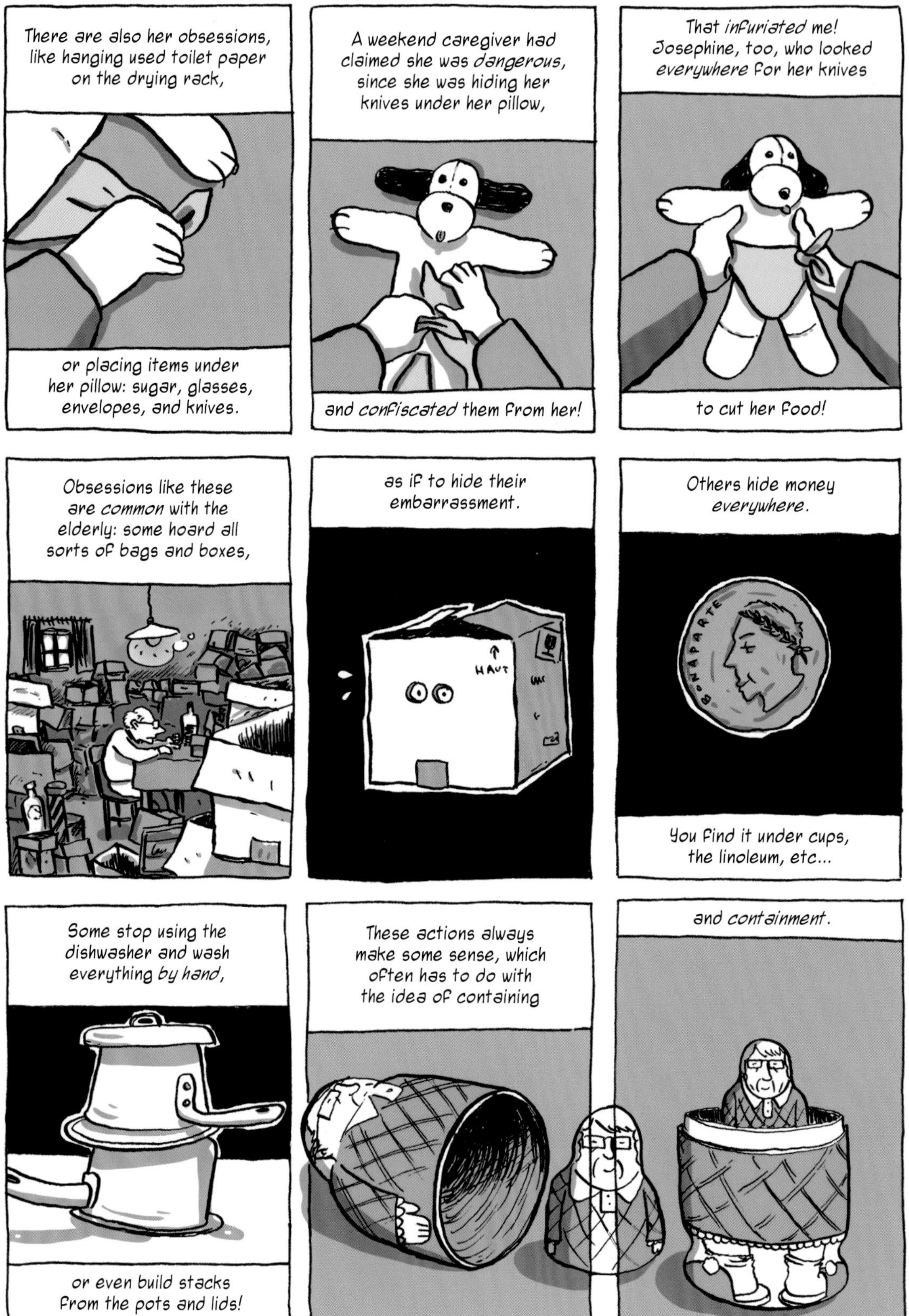
There are also her obsessions, like hanging used toilet paper on the drying rack,
or placing items under her pillow: sugar, glasses, envelopes, and knives.
A weekend caregiver had claimed she was dangerous, since she was hiding her knives under her pillow,
and confiscated them from her!
That infuriated me! Josephine, too, who looked everywhere for her knives
to cut her food!
Obsessions like these are common with the elderly: some hoard all sorts of bags and boxes,
as if to hide their embarrassment.
HAUT
Others hide money everywhere.
BONAPARTE
You find it under cups, the linoleum, etc...
Some stop using the dishwasher and wash everything by hand,
or even build stacks from the pots and lids!
These actions always make some sense, which often has to do with the idea of containing
and containment.

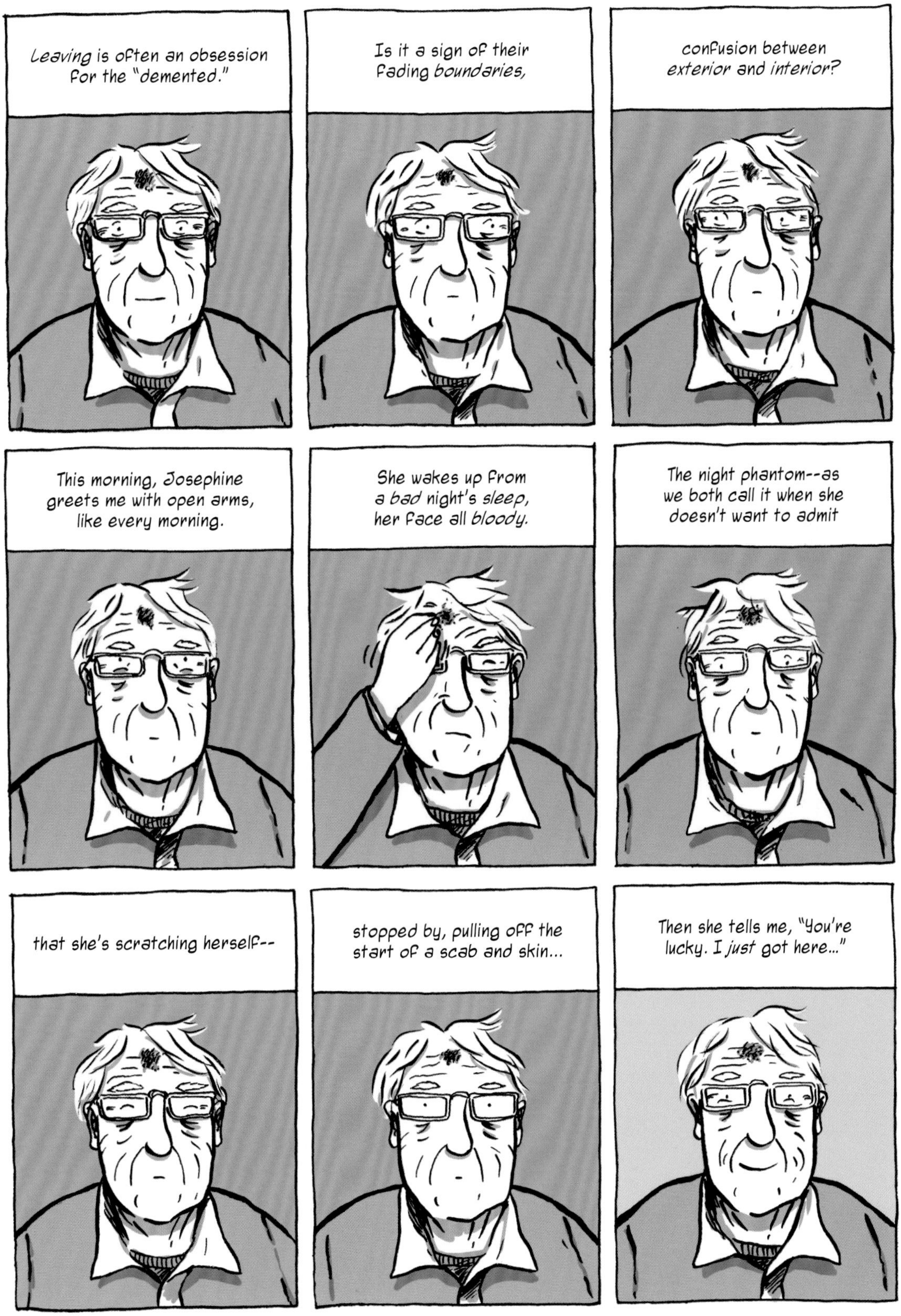

Leaving is often an obsession for the "*demented.*"
Is it a sign of their fading *boundaries,*
confusion between *exterior* and *interior?*
This morning, Josephine greets me with open arms, like every morning.
She wakes up from a *bad* night's *sleep,* her face all *bloody.*
The night phantom--as we both call it when she doesn't want to admit
that she's scratching herself--
stopped by, pulling off the start of a scab and skin...
Then she tells me, "You're lucky. I *just* got here..."

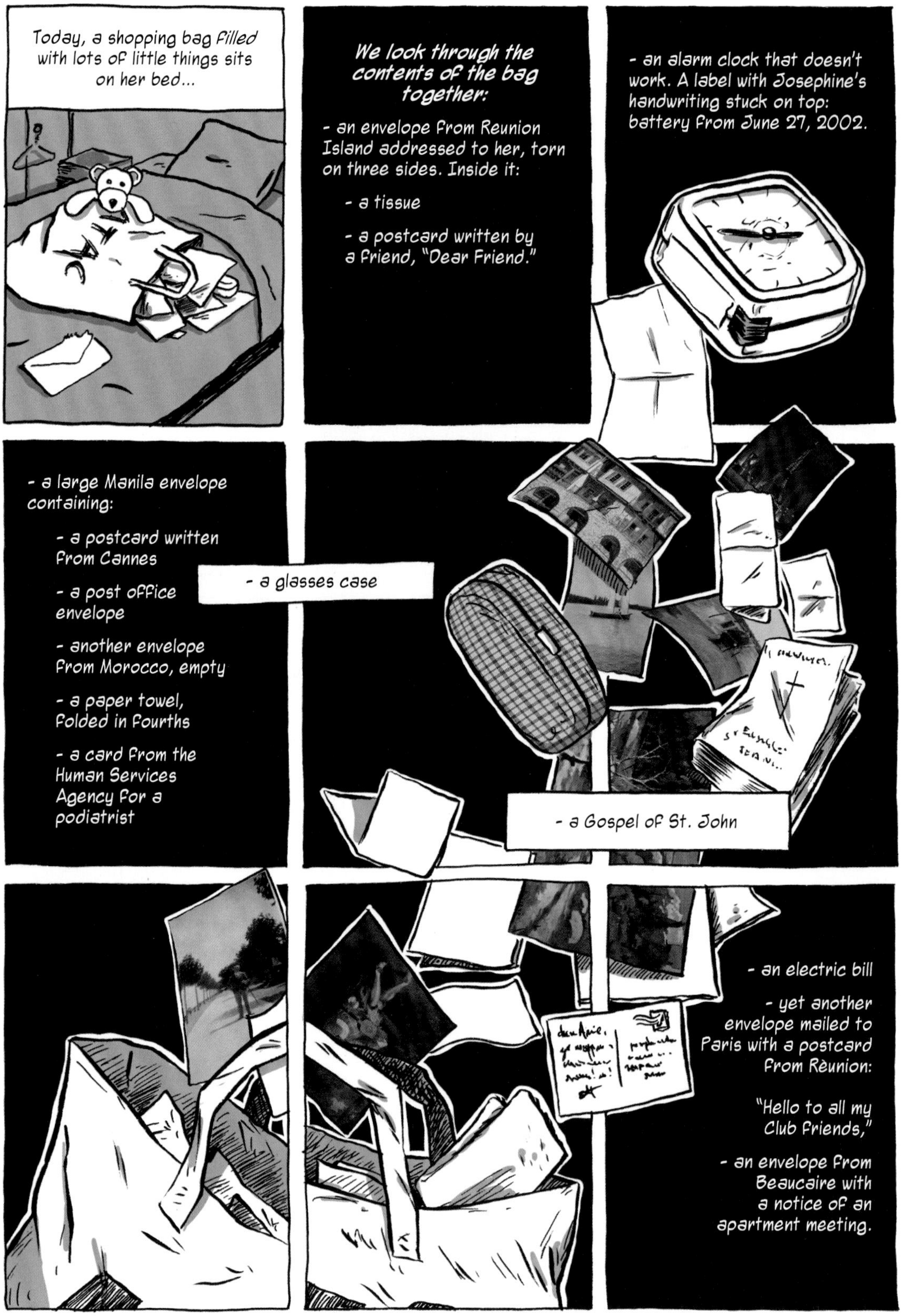
Today, a shopping bag *filled* with lots of little things sits on her bed...
We look through the contents of the bag together:
- an envelope from Reunion Island addressed to her, torn on three sides. Inside it:
- a tissue
- a postcard written by a friend, "Dear Friend."
- an alarm clock that doesn't work. A label with Josephine's handwriting stuck on top: battery from June 27, 2002.
- a large Manila envelope containing:
- a postcard written from Cannes
- a post office envelope
- another envelope from Morocco, empty
- a paper towel, folded in fourths
- a card from the Human Services Agency for a podiatrist
- a glasses case
- a Gospel of St. John
- an electric bill
- yet another envelope mailed to Paris with a postcard from Réunion:
"Hello to all my Club friends,"
- an envelope from Beaucaire with a notice of an apartment meeting.

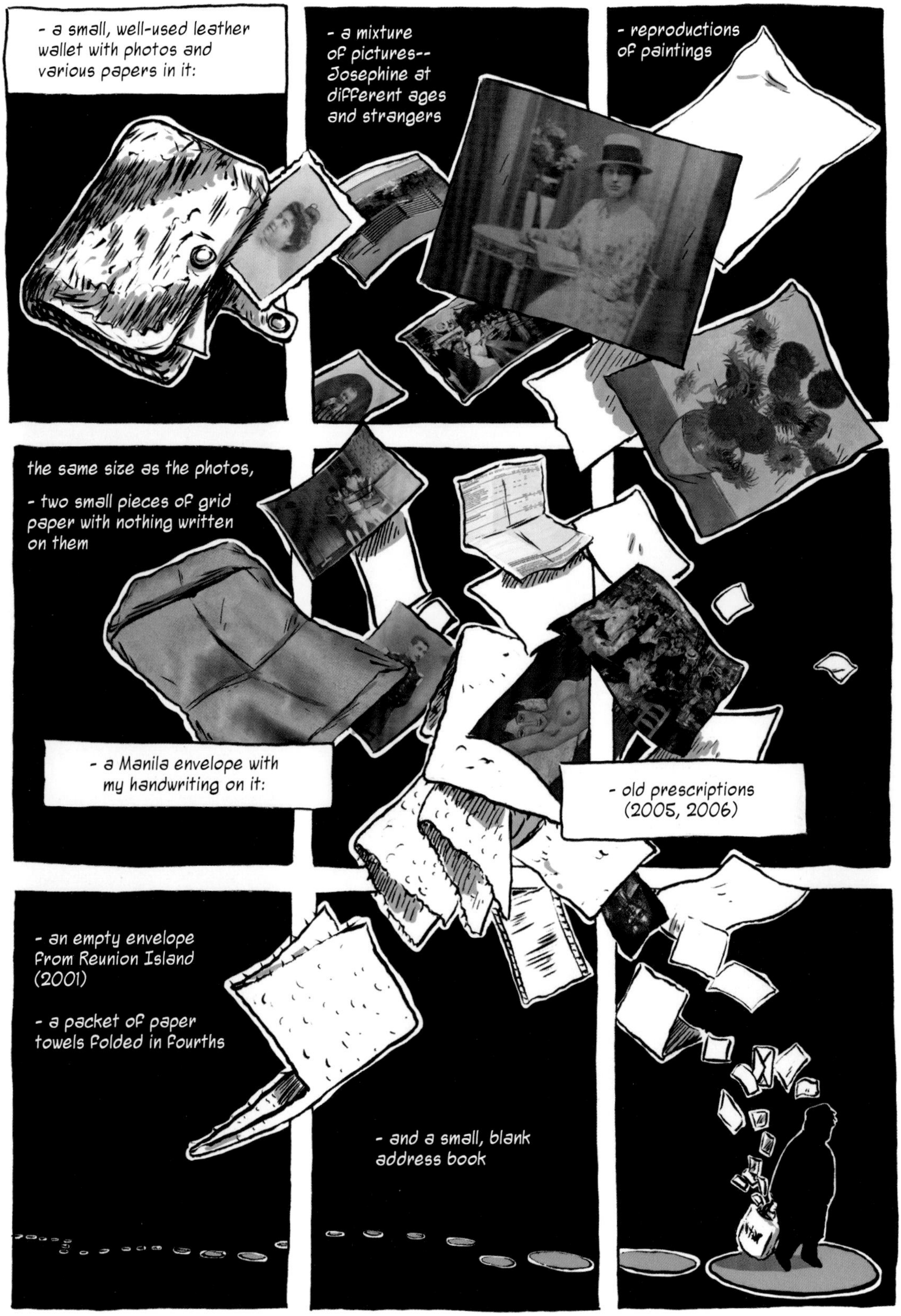
- a small, well-used leather wallet with photos and various papers in it:
- a mixture of pictures-- Josephine at different ages and strangers
- reproductions of paintings
the same size as the photos,
- two small pieces of grid paper with nothing written on them
- a Manila envelope with my handwriting on it:
- old prescriptions (2005, 2006)
- an empty envelope from Reunion Island (2001)
- a packet of paper towels folded in fourths
- and a small, blank address book

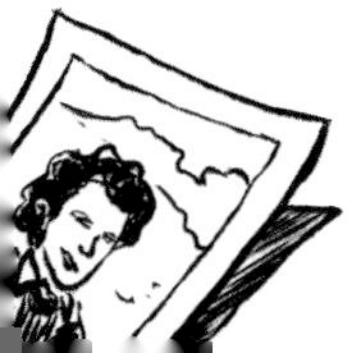

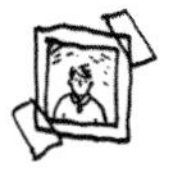

It's a strange collection of items...

related to everything gathered there, like little fragments of life,

an unlikely passport for *braving* her (often) *imaginary* trips.

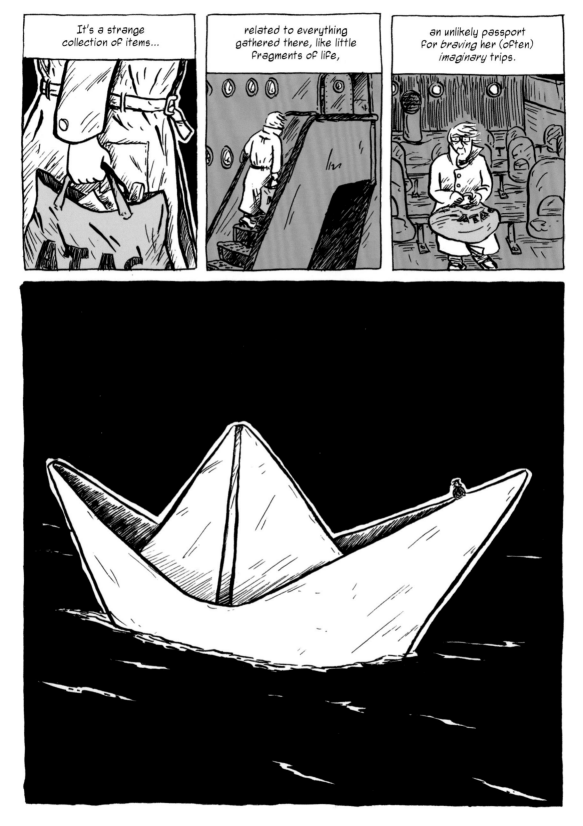

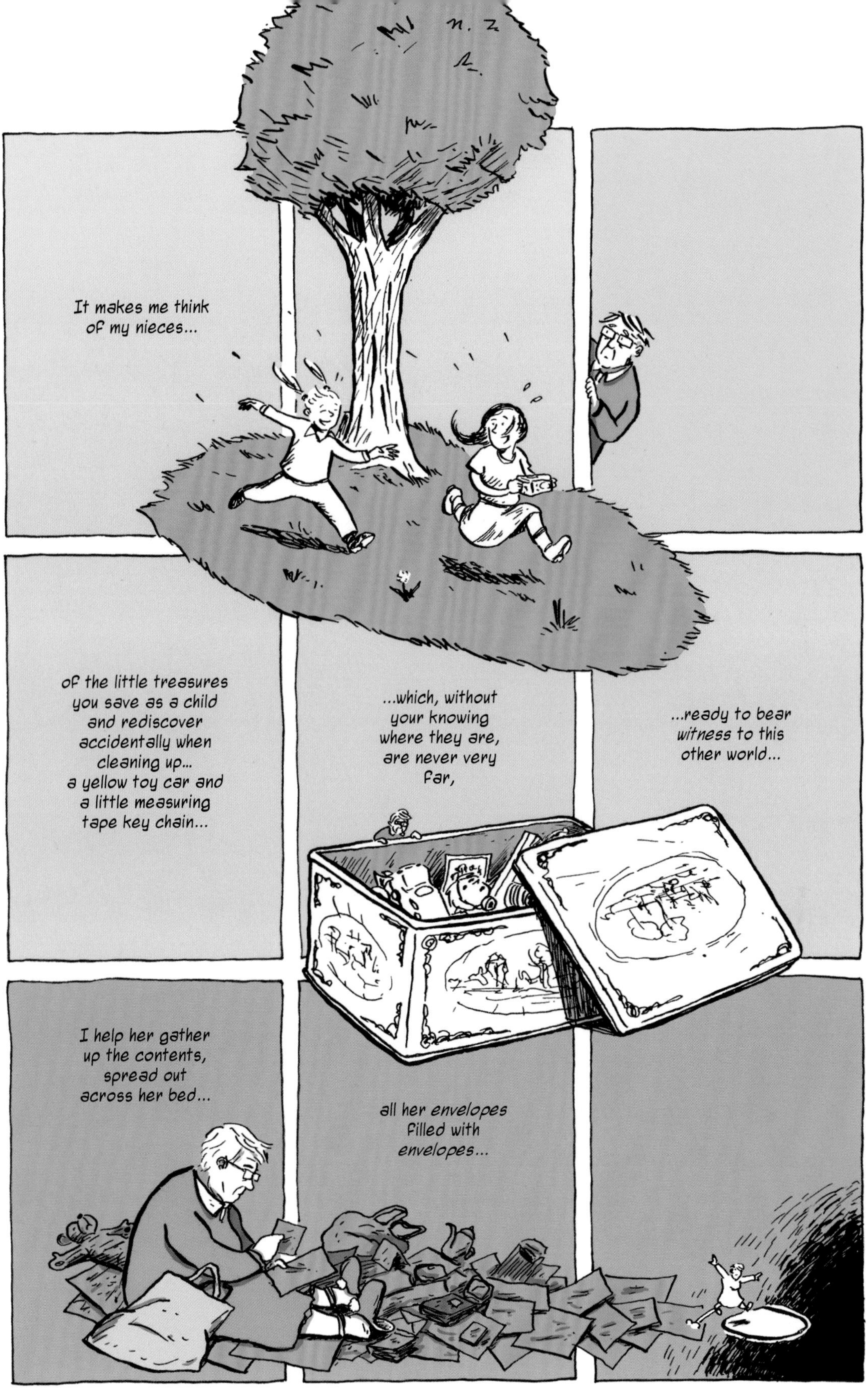
It makes me think of my nieces...
of the little treasures you save as a child and rediscover accidentally when cleaning up... a yellow toy car and a little measuring tape key chain...
...which, without your knowing where they are, are never very far,
...ready to bear *witness* to this other world...
I help her gather up the contents, spread out across her bed...
all her *envelopes* filled with *envelopes*...

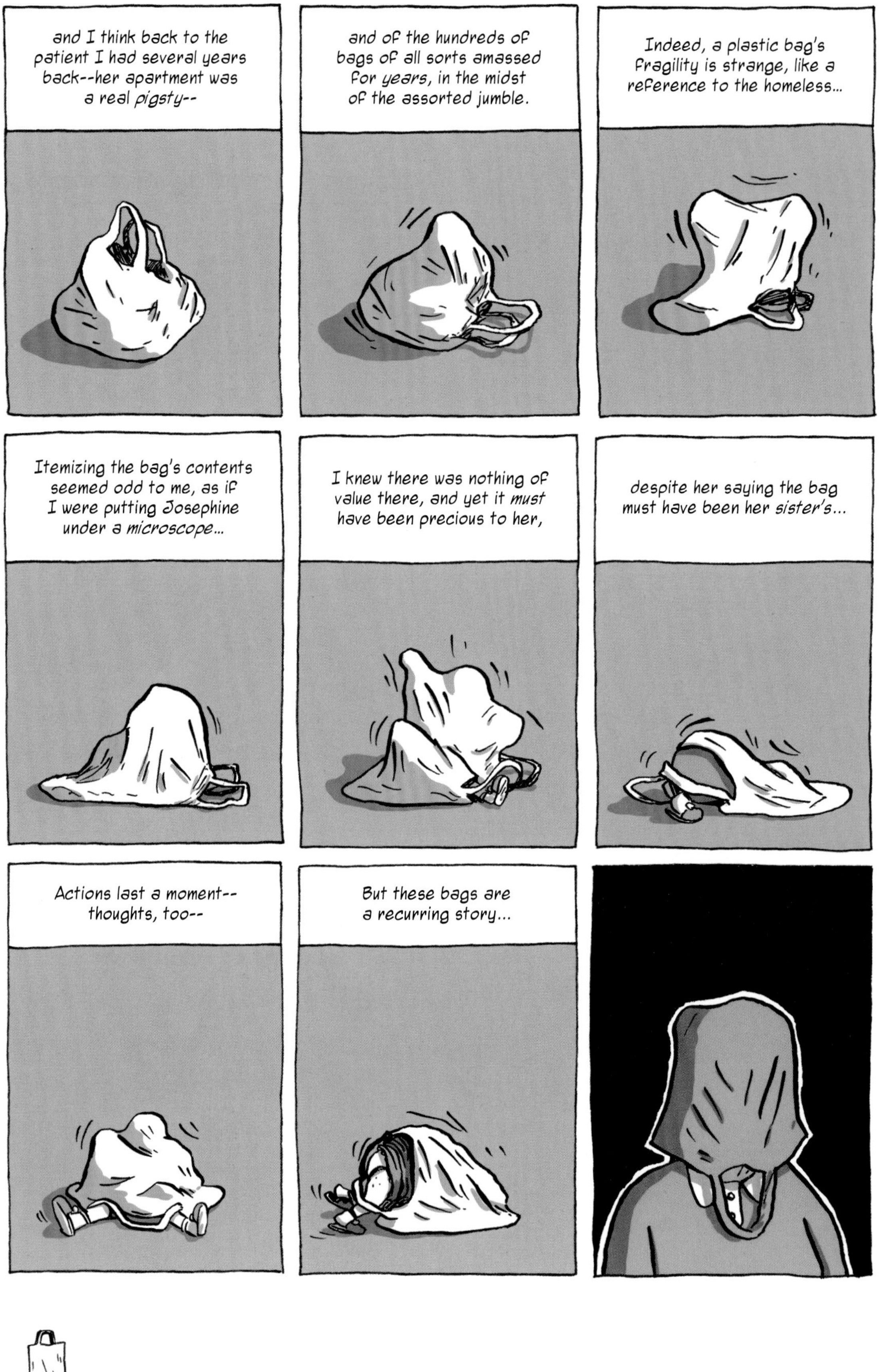
and I think back to the patient I had several years back--her apartment was a real *pigsty*--
and of the hundreds of bags of all sorts amassed for *years*, in the midst of the assorted jumble.
Indeed, a plastic bag's fragility is strange, like a reference to the homeless...
Itemizing the bag's contents seemed odd to me, as if I were putting Josephine under a *microscope*...
I knew there was nothing of value there, and yet it *must* have been precious to her,
despite her saying the bag must have been her *sister's*...
Actions last a moment--thoughts, too--
But these bags are a recurring story...

I've been going regularly to Josephine's for more than three years;

Soap?

oddly enough, she always surprises me. I never get bored when I'm around her.

Pssst...

Hmm?

In a certain way, she's part of my life, while keeping her role as patient.

"Master Crow ..."

I can't explain why she affects me so much:

Master Crow, in a tree was perched
Holding a piece of cheese in his beak
Master Fox, by the smell enticed,
Roughly like this, began to speak:
"Hey, good day, my fine Master Crow
How fine you look. And handsome,
Without a lie, truly you ...
is like [...]
Then you're ...
On hearing ...
And to sh...
Opened

her fragility, sense of humor, and remarks create a unique link between us.

...

Where'd that come from?

Three years made up of moments of calm...respite, as the disease progresses,

but also of rough times-- forgetting, delirium, and hallucinations,

wherein it's taken all my effort to keep her "out of danger,"

and bring her back to reality.

*La Fontaine's tale of *The Fox and the Crow*.

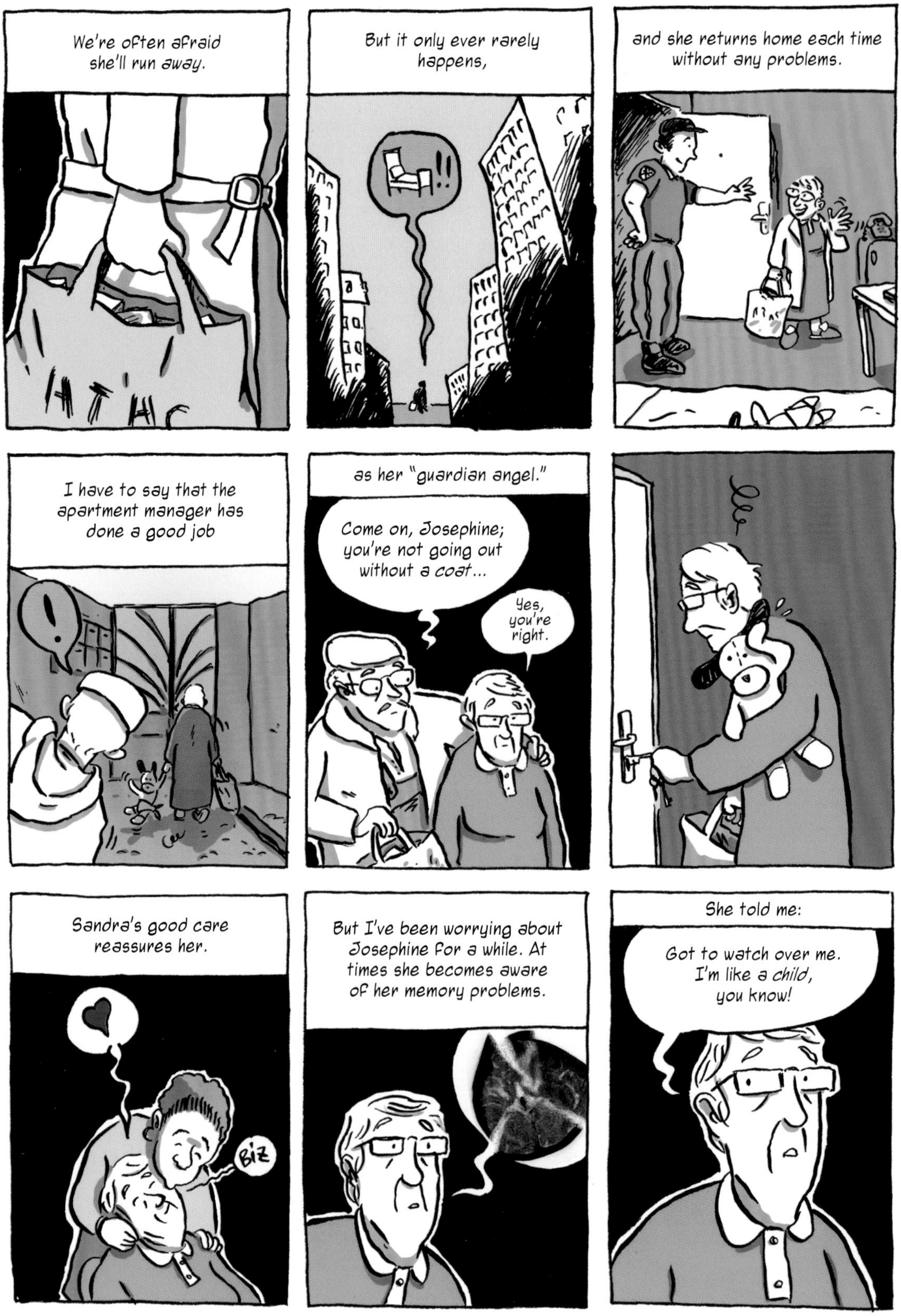
We're often afraid she'll run *away*.
But it only ever rarely happens,
and she returns home each time without any problems.
I have to say that the apartment manager has done a good job
as her "guardian angel."
Come on, Josephine; you're not going out without a *coat*...
Yes, you're right.
Sandra's good care reassures her.
BIZ
But I've been worrying about Josephine for a while. At times she becomes aware of her memory problems.
She told me:
Got to watch over me. I'm like a *child*, you know!

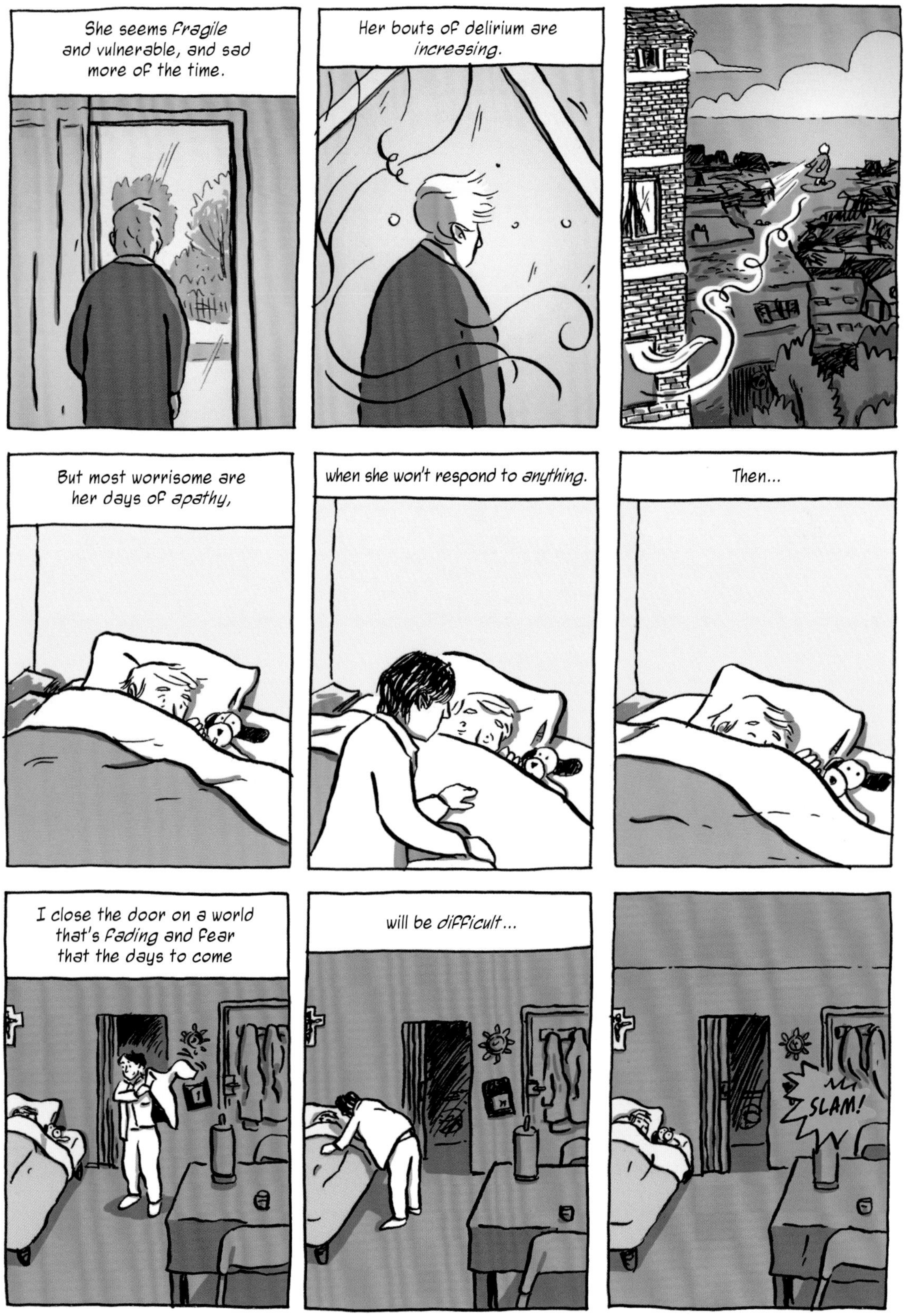
She seems *fragile* and vulnerable, and sad more of the time.
Her bouts of delirium are *increasing*.
But most worrisome are her days of *apathy*,
when she won't respond to *anything*.
Then...
I close the door on a world that's *fading* and fear that the days to come
will be *difficult*...
SLAM!

Days of Nothing

The days when Josephine stays asleep in bed-- when it's difficult, even *impossible*, to rouse her from her *lethargy*--can be called "Days of Nothing." It's as if a *thick fog* has blanketed her thoughts: nothing comes out.

Everything is hard; fatigue has the upper hand...

Fatigue with *everything*: living, moving, speaking...

During these times, there's no choice but to leave her alone and try to create a *cocoon of comfort*...

Cover her up, give her the fruit juice she likes...and wait for her to awaken...

It's a kind of inevitable *hibernation*, as if the world were too much.

It feels odd--no longer the same. No more jokes. Nothing else emerges.

A slow descent into withdrawal...

This generally lasts a day, scarcely more...

The next morning, a cheerful Josephine gets out of bed!!

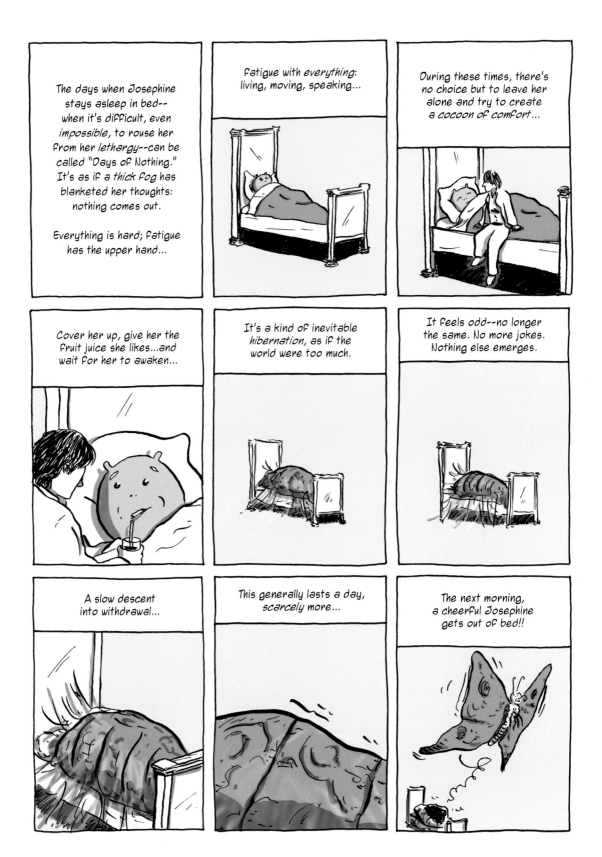

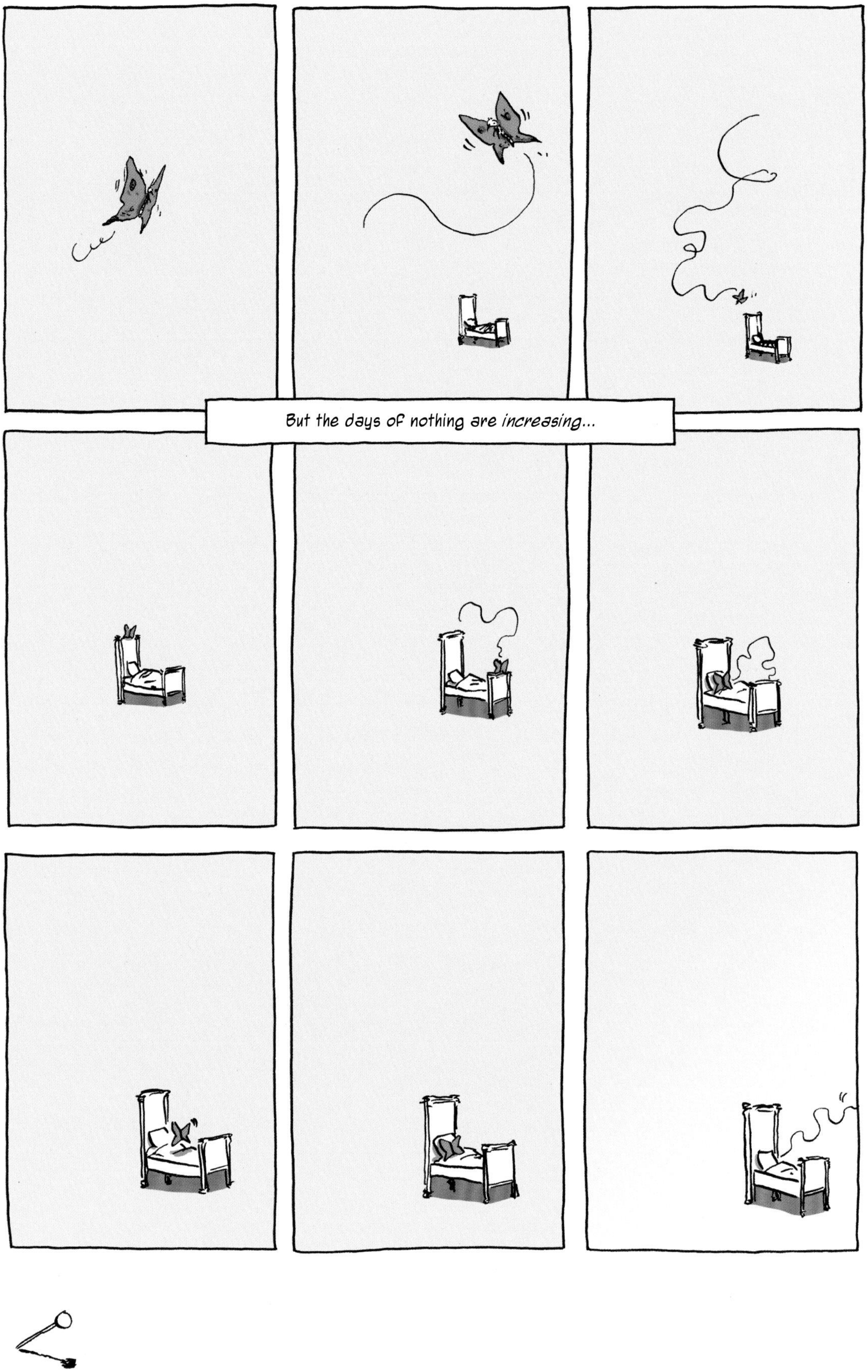
But the days of nothing are *increasing*...

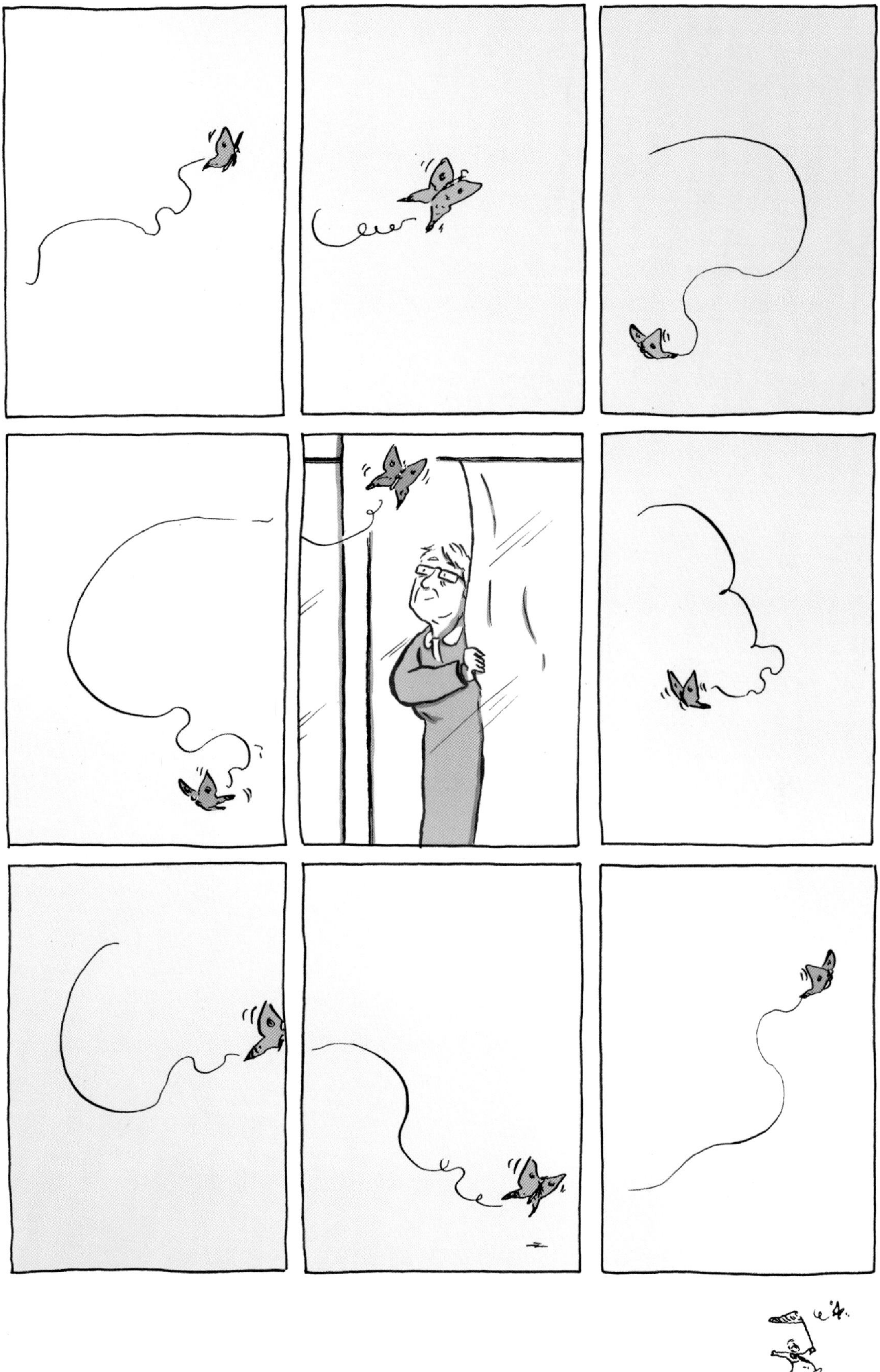

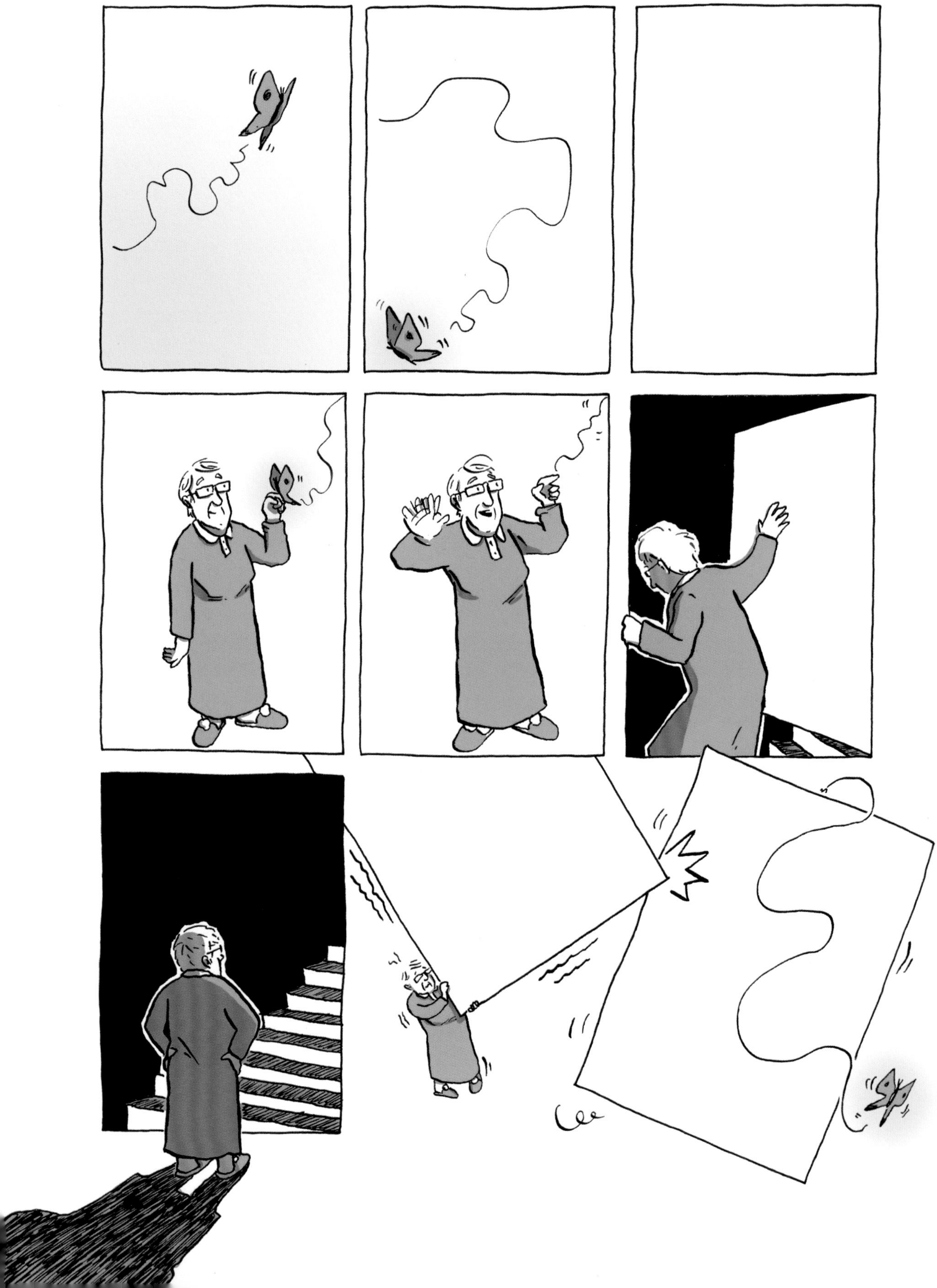

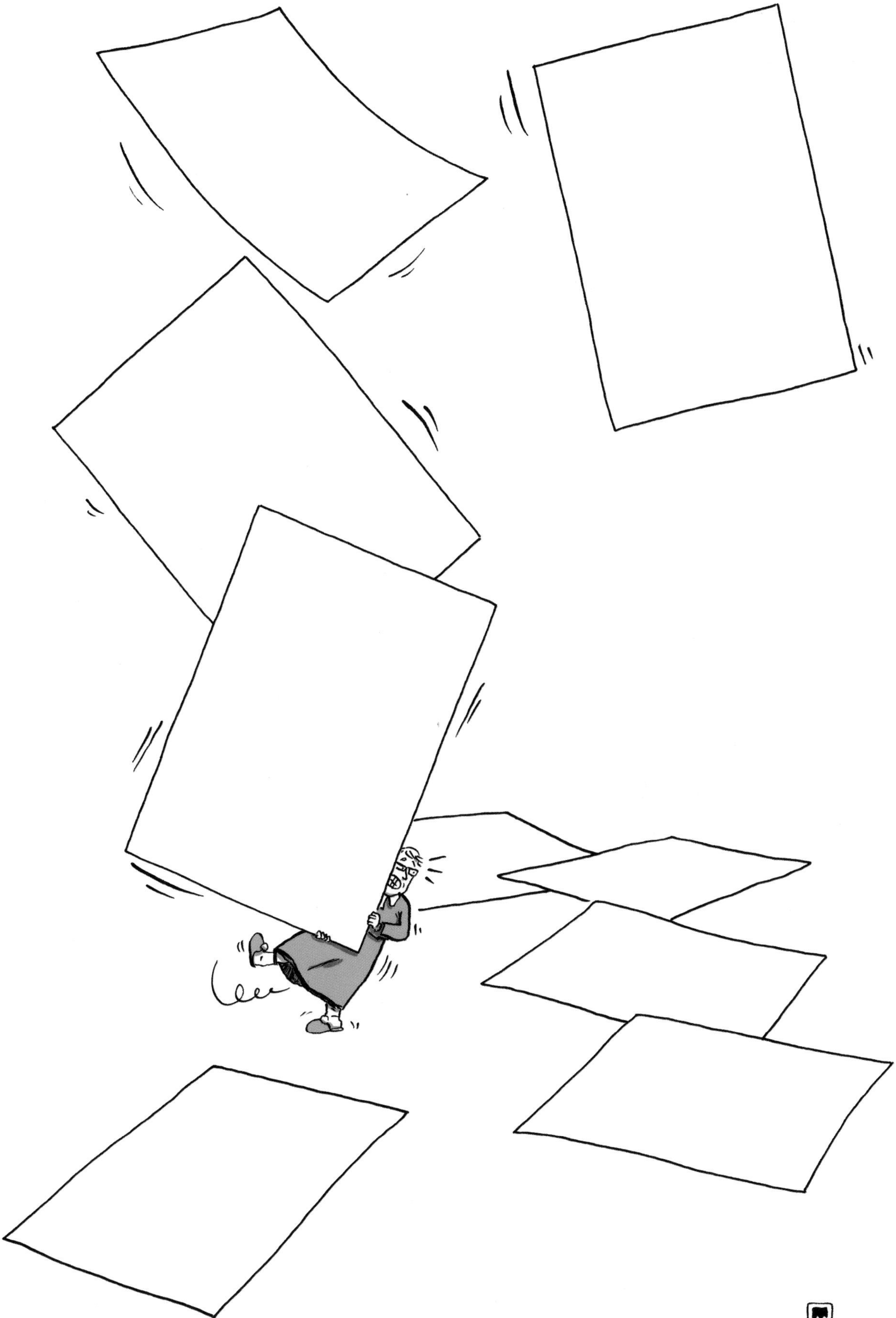
FRAGIL

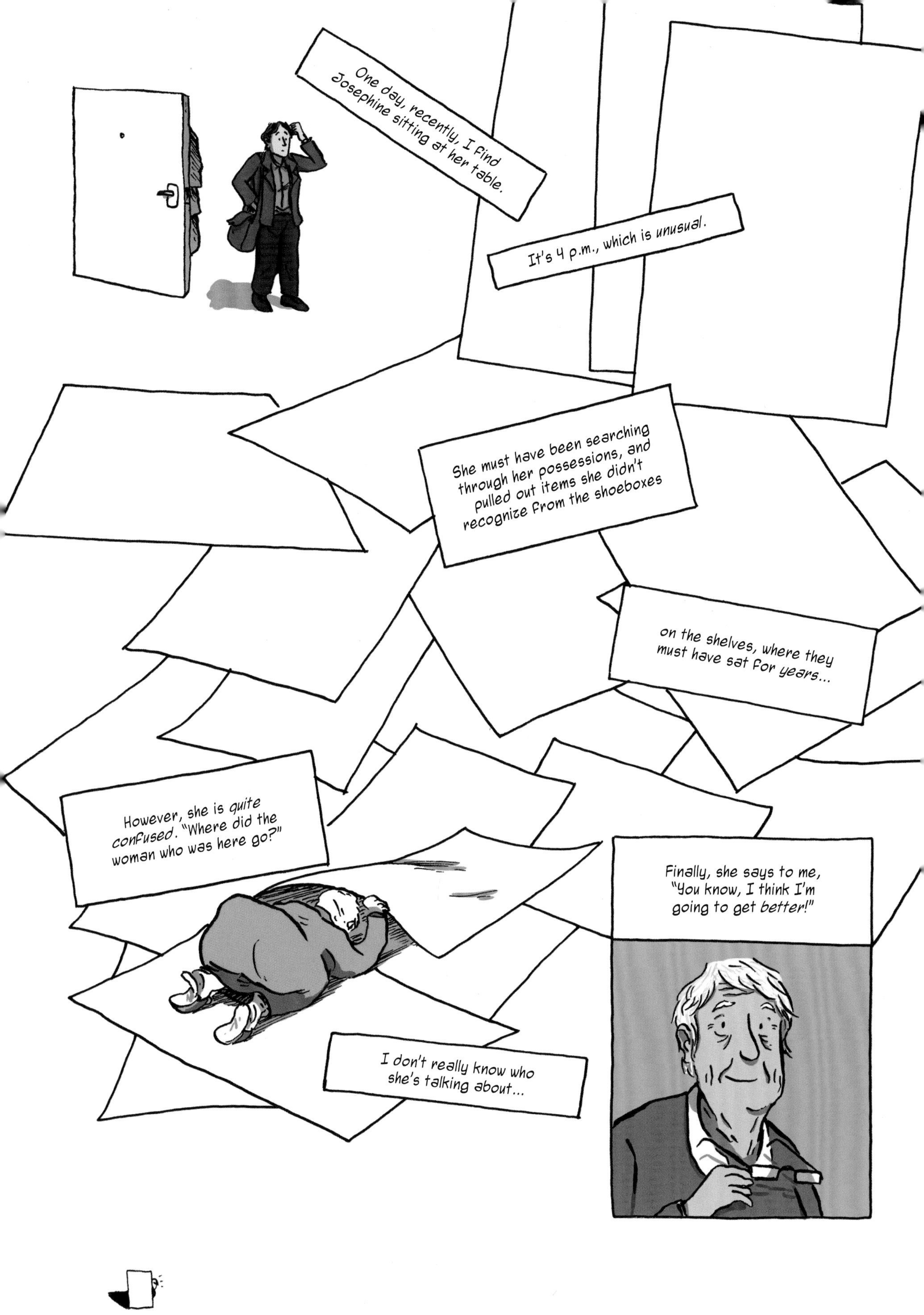
One day, recently, I find Josephine sitting at her table.
It's 4 p.m., which is *unusual*.
She must have been searching through her possessions, and pulled out items she didn't recognize from the shoeboxes
on the shelves, where they must have sat for years...
However, she is *quite confused*. "Where did the woman who was here go?"
I don't really know who she's talking about...
Finally, she says to me, "You know, I think I'm going to get *better*!"

*But Josephine
didn't get better.*

And the emptiness...

One day, when I open the door to her apartment, Josephine has disappeared.

It is 9 a.m. I search everywhere in disbelief. But nobody is there.

Everything is tidied up, as one does before leaving: the bed made, the kitchen door closed, the table cleared, the clothes from the day before where I'd left them.

The image of her empty bed

seems unbelievably

violent.

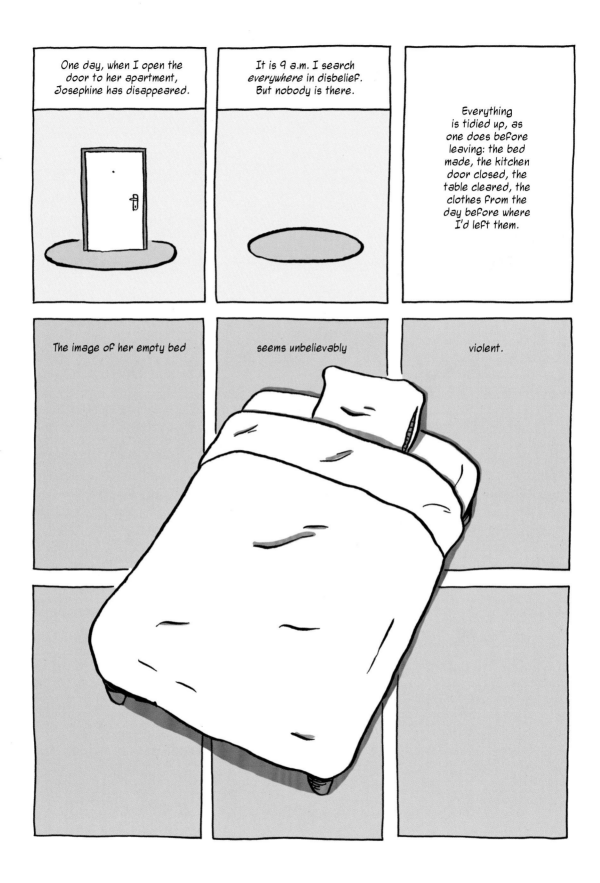

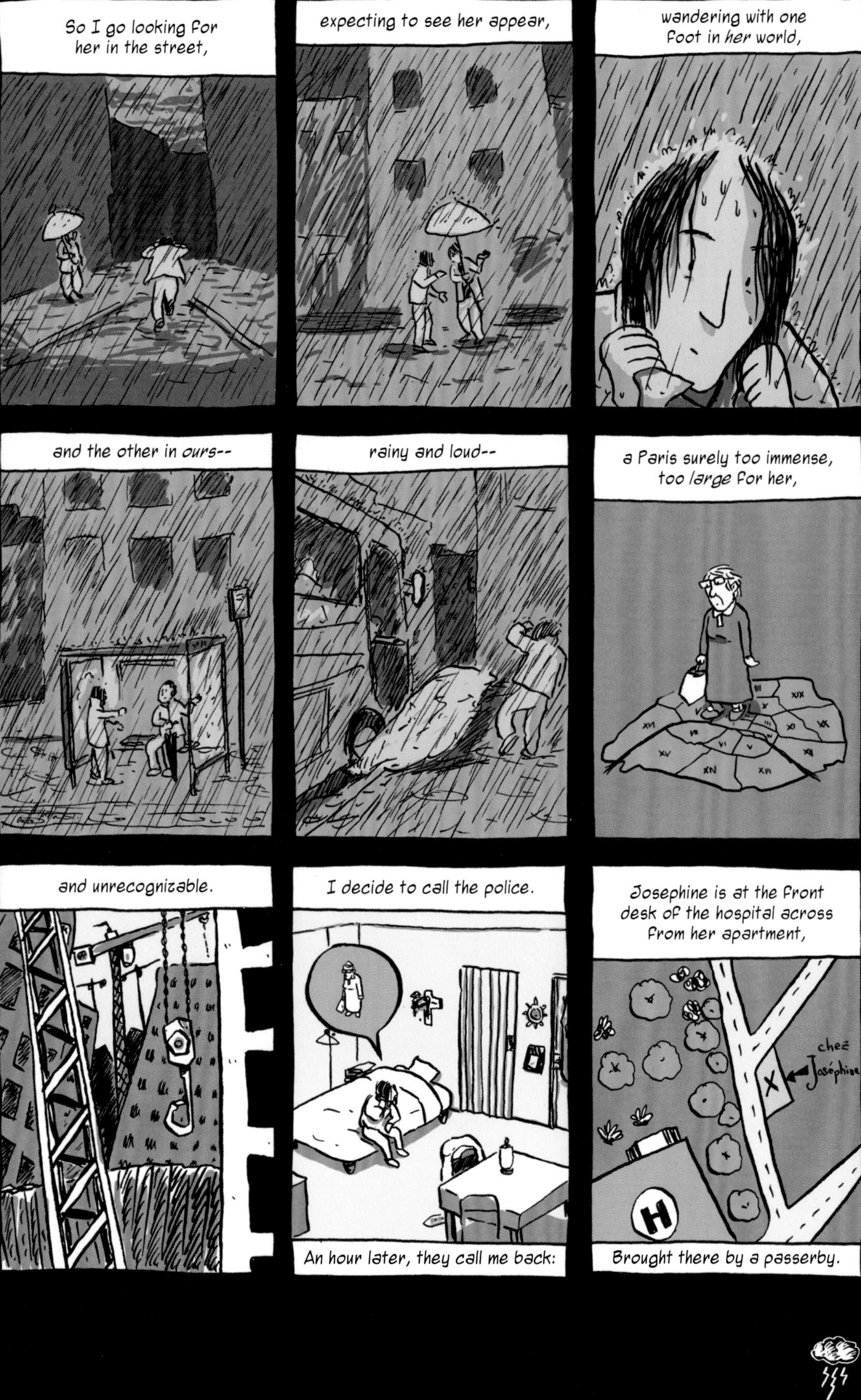
So I go looking for her in the street,
expecting to see her appear,
wandering with one foot in *her* world,
and the other in *ours*--
rainy and loud--
a Paris surely too immense, too *large* for her,
XIX
XX
XV
XIV
XIII
XII
and unrecognizable.
I decide to call the police.
An hour later, they call me back:
Josephine is at the front desk of the hospital across from her apartment,
chez Joséphine
H
Brought there by a passerby.

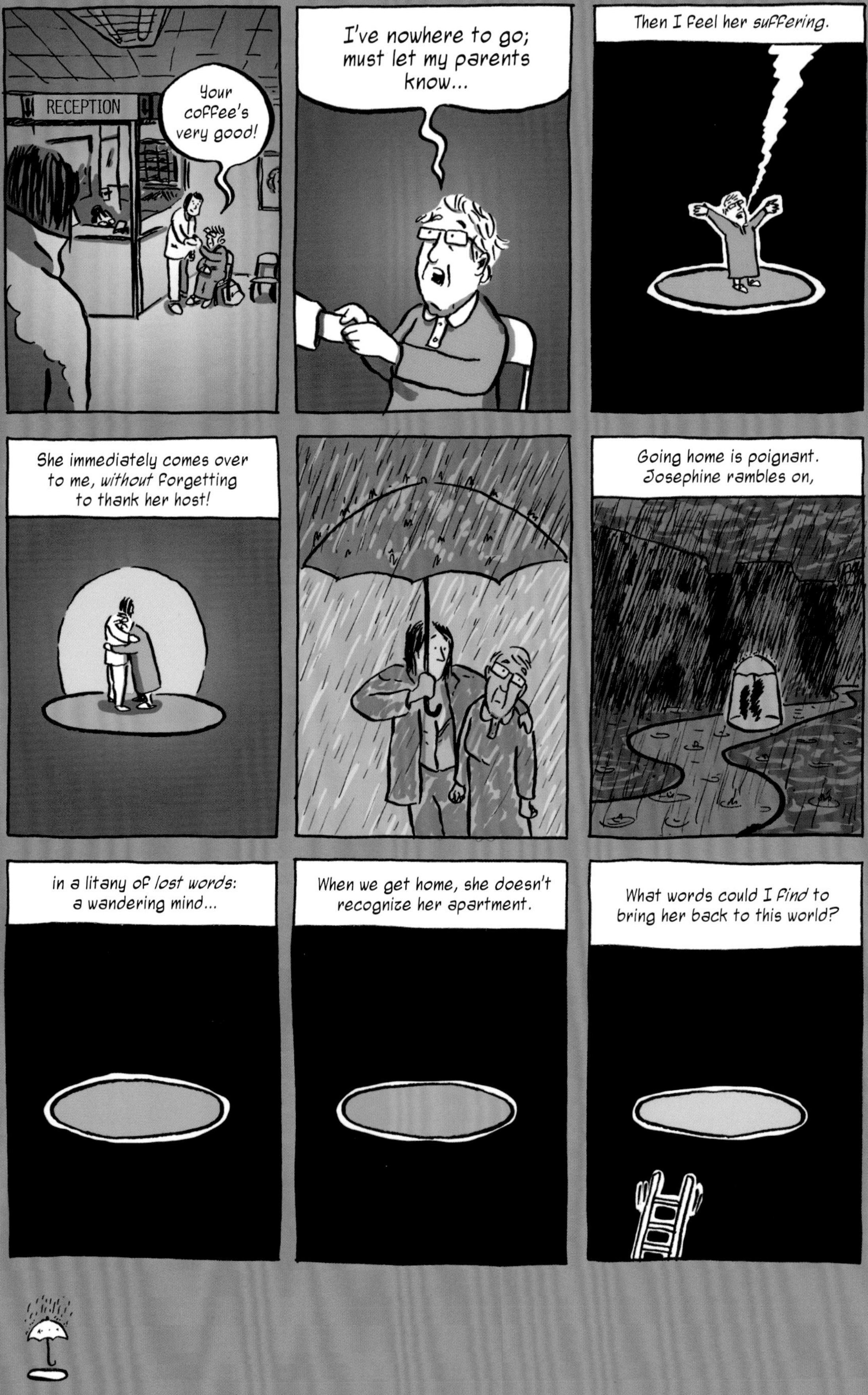

RECEPTION
Your coffee's very good!
I've nowhere to go; must let my parents know...
Then I feel her *suffering*.
She immediately comes over to me, *without* forgetting to thank her host!
Going home is poignant. Josephine rambles on,
in a litany of *lost words*: a wandering mind...
When we get home, she doesn't recognize her apartment.
What words could I *find* to bring her back to this world?

...returns

And then, without our really knowing, the end intrudes,
approaching with muffled steps.

All the signs are there. We recognize it, but we don't
yet know what form it will take.

The relentless, recurring emptiness we encounter
sometimes draws me in, and I no longer know
what is good for Josephine:

staying home or going to a retirement home.

Will her world feel different in a place with more people?
Can we chase away her ghosts
or will they overwhelm her even more?

Eventually, there is no longer a choice.
One Sunday, a caregiver calls 911, panicking
at seeing Josephine so ill.

The doctor hospitalizes her.

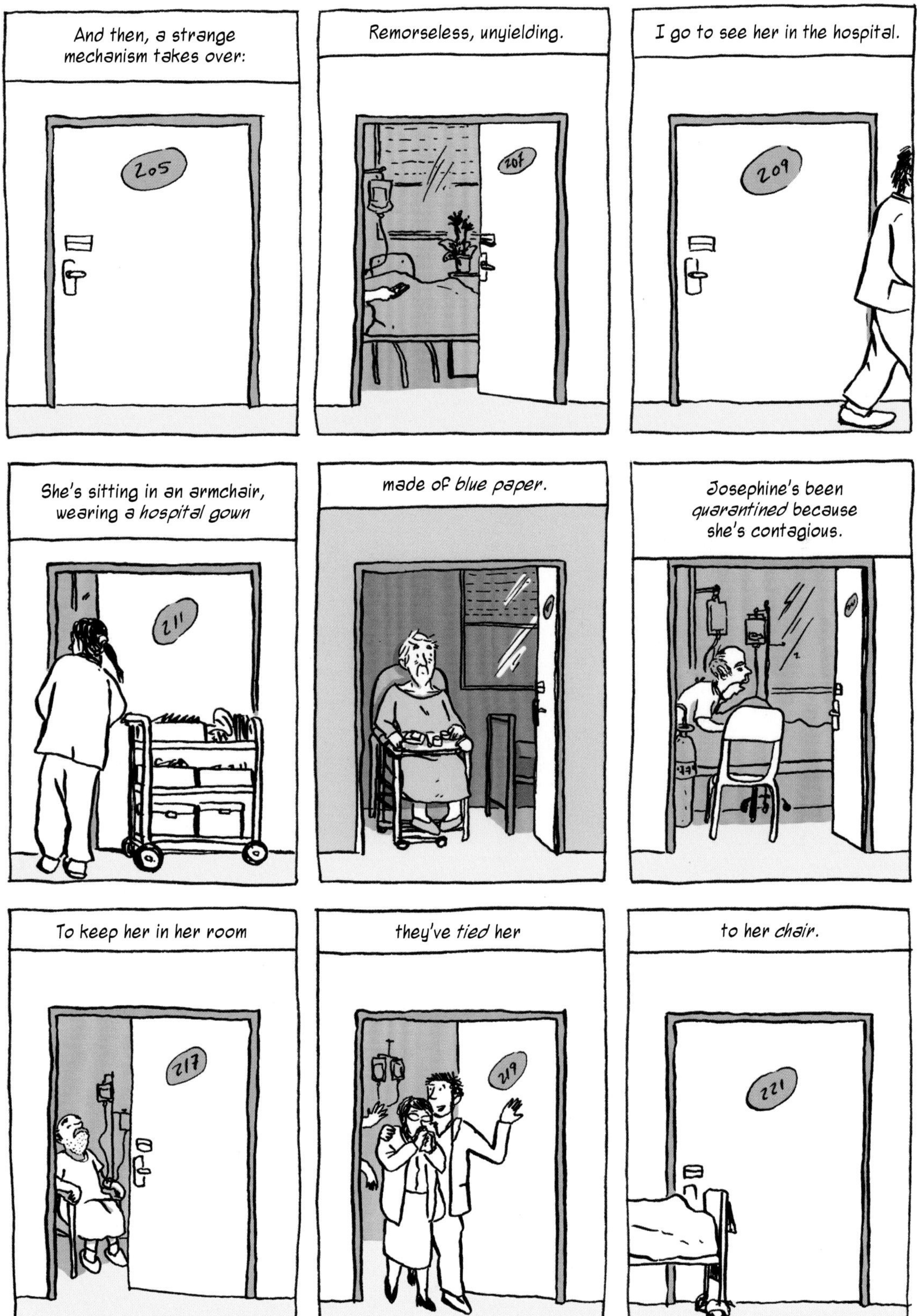
And then, a strange mechanism takes over:
Remorseless, unyielding.
I go to see her in the hospital.
She's sitting in an armchair, wearing a *hospital gown*
made of *blue paper*.
Josephine's been *quarantined* because she's contagious.
To keep her in her room
they've *tied* her
to her *chair*.

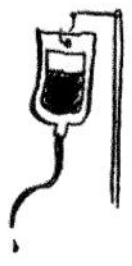

It's mealtime. There's a tray before her:

mashed potatoes, yogurt, fruit.

Nothing's been touched. The potatoes are cold.

The staff has many *other* Josephines to feed,

and very little time

to devote to each patient.

She takes a few spoonfuls, but soon stops.

As at home, she eats slowly.

I imagine the tray often goes back nearly untouched.

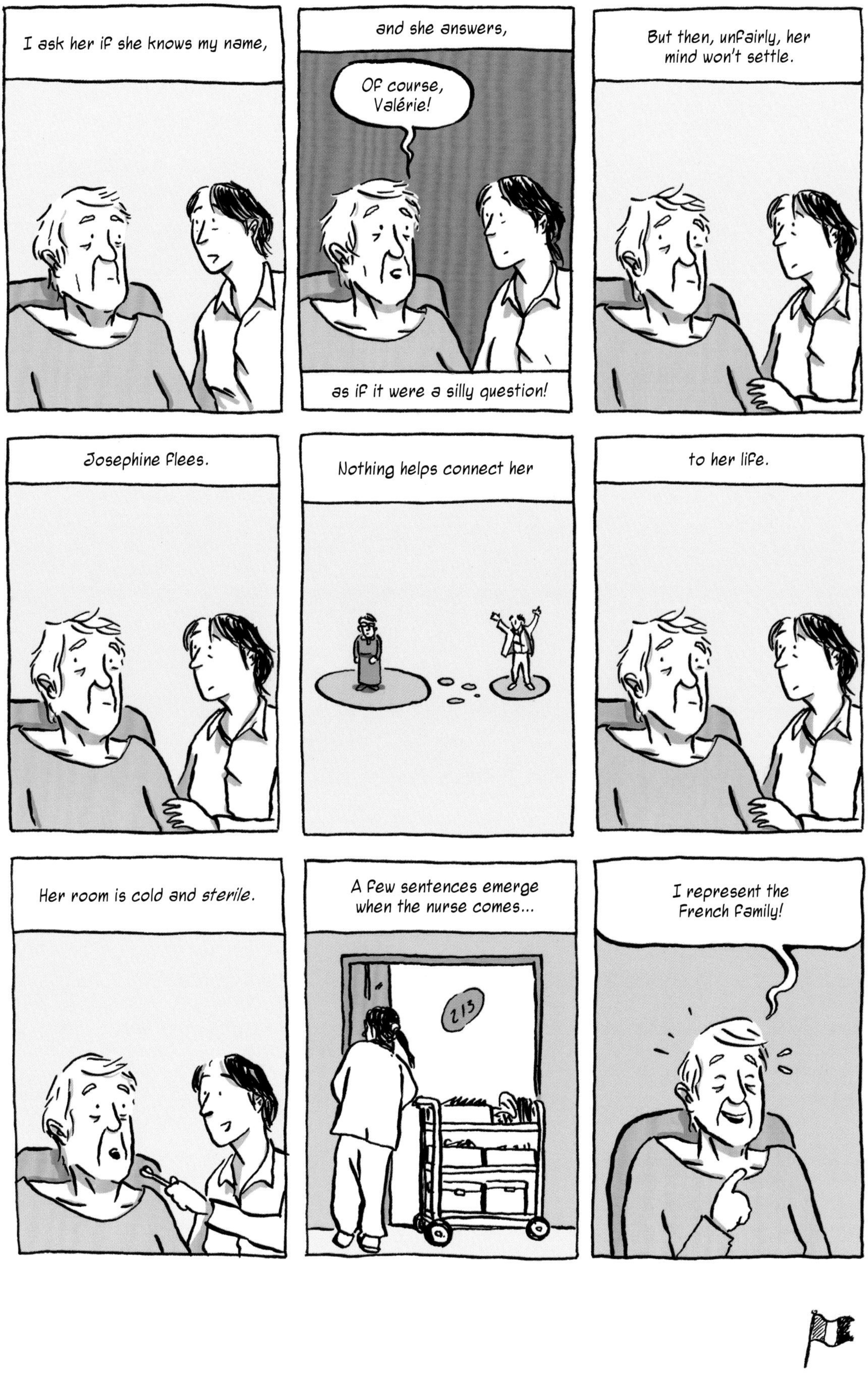

I ask her if she knows my name,
and she answers,
Of course, Valérie!
as if it were a silly question!
But then, unfairly, her mind won't settle.
Josephine flees.
Nothing helps connect her
to her life.
Her room is cold and sterile.
A few sentences emerge when the nurse comes...
213
I represent the French family!

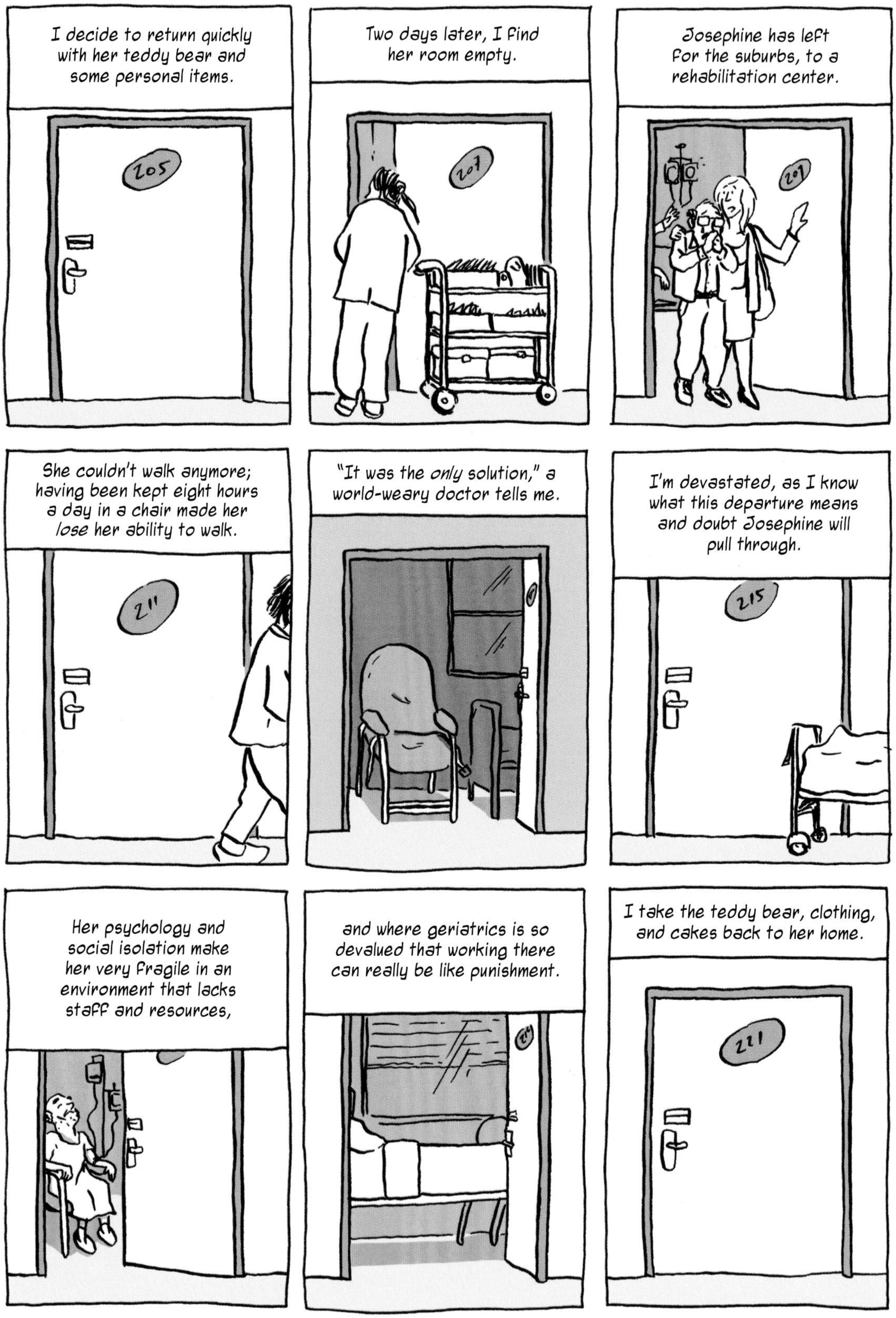
I decide to return quickly with her teddy bear and some personal items.
Two days later, I find her room empty.
Josephine has left for the suburbs, to a rehabilitation center.
She couldn't walk anymore; having been kept eight hours a day in a chair made her *lose* her ability to walk.
"It was the *only* solution," a world-weary doctor tells me.
I'm devastated, as I know what this departure means and doubt Josephine will pull through.
Her psychology and social isolation make her very fragile in an environment that lacks staff and resources,
and where geriatrics is so devalued that working there can really be like punishment.
I take the teddy bear, clothing, and cakes back to her home.

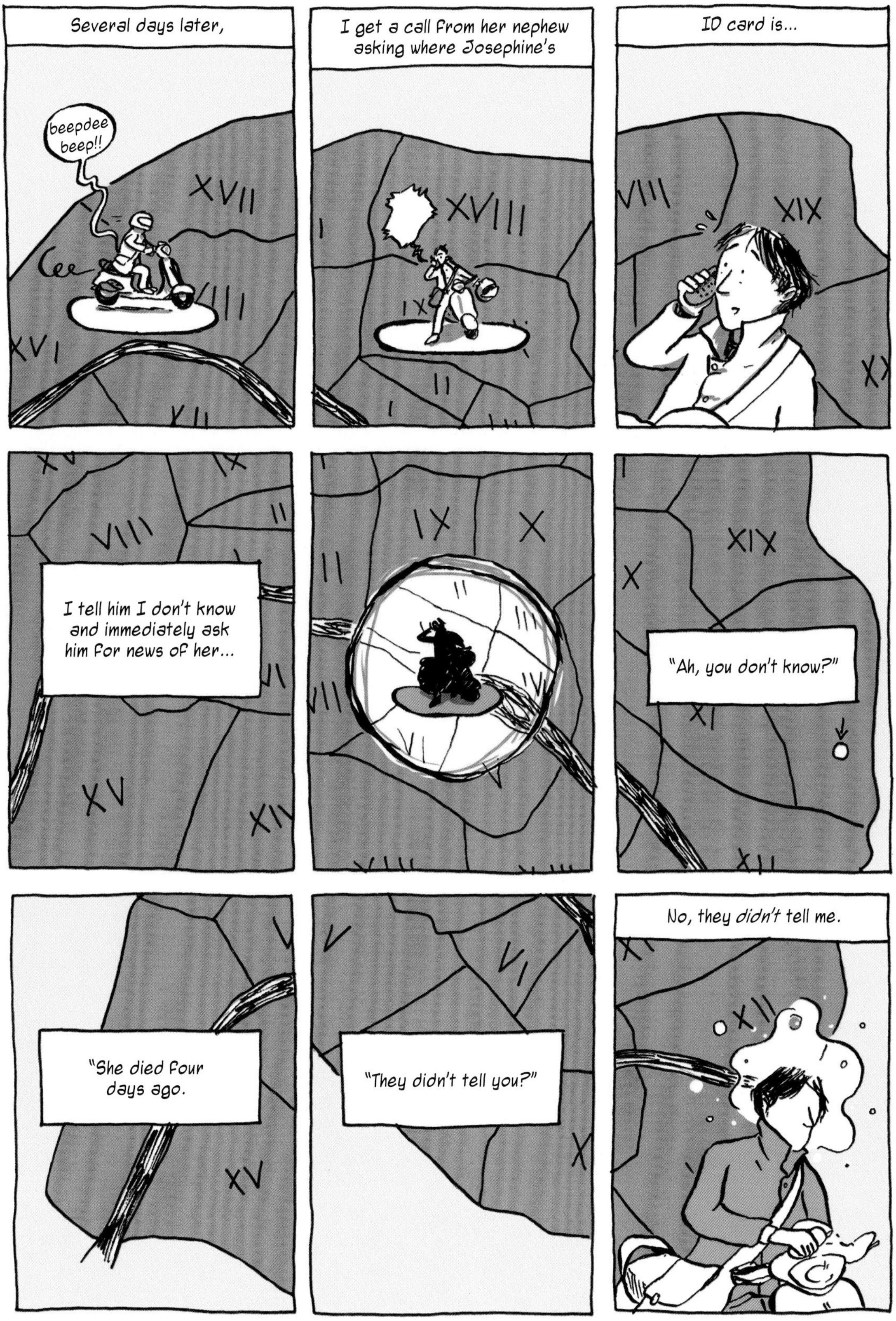
Several days later,
beepdee beep!!
I get a call from her nephew asking where Josephine's
ID card is...
I tell him I don't know and immediately ask him for news of her...
"Ah, you don't know?"
"She died four days ago.
"They didn't tell you?"
No, they *didn't* tell me.

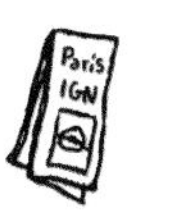
Paris
IGN

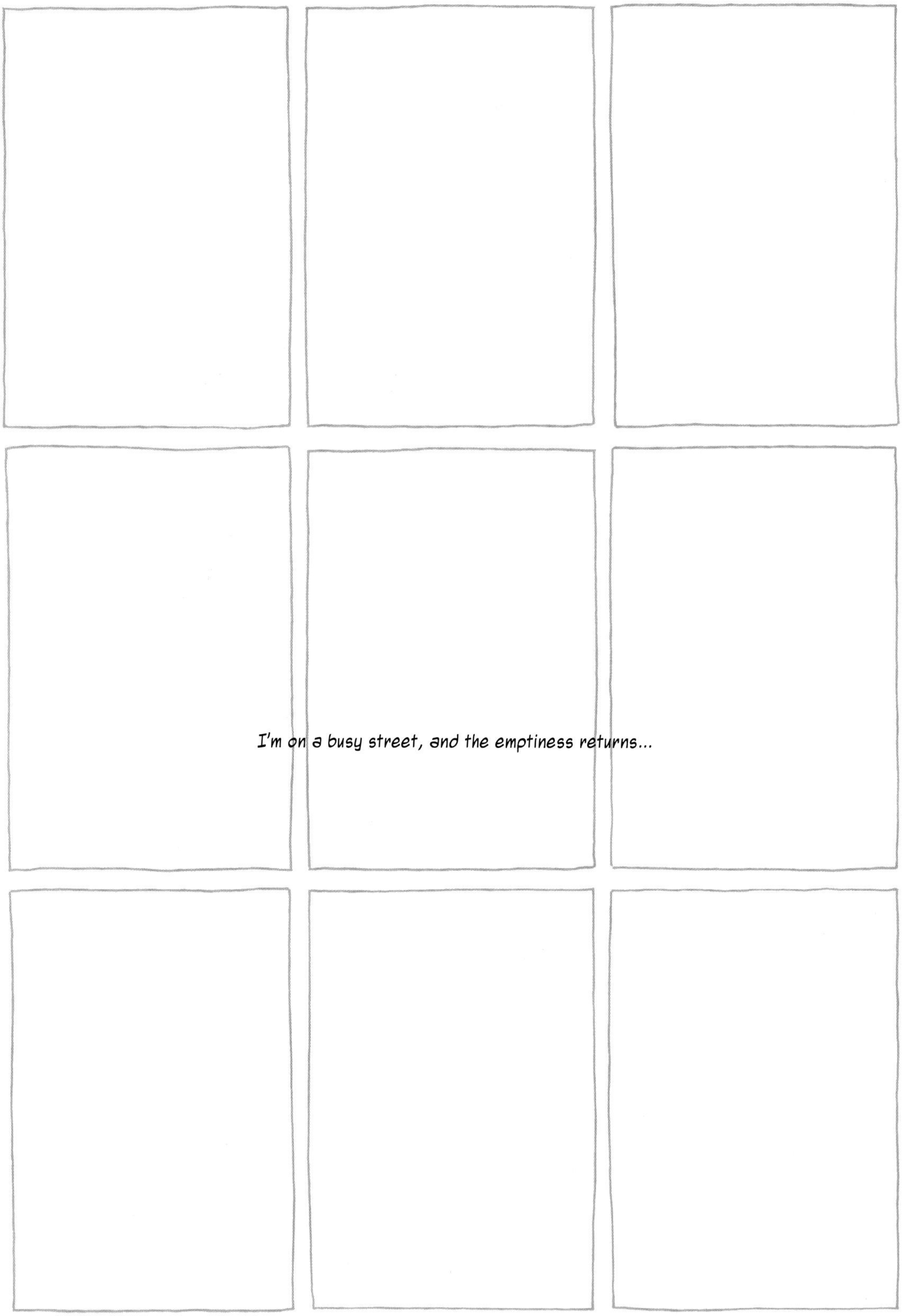
I'm on a busy street, and the emptiness returns...

I'm like a piece of wood:
I look at the sky and the clouds,
And I feel nothing.

These are the words of a patient this morning--stretched out on her bed, gazing towards the sky. I thought of Josephine, of those few years we spent close to each other.

I thought they were speaking about the same world, one with other anxieties and other symptoms.

I thought of this world that's too empty and too full, that Josephine observed from her bed, of her life that was limited to the rectangle of her apartment, filled with ghosts and fear, and with no reason to live.

Working with Josephine was a major event in my career as a nurse. I felt an indescribable feeling of resemblance, an affinity that we seldom encounter in life.

I was lucky to meet her. This woman who called herself the daughter of Arsene Lupin*! Humor was our language, our playground and our connection. She was funny and amazingly alive, despite the problems she faced. Josephine made me question what was important and helped me think better of my work, keeping me from losing myself in passivity and indifference.

In telling this story, I wanted to say that we should never give up when faced with behavioral disorders that can seem so destabilizing for us "healthy" people. We always have to look for the link, the door that gives us access to another person.

And then, we should be willing to be deeply moved by the "girl with green eyes!"

"Scout's honor!"

Valérie Villieu

*Gentleman Thief, Master of Disguise, and Hero of a series of novels by French author Maurice Leblanc.

Alzheimer's Disease is a type of dementia that causes problems with memory, thinking and behavior. It is a progressive disease, meaning symptoms gradually worsen over time, often becoming severe enough to interfere with daily life. According to the Alzheimer's Association, 5.8 million people have Alzheimer's in the U.S. alone, and caregivers will have provided an estimated 18.5 billion hours of care in the year 2019.

Currently, there is no cure for Alzheimer's Disease, but treatments for symptoms are available and research continues. Although current treatments cannot stop Alzheimer's from progressing, they can temporarily slow the worsening of dementia symptoms and improve quality of life for those with Alzheimer's and their caregivers. Today, there is a worldwide effort under way to find better ways to treat the disease, delay its onset, and prevent it from developing.

Learn more at alz.org.
24/7 Helpline: 800.272.3900